"I'm not a liar!"

r words, Greg was off the couch and walking
rd her as if to settle her again. But Eliza didn't
to be settled.

ck of this, Greg. I'm sick of being mistaken for
victim. I want this to end. I want all of it to end."

will. Once we find out who was in your house
. Once you get your memory back."

ne was gentle and reassuring. She didn't want
e and reassuring. She didn't want a lecture by
halmers on how everything was going to be
when clearly it wasn't.

anted to feel something different. She wanted
the person controlling her fate. She wanted...

g two determined strides toward him she lifted
ms around his neck. "This," she whispered
t his lips. "This is what I want."

Dear Reader,

I've had the idea of a human lie detector as a character for some time. Guys like the one in *The Mentalist* whose powers of observation—because, really, that's all that skill is—are just better than anyone else's. Almost like a modern-day Sherlock Holmes. I knew Greg was that character. I mean, what better skill to have as a psychologist than the ability to really "see" the person you're trying to help?

Until it all goes wrong for Greg, of course. It was at his lowest moment when I had to imagine the heroine who might come along and save him. A heroine who needs a little saving herself. I thought, how does a woman keep her secrets from a man who can see everything about her? The answer was simple. She couldn't have any secrets. So I made her a blank slate.

This is my amnesia story, and while maybe it's been done before, this is my attempt. I hope you enjoy Greg and Liza's story.

I've lived with these characters who have ties to the Tyler Group—*One Final Step* (October 2012), *An Act of Persuasion* (March 2013) and *For the First Time* (October 2013)—for so long that I wasn't quite ready to leave them. So I've written two novellas with some of the secondary characters: Elaine, Chuck, Sophie and Bay. Look for the digital book with both stories available now!

I love to hear from readers. Feel free to reach out to me at www.stephaniedoyle.net or on Twitter, @StephDoyleRW.

Happy reading!

Stephanie Doyle

STEPHANIE DOYLE

Remembering That Night

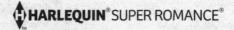
HARLEQUIN® SUPER ROMANCE®

Recycling programs
for this product may
not exist in your area.

ISBN-13: 978-0-373-60834-8

REMEMBERING THAT NIGHT

Copyright © 2014 by Stephanie Doyle

Printed in U.S.A.

ABOUT THE AUTHOR

Stephanie Doyle, a dedicated romance reader, began to pen her own romantic adventures at age sixteen. She began submitting to Harlequin lines at age eighteen, and by twenty-six her first book was published. Fifteen years later, she still loves what she does, as each book is a new adventure. She lives in South Jersey with her cat, Lex, and her two kittens, who have taken over everything. When she isn't thinking about escaping to the beach, she's working on her next idea.

Books by Stephanie Doyle

HARLEQUIN SUPERROMANCE

SILHOUETTE ROMANTIC SUSPENSE

SILHOUETTE BOMBSHELL

Other titles by this author available in ebook format.

PROLOGUE

"All in."

Greg looked at his opponent across the table. He watched the man's eyes drop to the table. Watched him slow his breathing. Watched him try to erase every visible tell.

A regular poker player with years of experience no doubt. The old man had to be nearing seventy if he hadn't already gotten there. His face was weathered. His teeth a hard yellow from years of smoking. Yeah, Greg was fairly certain this wasn't his opponent's first time in Atlantic City. It probably wasn't even his first time putting what amounted to over ten thousand dollars up for gamble.

If Greg folded his cards, he would still leave the table up several thousand dollars. If he called and lost, he would lose both his stake and his day's earnings. How many hours of play time was it? Ten? Twelve? He'd lost track at some point, but it sure would be a shame to have wasted all that time for nothing.

If he called and won then the world was his. At least for a moment.

Greg reached for his glass and took a shot of the subpar Scotch the casino provided. At one time in his degenerate life he would have insisted on only the best. Given his faithful patronage, the managers would have seen to it immediately. Plus they would have comped him a room and a meal, as well. Back in his Vegas days.

Before they'd figured out who he was. Before they'd ejected him.

Now AC was his last remaining haunting ground. The Grande was the last casino he could still play in. Once it ended for him here—and it would end because it always did—he would have to find Native American reservations nearby or private high-stake games.

Pathetic.

"Well? Are we doing this?"

His opponent was getting impatient. The man had asked the question with a laconic ease. Not a tremor in his voice. Not a measure of fidgeting in his body to give away his thoughts. No, he'd done a good job controlling his body language.

It was a shame he'd never really had a chance. Not against Greg.

Because Greg didn't fold and walk away. Greg didn't call and lose ever. Greg only ever called and won because Greg knew the outcome of the game before he placed the bet.

The man was bluffing.

"Call."

Then it happened. The man's lip twitched, his nostrils flared. He turned over one ace, which paired the turn, giving him a pair. His other card was a valueless ten.

Greg turned over his pocket jacks which wouldn't have won had there not been another jack on the board. Trips beat a pair every time.

The dealer acknowledged the cards, pushed the chips toward Greg and there it was. That feeling of satisfaction.

It didn't come from winning. Or from the money. It came from knowing that he'd been right. Again. That was his only thrill. That was what kept him coming back, day after day.

Tired of sitting and playing, Greg figured he'd had enough for one day. He piled his chips into a plastic holder. "Nice hand," he offered his opponent, but the man only sneered at him.

He cashed in his chips and bundled the large bills into a roll he shoved into an inside pocket in his leather coat. He left the poker room, found the elevator to the parking garage and as he traveled up to the second level he wondered what time of day it was.

What time had he started? In the morning but not so early. It had to be night. Not that it mattered. He'd go home, shower, maybe sleep for a few hours and then do it all over again. Whether he did that during the day or at night wasn't a concern.

It was quite a ritual he'd carved out. He'd make the drive from Philadelphia to AC. Find a table of players. Then read them until he could tell when each one was lying. In poker once you knew someone was bluffing—really knew it—all you had to do was wait for the cards to fall your way and then take them.

He wouldn't call it cheating. Poker was a game of skill after all. If a person could defeat Greg's particular lie-detecting skills, then Greg would lose. So far that hadn't happened.

What a freaking awesome life he had.

Greg put his head down and hunched his shoulders slightly to diminish his height as he made his way to his car. AC wasn't a safe city but the casinos prided themselves on keeping the criminal element out of their rooms and garages. As long as you didn't venture out onto the streets or to the dodgy end of the boardwalk you were as safe as you would be in any major city.

Still, a man with over ten thousand dollars in cash in his pocket couldn't be too careful and anything he could do to keep from standing out was smart. Despite keeping his head down, though, he kept his ears open. It's why he heard the clicking sound of shoes hitting cement and felt the hair on the back of his neck rise before someone called his name.

"Mr. Chalmers? A word with you please."

Greg pulled out his keys and hit the lock button.

Two rows up he could see his car lights flash on. He drove a black Porsche 911 because a man had to do something with all his winnings. Sadly he knew he wasn't going to make it to the car. Two rows away was probably one row too far.

The clicking shoes sped up and in an instant two men were standing between him and his escape. Two very large men with thick necks and beefy hands. He'd met their type before. At the Bellagio and the Wynn in Vegas.

At the Borgata in AC and the Golden Nugget just last week.

"Guys, it's been a long day. I just want to go home."

Thick Neck number one stepped forward. He had a short forehead, buzzed hair and a nose that had been previously broken. He wore a black suit and a tie that looked as if it struggled to maintain its hold on his bulging neck.

"Sir, my name is Victor Lario, I run the security for this establishment. It's come to my attention you had a pretty good night tonight."

"Yep. Great night. Great service. Love the buffet. I'll be back." Greg tried to step around him, but both men repositioned themselves to block his path.

"Sir, it's our understanding that you have a good night every night you are here. Never down. Always up."

Greg sighed, falling back on a familiar answer to

explain his success. "It's poker, not blackjack. I play the people and I win."

"Yeah. It's poker. That's what I thought, too. I thought maybe you were one of those World Tour guys, you know. So I looked you up."

Ah yes, Greg thought. 'Twas the price of needing a casino complimentary card for the extra perks, like free access to the all-you-can-eat buffet. He'd been required to provide identification. When he'd handed over his ID he'd felt that moment of panic, but the girl issuing him the card hadn't been inspired to do any kind of background check. Probably because Greg looked more like a psychologist in his sweater and jeans and less like a professional gambler.

When she'd handed him back his license a few days ago with the card and a wish for good luck, he told himself this time would be different. He'd promised himself this time he would keep his head low. This time he would spread out his visits to not attract attention.

He'd failed. Just like he had the last time. And the time before that.

"Seems Vegas kicked you out of every casino on the strip not even a year ago. Then I checked with a buddy of mine at the Borgata and you're not wanted there, either."

"I know. You can't imagine the complex it's giving me being so unwanted."

The two men stepped forward in the ominous way

thugs have of silently delivering the message that they didn't appreciate sarcasm.

Greg held up his hands. "If I agree to go peacefully and never come back, can we end this now?"

Victor cracked his knuckles. So cliché, Greg wanted to tell him.

"I'm afraid that's not going to be possible, Mr. Chalmers. It's important you understand how seriously we deal with the matter of cheating at our establishment."

"It's not cheating."

It was the last thing he was capable of saying as Victor drove his beefy hand into his midsection.

This, Greg decided, was not going to end well.

CHAPTER ONE

"WE DIDN'T KNOW WHO ELSE to call. We've never seen anything like this before. We saw your name in the paper regarding a case you worked on with the Philadelphia P.D. We figured maybe you could help us, so we reached out to Ben Tyler."

Greg was standing in the lobby of what was the Brigantine Police Department thinking he was less than fifteen minutes away from Atlantic City. So close he could smell the salt in the air from the ocean. A cold sweat broke out on his brow and he considered how lucky he was that no one would notice with almost 90 percent humidity in the air.

The Jersey Shore, even in the waning days of summer, was no joke.

"How do you know Ben Tyler?"

The sheriff shrugged. "Everyone in law enforcement around here knows Tyler. He has resources that can be helpful for any number of cases. Also we recently worked with a former colleague of his on a cold case, Mark Sharpe. You know him, too?"

"Sad to say I do."

Ben Tyler was the head of the Tyler Group, a

troubleshooting organization that pulled together some of the best minds in many different areas, including political strategy, criminal investigation, law, computer technology and well…him.

Tyler was Greg's boss, for lack of a better word. Ben offered him various different jobs and Greg had the option of which ones he wanted to take. Which were all of them because they paid his bills. As for Mark, Ben's former colleague in the CIA, Greg tried to avoid him as much as possible, which wasn't easy because Mark and Ben seemed to be actual friends now.

Anytime the two of them were together, Mark would ask Greg to play poker with him because he wanted to see if he could bluff him. Nobody could bluff Greg. It was why the police had called him.

"Greg, are we doing this or what?"

Greg turned and found his roommate, Chuck, the man he credited with keeping him gambling sober for the past year, leaning over the lobby's counter trying to flirt with the young woman seated behind it. He was pointing to things on her computer, no doubt trying to enlighten her on more efficient ways to use the equipment.

Greg had told him dumping computer knowledge on women wasn't the best way to impress the ladies, but it was the only game Chuck had. Greg had to admit it actually worked sometimes. Lately, Chuck had had his fair share of female company.

Apparently computer nerd was the new hot.

Greg had asked his roommate to come along for the ride so that, in case his willpower faltered, someone would be there to back him up. He wasn't sure if Chuck's impatience had to do with the girl's lack of interest or if he was concerned on Greg's behalf.

Even Ben admitted he had hesitated before calling Greg for this particular job. He'd mentioned the case. Mentioned the location. Mentioned his concerns. Then asked, actually asked, if Greg thought he was up for it.

Up for it?

Screw that. He hadn't gambled in over a year. He could freaking handle a trip to the beach even if it was one town over from AC. He'd snarled at Ben and told him yes he could handle it. Then he'd hung up the phone and told Chuck to put on some real pants. Chuck preferred spending his days in their waterfront loft that overlooked Penn's Landing in clothes he referred to as his comfy-womfies. His assertion: a man who spent his life mostly on his ass in a chair in front of a computer needed to be comfortable. So pajamas, sweats and the occasional stretchy pants he referred to as men's yoga pants, were the norm. Some of them actually had small animals on them.

Since Greg refused to be seen out in public with him like that, anytime they went anywhere together he forced Chuck to wear jeans. While Chuck insisted they pinched—although at five foot six and barely a hundred and fifty pounds, Greg didn't know what the jeans were pinching—he usually agreed to put them on. Greg also tried to tell him that women didn't have sex with men who wore comfy-womfies in public.

"Can I see her?"

The sheriff nodded and escorted the two men back through a room that hosted a bunch of cubicles. They reached a door that led to a short hallway that ended in another door. No elaborate two-way mirror for a small town sheriff's office. Just a window that looked into a small room furnished with a stark wood table and two folding chairs.

The interrogation room.

Sheriff Danielson pointed to the door and Greg walked over and stooped a little to look through the window.

She was sitting in a chair, her shoulders slumped, her eyes dull, her demeanor defeated. Long, nearly white blond hair almost touched the table in front of her. Despite her posture, Greg could determine she was young, maybe late twenties early thirties, and slim in a charcoal-gray short-sleeved dress.

She might have been really pretty had it not been for all the blood.

"Okay, tell me the situation again. Ben gave me the details you told him, but I would like to hear them from you directly."

The sheriff nodded. "Officer Hampton was out on his normal patrol. He spotted her walking along the highway in the early morning. As he approached her he could see she was covered with blood. He pulled over, assessed that she wasn't injured, but when he asked for identification she couldn't provide it. When he asked her name, she said she didn't know it. When he asked her what happened—"

"She couldn't remember it," Chuck said, finishing the sentence for the sheriff. "Cool."

Greg gave him a severe look. "You want to wait outside?"

"I'm bored."

"Play a game on your phone. I'm working."

"Fine. I'll stay here and be quiet. But no more than an hour. You need to be in and out. You follow?"

"Yes, Mom." Chuck was like a mother hen. And he'd brought him along for exactly that reason. Despite the fact that his roommate was younger than him by seven years, he had a way of grounding Greg that was beneficial to Greg's continued gambling sobriety. He was almost like a sponsor, except as far as Greg knew, the only thing Chuck had ever been addicted to was hitting on women.

"You want me to talk to her and tell you if she's lying."

"It's a start. I don't really have any grounds to hold her on. She wasn't carrying a weapon. There is no crime that we know of, except someone is walking around without a lot of blood. For all we know that might be a deer she hit with her car. If you tell me she's lying, I'm going to come up with something to hold her for at least another twenty-four hours. Otherwise I don't know what I'm going to do with her."

"The hospital would be a good start."

"But she's not hurt."

"Sheriff, if her brain is not working, she's hurt."

He seemed to consider that. "True. Man, you don't think this is one of those bumps to the head that caused this?"

"Since bumps to the head that leave the victim this physically functional rarely cause memory loss, I'm going to say no."

"Maybe we should hit her on the head again and see if her memory comes back. You know like… what was that show? Was that *The Brady Bunch?*" Chuck asked.

"Gilligan's Island," Greg corrected. "And that idea is as ridiculous now as it was on the show. But thank you for your insightfulness."

"Dude, she's got amnesia. That's totally cray-cray."

"Chuck. You're almost thirty. It's time you stop talking like a teenager. It's only crazy if she's telling the truth. Which she most likely isn't. Sheriff, I don't know how much you know about memory loss…"

"Nothing. Which is why I called you here."

"It's highly unlikely. True memory loss like you're describing is usually associated with a traumatic brain injury. As I said, if she'd suffered such an injury it's unlikely she'd be upright and walking along a highway. Hysterical amnesia, which could be caused by a traumatic event, is most likely what she's trying to emulate. However, in most cases this form of amnesia is temporary and only affects one's memory of a particular period surrounding the traumatic event and not a person's whole life. Like a rape victim who forgets the attack, or a child who suppresses abuse."

"You think she's faking it?"

"Until I talk to her I can't be sure of course, but my guess is most likely. Which, if she's covered in blood, means it's a good bet she's hiding a violent crime and you should consider holding her."

"Hiding a crime by walking down a highway on a Sunday morning in a bloody dress? That's not exactly covert."

"She could already be strategizing a defense."

"Dude, you are so cynical," Chuck noted. "Sheriff, please understand my friend here doesn't believe anyone, ever."

Greg considered the veracity of that statement. Chuck wasn't exactly wrong. "Only because I know they are lying. Okay, let me talk to her. We'll see how good of a show she can put on for me."

"Will it matter?" the sheriff wondered.

Greg shook his head. "Nope. Pathological liar or a great actress. None of it will fool me."

THE DOOR OPENED AND SHE looked up. Another face. A man, a tall man with a kind face and dark curly hair that was too long and a bit ruffled. He wasn't wearing a uniform.

"Who are you?"

"My name is Greg Chalmers and I would like to talk to you, if that's okay."

No, it wasn't okay. He was going to ask her questions. Questions she didn't know the answer to. She closed her eyes and tried to breathe. She knew slow deep breathing was supposed to help. It was supposed to calm her.

She didn't know how she knew it. She just did.

He sat down, or more accurately folded himself into the chair across the table. She could see that his smile, while gentle, was wholly insincere. She didn't blame him for that. She was as skeptical as he was. This wasn't happening to her. This wasn't possible.

She couldn't even look down at herself because the bloodstains were still there and they were starting to make her nauseous. They'd given her a washcloth to clean her hands and her face, but the smell was still there. Also that hint of metallic flavor on her tongue as if some had gotten in her mouth. No matter how many glasses of water she consumed, it was still here.

Maybe that was what she was. A vampire. A hysterical idea, except it wasn't any crazier than what she actually was. A woman with no memory.

"Don't," she muttered before he could start. "I don't know what you want me to say."

"I want to ask you some questions."

"I know. I know this is a police station. I know this is blood on my dress. I know this. I don't...I can't... It's like...I can't even explain it."

"What's the first thing you remember?"

She closed her eyes. "The sound of the siren. I heard a siren and I thought to move out of the way. Then I realized I wasn't in a car. I was walking. I stopped and the officer got out of his car and approached me."

"He asked you for identification."

"I didn't have my purse."

"Normally you do, though?"

"Of course. I carry a purse. I can't ever find my keys in it. It's big. I have a big purse and the keys are always at the bottom. I know that. I know that's true."

She couldn't see the purse in her head. She could only recall the sensation of digging in it with her hands. The jingling sound of keys. She struggled to latch on to that. Willed herself to see something, any picture in her mind of her purse or her wallet and where they might be. But there was nothing. Just this small room and this man with the eyes that didn't match his face. They were brown, but they weren't nice. Not like his smile or his casual attire or the way his body relaxed into the chair. It all suggested he was a laid-back person. A nice guy.

But his eyes weren't nice. They were…cold.

She started hyperventilating.

"Hey, calm down. Deep breaths."

She nodded. She felt like that phrase had been her mantra at one point. "Deep breaths," she repeated. "Deep breaths." She tried to take one after each time she said it. Her lungs slowed.

"Okay. That's better. Now can you remember anything else? Any detail. Like your big purse or maybe a favorite place. Any small detail might help us find out who you are."

She looked at him then. At his eyes that were pinned on her face and then moved to her hands, then back to her eyes.

"You don't believe me." She couldn't say how she knew, but she did. It was as if he didn't care about the answer she gave, only how she said it. "You think I'm a liar."

"No. I'm only trying to help you."

She shook her head. There was no help in this room. The officer wanted to help her. When he found her on the side of the road he was worried she was hurt. Worried she was in pain. She knew what it felt like to have someone want to help her.

"You're lying."

He shifted then as his lean body worked to find

a more comfortable position in the chair. "Why do you think so?"

"Because your eyes are…mean. I'm sorry if that's harsh. But you're sitting there like you're relaxed, but your eyes don't match. They're almost cruel. So I think you're lying. You think I know who I am. What happened."

After a moment, he shrugged. "Yeah, I do. I think amnesia is very rare, especially to the extent you're claiming."

Amnesia. It was a ridiculous word. A word from daytime TV and silly sitcoms. Bad fiction books.

It wasn't real. It couldn't really be happening to her. "I agree with you. That isn't possible." This was just a temporary lapse. A crazy event that would be reversed in a minute when her life and her name and this morning came back to her.

"Then tell me what your name is."

He said it so gently. As if he was helping her to say the thing she really wanted to say. And she really did want to say it.

My name is…

My name is… And I'm from…

My name is…

She closed her eyes and pushed her brain to function. She did math in her head. Odd numbers she added together easily. Multiplication tables. Eights. Nines. Twelves. She knew that without effort. She thought of books. She knew who Harry Potter was.

He was a wizard. With friends. The books were about magic.

Movies. *The Sound of Music*. When Maria finally kisses the captain. She knew that was her favorite scene.

My name is...I like The Sound of Music *and Harry Potter.*

She met the man's eyes, the scary ones, and shook her head.

"I don't know it. I don't know my name. Please help me. Please, please help me."

GREG SHUT THE DOOR BEHIND him carefully, silently. The sheriff's eyebrows were almost off his head waiting for his assessment.

"Well?"

"Yeah, what's the word, Cruel Eyes? That's totally your new nickname, by the way."

Chuck was laughing at his own joke, but Greg didn't think it was funny. *Mean* and *cruel*. He'd never had those words associated with him before. He'd spent his life making people comfortable with him, getting them to open up to him. He'd been a support and comfort to people for years when he'd been a psychologist.

Only he wasn't a psychologist anymore. Now he was a cynic. A cruel one, apparently.

"I don't know."

"What? I thought you were an expert in this stuff," the sheriff complained.

Chuck snorted. "Come on. You know she's lying. You said it."

"No, I only think she's lying. And that's based on the statistical improbability of her condition. However, physically she showed no signs of it."

Chuck let out a whistle. "But that's almost impossible to do, isn't it?"

"It is. Unless she's a sociopath or so completely delusional she doesn't believe she's lying. Which is, statistically speaking, also unlikely."

"Buddy, I don't care about the damn statistics. Does this girl not know her name or what?"

Greg turned and looked through the window again. She was still sitting the same way. Only, if anything, she looked even more defeated. Because when she'd asked him to help her, he'd gotten up and left her instead.

He didn't help people anymore. Except the need, the physical need, to spend more time with this woman, to dig deeper into her brain, was almost as strong as the pull of the casinos not fifteen minutes down the road.

In fact it was stronger.

Did she know her name? Could she have done something no one else had succeeded in doing before? Fabrication was easy. Controlling a physiological response to it was not.

"What's your gut say?"

Greg turned to the sheriff, struggling a little to take his eyes from the woman on the other side of the window. It wasn't conceivable. It wasn't likely. But he couldn't ignore the evidence because he didn't like it. Because it didn't fit with what he expected.

Instinct, intuition. Greg hated these words. While psychology was a difficult science it was still a science. Greg relied on it and the body's physical response to stimulus. Based on the data, he could only come to one conclusion.

"She could be telling the truth."

CHAPTER TWO

"TELL ME AGAIN WHY WE did this."

Greg and Chuck sat outside the treatment room in the only hospital in Brigantine. A small facility, it mostly responded to severe sunburns, stomach irritations from too much cotton candy and the unexpected illness or accident that happened while families were on vacation. Brain trauma was no doubt outside their specialty but Greg thought their mystery woman should at least be looked at by a physician. Just because she was speaking with ease and moving without restriction didn't mean there couldn't be the possibility of some type of brain event. He'd volunteered to take her and the sheriff gratefully allowed it.

The truth was the small-town sheriff had no idea what to do with the woman. Especially given no crime had been reported that he knew of. Even though they couldn't charge her with anything, she did volunteer to have her fingerprints taken, if only for the hope of identification. If she was a teacher she would be in the system.

Or if she was a criminal.

She also agreed to let them cut a small piece of her bloodstained dress. That way she could leave wearing it, and if the police needed to they could get a blood type and DNA from the cloth. Greg thought a lawyer might object, but she had willingly agreed to whatever the sheriff wanted.

As if it didn't occur to her that she might be guilty of anything.

"It's a Sunday. We've got nothing else to do," Greg said in response to Chuck's question.

"Dude, speak for yourself. I could be working. Programming my next app. Making my next million."

"The world does not need another 'Shoot the Squirrel' update."

"That's the point of apps. You don't *need* them. In my next version I was thinking of making the squirrels rabid. So if you don't shoot them in time, they attack with foam coming out of their mouths."

"Awesome. Please let me pay ninety-nine cents for foam-mouthed squirrels."

"Don't hate the programmer, hate the game."

"It's the nice thing to do," Greg said trying to convince himself there was nothing more going on between him and this woman than a chivalrous act. It wasn't as if he was trying to save her or anything. Just maybe…help her. A little. Which he didn't really do anymore, but he was making an exception for her.

Why her?

Annoyed with himself, Greg stood. "She's lost, helpless. You're never going to get anywhere with women if you don't recognize that when the needy, helpless ones come along, you have to step up your game."

"Hey, I get everywhere with women. I have no problem with you stepping up and playing knight to this damsel in distress. If you think she's really in distress."

"She might be," Greg said ambiguously.

"See, that's my point. You are never on the fence. Why are you now?"

"Because hysterical amnesia is really hard to accept, but her body wasn't conveying the tells normally associated with someone lying."

"Do you hear yourself? You sound like a politician."

Exactly. He wasn't willing to commit to an answer. He didn't want to say she was telling the truth only to look ridiculous for having bought into such an incredulous story. However, he couldn't say she was lying when he didn't see any evidence of it.

He suddenly had a new appreciation for politicians. Saying something without saying anything wasn't easy.

Chuck was staring at him. Greg could feel it, but he didn't want to acknowledge it. His roommate's hazel eyes were like beacons of suspicion.

"You've got the hots for her."

Greg closed his eyes. "Why does it always come down to sex with you?"

"Because I'm a man. Hey, I get it. She's smokin'. Or would be if she wasn't rocking the Carrie look, but seriously, man, do you really want to go there with a babe who has issues like she does?"

"You are ridiculous," Greg stated unequivocally. "I refuse to comment further."

It was at that point that *she*—because they had no other name for her—emerged from a hallway and walked over to them. She gave a little wave as if she appreciated that they'd waited for her. As if they were her friends. Which, considering that the number of people she knew in the world had been reduced to the officer who found her, the sheriff who questioned her and them, wasn't all that wrong.

Greg met her halfway. "Well?"

"They took a CAT scan but didn't find any evidence of a bleed. No bumps, either," she said pointing to her temple. "And they gave me a concussion test, you know, look up, look down, that kind of thing. The doctor seemed to think I was fine physically. I didn't know which day of the week it was, but I know who is president. Which is weird."

Greg nodded. So it was back to hysterical amnesia, most likely brought on by an event. Given that she was rocking the "Carrie look," as Chuck had previously pointed out, the odds were it had been a fairly traumatic event.

"Did he have any suggestions?"

"There is a specialist at Thomas Jefferson he wants me to see. He said he would call and see if he could get me an appointment tomorrow. It's a hospital in Philadelphia…."

Her voice trailed off and Greg could see the panic start to take over as the ramifications of what she was saying sunk in. She had no car, no money, no identification. She had no way of getting herself to Philadelphia without hitchhiking.

She didn't even have a change of clothes. Or a way to clean the ones she had.

"We'll take you." The words were out of his mouth even as her breaths grew faster and shorter.

She looked at him. "Why would you do that? You don't know me."

"I can't wait to hear this," Chuck said coming up behind him.

"Being a good citizen isn't enough?"

Her suspicion was evident. What was less obvious was the bone-deep fear she was trying to keep at bay, but Greg could see it. "I think I should go back to the police. If they find something out about me…"

"Listen, the sheriff doesn't have any place to hold you unless it's in a cell. They already took your prints to run them through the database. If anything hits they will let me know. You trusted us enough to get in a car with us to take you to the hospital. If we were going to hurt you we could have done it then.

You need a free place to stay, a shower, a change of clothes and a meal."

"And you're going to give me all that? For no reason?"

"Not for no reason. I can't fully establish if you're lying or not. If you are, then you're doing so because you committed a crime and you should be watched by someone. If you're not, then you're a fascinating case I would like to explore some more."

"I'll bet." Chuck snorted.

Greg slapped him upside the head.

She looked between the two men. "You're asking me to trust you when you don't trust I'm telling the truth. That doesn't make sense. To go back to your place with you..."

"Both of us," Chuck interrupted. "We live together."

Her lips firmed and she shook her head. "I forgot my name. It doesn't make me an idiot. Going to your home is different than getting in a car when the sheriff knew I was with you."

"I'll call the sheriff again. Do you have any choice?"

"Maybe you could drive me around. Back along the highway to Atlantic City. Maybe I'll see something or remember something."

"I'm not going to Atlantic City," Greg told her. He'd pushed it enough as it was. Not that he was fighting any serious urge to gamble. She had become enough of a distraction to take his mind off that. But he was definitely feeling on edge. With her, with the situation. Even with what he was offering.

He could tell himself she was just a lost person he was trying to help out. A nice gesture. Something anyone might do for a fellow human being in need.

It was a lie. He wanted to know if she was telling the truth. He wanted to know where the blood came from. He wanted to know what type of horrible event might have overcome her to the point of erasing her mind. Her memories.

If that was the case, he wanted to cure her and he hadn't cured anyone in a really long time. Intellectually, he told himself he should resist the temptation. He didn't cure people anymore. Instinctively, he couldn't help himself.

"Do either of you know a woman you could call?"

Chuck snorted. "Babe, there are plenty of women I could call. Like on a dime. Drop of a hat. I hit some digits and bam, next thing you know my doorbell is ringing."

She looked at him skeptically, and then turned to Greg. "Someone you know well. Someone I could ask about what kind of people you are. I have nothing to go on but my gut here. So if I could talk to another woman, have her tell me what kind of men you are, then it would ease my mind."

Chuck was shaking his head but Greg nodded. He took out his cell and went to his favorites page.

Mark's wife, JoJo, was his first choice. While Mark might be a thorn in his side, his wife had become one of Greg's favorite people. He hit her number and waited.

"Yo, what's up?" she answered.

"You in the middle of something?"

"No, Mark and Sophie and I were about to put on a movie and gorge ourselves on popcorn. Why?"

"Who is that?"

Greg could hear Mark asking in the background.

"Tell him it's your lover," Greg said wanting to do anything that might push Mark's buttons.

"You want to get shot? You do remember he's former CIA."

Greg knew. It was a risk he was willing to take. "Tell him anyway."

"I will not. I like you too much," she teased.

"Listen, I have someone here. A woman. She's in trouble and I've offered to help her out. But she obviously doesn't know me or trust me. She would like to talk to someone I know."

"Oh, this sounds promising. Put her on."

Greg handed over his cell phone. "Her name is JoJo. She and her husband are people I've worked with."

She took the phone and said hello. "Mostly I want to know if I can trust him and his friend Chuck."

It sounded to him as if JoJo was doing a lot of explaining. He could hear her talking on the other end of the phone but couldn't distinguish exactly what she was saying. Greg figured it would be a yes-or-no answer, but apparently JoJo felt she had to say more.

"And his friend Chuck?"

Greg watched her frown and could only imagine JoJo's take on Chuck. They had a met a few times through different events at Ben's house. No doubt Chuck would have introduced himself by hitting on JoJo before realizing she was married. Hopefully, JoJo would have seen through it and concluded that Chuck was all talk and a decent guy at heart.

Which was mostly true.

Finally, she said thank-you and handed the phone back to him.

"Did you tell her what a knight in shining armor I am?" Greg asked JoJo.

He was teasing but there was a pause for a second and then he heard a small hiccup. JoJo had turned into such a sap since she and Mark had married. "Yeah. I did. Because you are. You try not to be, I know. But I'll never forget what you did for me. So yeah, I told her she could trust you."

What he did for her? A few conversations. A few walks in the park. It wasn't as if he'd given her therapy to help her overcome the tragic death of her sister and her subsequent split with her family. He didn't do therapy anymore. All he'd really done was listen.

Not long after that though, she was ready to move

on in her life with Mark. Who, beyond all reason, made her ridiculously happy. Go figure. Sometimes there was no accounting for taste.

"Thanks."

"You're going to call me or Mark tomorrow and tell us what's going on, right?"

Mark and JoJo worked as private investigators. Mostly they specialized in criminal cold cases but he imagined they would be tempted to take on something a little more current if it meant giving him a hand.

First he had to know if a crime had occurred. Second, he needed to find out who *she* was.

"I'll let you know when I know something. I promise."

Greg shoved the phone in his pocket. "Satisfied?"

She nodded. "She said I could trust you."

"And me, too," Chuck chimed in, "right?"

The woman smiled shyly. "She said you were a bullshit artist and I shouldn't believe half of what comes out of your mouth."

Chuck's jaw dropped. "I thought JoJo liked me."

"She also said beyond the bullshit was a sweet guy."

"Sweet?" Chuck groaned. "I hate being sweet!"

Greg laughed. "But you are sweet. Okay, let's ditch the hospital. I'll call the sheriff and let him know you're staying with me."

Greg started to turn but *she* reached out and grabbed his arm. "Why are you doing this? Really?"

"Really? I have no flipping idea. But it's not like I had anything better to do on a Sunday."

SHE LOOKED IN THE STEAMED-UP mirror. "Amanda. Amy. Alice. Alison."

The names triggered nothing. She tried again. "Beth. Betty. Barbara. Bonnie."

Maybe if she had one of those baby books. She could go through it alphabetically and wait until something jumped out at her. Then, once she remembered that one critical piece of information, everything else would fall into place.

She took a step back from the mirror and looked at her body. Despite her lack of memory it didn't feel foreign to her. The three oddly placed moles on her chest actually looked familiar. She touched them and drew a line between the one in the center, the one that hovered over her right breast and the one that hovered over her left. As she made the triangle, it was something she felt she'd done before.

Her very own body art.

She'd already checked for any scrapes or wounds. There was nothing she could see. Twisting around in the mirror she didn't detect any obvious marks on her back. That gave her relief. At least she wasn't the product of some type of abuse. Not a victim.

Then why did whatever happen to you take your memory? Your life?

"Excellent question," she muttered. But at least she was starting to understand the way she thought about things. She was cautious in nature. Which again felt right. Cautious women were smart women. They didn't jump feetfirst into unknown territory. They were thoughtful and patient and wise.

Even standing naked in some strange man's bathroom, she felt she'd handled the situation as best she could. She was at the mercy of human kindness with no memory, no identification and no money.

Greg Chalmers had offered to help her, but she hadn't just accepted it. She'd questioned it. She'd gotten a reference from a woman.

This made her careful. She liked the idea of being a careful person. It soothed her and gave her back a little of her control.

Glancing at the toilet, she looked at the jeans and T-shirt she had placed on the lid. Greg's clothes that he suspected would fit. The jeans had her a little worried. Yes, he was taller than she was, but he had no hips.

Staring back in the mirror, hers weren't anything to write home about, but even a woman with no hips sometimes found herself stuck in boy jeans. However, the option of putting her own clothes back on wasn't available. They were being washed, including her panties and bra. She'd never been so happy to strip out of clothes as she was when she arrived at Greg's apartment.

A knock on the door startled her. She jumped then, checked to see that she'd locked it, which she knew she had because after she'd locked it, she'd tested it twice.

"How are you doing in there?"

Greg. He sounded worried. Maybe she had spent an overly long time in the shower, but the need to feel clean, really clean, had pushed her to stay under the hot stream of water until it had run lukewarm.

"Okay."

"You must be hungry. I'm making spaghetti."

At the mention of food her stomach rumbled. "I'll be out in a minute."

"Good."

She scrambled into his jeans and gave a sigh of relief when they buttoned and zipped. Her butt was snug but that was to be expected when the owner of the jeans didn't have one of those either. The T-shirt was a thick cotton and navy blue. She tucked it in and bloused it a little to create a loose effect. Satisfied she didn't scream "here are my boobs, please look at them" she was ready to leave the safety of the bathroom. She'd already used a comb to untangle her hair and tie it up into a knot that would hold as long as it was still wet.

The two men were already in the kitchen. Greg was using prongs to dish out pasta and then handing

Chuck a big bowl of what appeared to be sauce and meatballs. A green plastic container of cheese and a basket of white square bread she was pretty sure came out of a plastic bag sat on the table amongst the dishes.

This was wrong. Dinner was not being served properly. Instinctively, she knew that.

"You know if you pour the pasta back into the pot where the gravy is cooking, it will take on some of the flavor. Then you can serve it already mixed together."

They looked at her for a moment as if she was an alien, but then Greg nodded. "That's a good idea. We'll try that next time."

She approached the table and sat down. She wanted to be grateful. She *was* grateful. The shower, the clothes, the feeling that there was a place in the world for her to be. She owed these two men everything.

But, seriously, how could they call that tasteless white stuff that Chuck was spreading an inordinate amount of butter on bread?

Greg piled some pasta on her plate and handed her the gravy. She took two big meatballs, what she imagined was a hunk of sausage, and mixed it in with her pasta. She sprinkled the cheese from the container on top of her plate, disappointed that the powdery substance didn't melt properly.

Without expressing her dismay, she ate. It didn't

matter that it was fake cheese and sauce from a jar. It was food. They were kind to be giving it to her. She would never forget this meal for as long as she lived.

Silence reigned over the table as the two men dug in. They both ate as if they were starving and, given how thin they were, maybe they were.

She looked to Greg and the thought popped out of her mouth before she could think better of it.

"You're one of those tall, lean men who can eat whatever you want, aren't you?"

He nodded around a mouthful of pasta.

"And Chuck, I bet you eat junk food all day long but never gain any weight."

He smiled as he bit into his butter-covered bread.

She smiled and stood up, leaving the napkin she'd placed on her lap on the table. "Do you have a spoon?"

Chuck's eyebrows rose. As he cut his pasta with a fork and knife, he shook his head. "What do you need a spoon for?"

"Third drawer over from the sink," Greg offered.

Taking his direction, she found the utensil she was looking for and sat down again. With precision born of practice she lifted the pasta onto the fork, braced it against the spoon and twirled it until it was a perfectly neat bite.

After a few mouthfuls, Chuck got up from his seat and also found a spoon. Greg, she noticed did not, preferring to brace the fork against the plate and spin it. She might have protested if it was china, but the everyday dishware was made of sturdy material.

You used to eat pasta off of china.

The thought was the barest whisper along her brain.

Think! When? Where? With whom?

"We need a name for you."

The question startled her out of her thoughts.

"We can't keep calling you 'hey, you.'"

She tried a faint smile. "I'm fairly certain 'you' is not my name."

"What about Jane?" Chuck proposed. "You know, like Jane Doe."

She frowned. "Jane. A little unoriginal, don't you think?"

"Would you rather be Bunny or Cherry or something?" Chuck asked.

"No. I choose not to sound like someone who made her living dancing with a pole." She stopped herself then. "That sounded really snobbish, even to my ears. I don't know why I said that."

"Maybe you know girls named Bunny and Cherry and they are strippers," Greg allowed.

"I hardly think I spend my time around strippers." She was offended. Then she realized how snobbish that had sounded, as well. For all she knew she was a stripper. Maybe it was the only way she could afford to make rent, pay for food and take care of her child.

Oh my God! Do I have a child?

"Stop with the what-ifs," Greg told her. He reached over and grabbed her hand. "Your breathing is accelerated, your pupils are dilating. You're in a mild stage of panic. Stop wondering about what you can't answer. Take five deep calming breaths and then concentrate on eating."

It was the way he said it. As though he was a doctor ordering two aspirin and a follow-up call in the morning. She did as he directed without thought and then went back to her bland pasta meal.

"For now we'll call you Jane."

Jane sighed and felt tears well up. It wasn't her name. She knew it. Instead, she worked on her breathing and forced down her tears. "It doesn't feel right."

Greg nodded, and it wasn't until then that she realized his hand was still resting warmly on top of hers. He made her feel safe, just with his touch. That was quite a gift.

"Okay. Then we know two things about you. Your name is not Jane…."

"What's the other?"

"You're the daughter of a wealthy Italian-American family."

CHAPTER THREE

HE WATCHED AS JANE SCRUNCHED her face in rejection.

"You can't possibly know that."

"You said the name didn't feel right."

"Yes, I know my name isn't Jane. It's the other part you can't know. Look at my hair." She unraveled the wet knot that was now partially dry and it dropped to nearly her waist. Long shimmering strands of blond on blond.

"Genetics is a crazy thing. I didn't say you were southern Italian, only that you came from an Italian family."

"Oh, here he goes." Chuck groaned. "He's about to Sherlock Holmes you."

"What?"

"Follow," Greg began. "You refer to the sauce as gravy, as do most Italian-Americans. You tried not to, but you winced at the bread and the container of cheese, which means you're used to finer Italian cuisine. You instructed us on how to properly prepare it, which means you have some expertise with Italian cooking. Your back isn't touching the chair and the paper napkin was spread on your lap in a manner that suggests you're used to using cloth. Also, you got yourself a spoon, which indicates you were raised in a house where manners were important. Manners are traditionally more important among upper-middle- to upper-class homes. Why I say you're wealthy is that you looked at me while I twirled my fork against my plate, and then you studied your own plate as if you were concerned for the surface. That suggests you eat on finer dinnerware, potentially china, and china for everyday eating suggests wealth."

Jane gasped.

"I know," Chuck said. "It's freaky. But he's usually right."

Greg watched her face, as she assimilated all the information he'd given her. Eventually, she nodded. "Okay. I guess that makes sense. I had the same thought about the china, too. And I hope you don't think I'm not thankful for the meal…but the white bread was a little off-putting."

"You just need to put a lot of butter on it," Chuck suggested as he reached for another slice.

"It's all just pieces, Jane. Put enough of them together and eventually they will start to paint a picture. When you see the picture it will make more sense."

She nodded and reached again for her fork and spoon.

Greg's cell phone went off and he pulled it out of

his back pocket. Only a number registered, but he recognized the area code.

"Excuse me."

He got up and walked as far away from the kitchen area as he could. The place he and Chuck inhabited was basically one large open space that comprised the kitchen and living area. Off that space were two bedrooms and a spiral staircase that led to a loft where Chuck kept all his technical equipment. By Philadelphia standards it was big and luxurious and something they never would have been able to afford without Chuck's squirrels.

Unless Greg walked into his bedroom and shut the door, there wasn't a lot of privacy for this type of conversation. He didn't want his actions to seem suspicious, but he was afraid he had no other choice. He had a fairly strong inkling who was calling.

Closing the door to his bedroom, he finally answered the phone. "Hello?"

"Chalmers? This is Sheriff Danielson. That girl still with you?"

Greg imagined Jane might take exception at the description of "girl." She might not know her birthday, but she certainly knew she was a grown woman. For that matter, so did Greg.

"Yes. She's still with me. I told you I would watch over her."

"Well, you're going to need to bring her back in for questioning. We'll need her clothes, too."

"What good is questioning her going to do if she doesn't remember any of the answers?"

"She's going to need to try harder."

Greg picked up on the ominous note in the sheriff's voice that implied he knew something. He wished the man would skip the dramatics and get to the point. This was probably the most excitement the sheriff had had in a long time. "Why is that?" Greg asked.

"There's been a reported murder. In Atlantic City. Witnesses report seeing a woman with long blond hair walking away from The Grande Casino early Sunday morning, covered in blood and wearing a gray dress. It's a pretty good bet that's our girl."

"Who was killed?"

"See, this is where it gets interesting. You ever hear of Hector D'Amato?"

Greg's stomach clenched. Sure he'd heard of Hector. The last time Greg had been in A.C. D'Amato's thugs had invited him—in a memorable way—to never come back. In one respect, he was grateful to them because that last beating put him over the edge. The pain of it had been nothing compared to the humiliation.

Besides owning and running one of the largest casinos in AC, D'Amato was rumored to be involved in drugs and prostitution. Only no criminal charges against him had ever been able to stick. D'Amato's assertion had always been that he was clean and his only crime was running a successful casino and having an Italian last name.

"Yeah, I know who he is."

"He's our victim. Found dead in the alley between his casino and the Plaza. A bullet through his skull. Lots of blood."

"You suspect our Jane Doe."

"That's the thing, she's not a Jane Doe anymore. Her name is Eliza Dunning. The witnesses who saw her walking away from the hotel knew her. She was an employee of The Grande, but the people we talked to implied there was more between her and D'Amato than that, if you get my drift."

Greg did and didn't like the feeling that came with it. A mobster's mistress? He couldn't picture it. Although, if she was present at his death—whether as a participant or a mere witness—it would be a pretty good basis for a traumatic reaction that could bring on hysterical amnesia.

If she was telling the truth.

"You've been with her all day. Do you still think she's telling the truth about not remembering anything?"

Greg thought about her reaction in the hospital. Then what she'd looked like coming out of the bathroom, clean of blood and wearing fresh clothes. He had seen relief. Because she felt like she was getting away with murder? Or because her hair was no longer coated with blood? It was hard to know.

"I can only tell you I can't detect any subterfuge. No physical signs of lying, anyway. Unfortunately, that doesn't mean she couldn't be the best liar there ever was." Good enough to fool even him.

She wouldn't be the first. Tommy, one of his former patients, held that tragic honor.

"You need to bring her back down."

"To AC?" That wasn't going to happen. Greg was never going back there. Ever. Chuck could go with her if she needed someone to take her.

"Yes. It's their case now. I let the detective know we found her and where she was staying. He's okay if you want to bring her down tomorrow. If she doesn't come willingly, he'll issue a warrant for her arrest and have the Philadelphia P.D. pick her up."

"She'll come down, though I'm not sure how useful the questioning will be."

"How useful does it have to be? She knew D'Amato. D'Amato was plugged in the face. She was covered with blood and found walking down a road twenty miles outside of Atlantic City. Seems pretty clear to me that she knows something about it."

Damn it. It did to Greg, too. "Okay. We'll have her there in the morning."

"Thanks. And, Chalmers, I would appreciate if you don't give her a heads-up about what will go down tomorrow. The ACPD deserve to be able to question her without advance warning, if you know what I mean. I can remind you, since we called you in, that you are a consultant to the police force…"

"You don't have to. I've got the message."

Greg ended the call and stared at the phone in his hand. D'Amato…really? He didn't see it. There was something in her face that was too open. Too unguarded to have survived being associated with him. Of course, that was assuming the rumors about his criminal behavior were true. To date no one had proved anything. Was she playing him? Had it all been a perfectly executed performance? A way to set up her defense when she was brought to trial? Hysterical amnesia. Greg wasn't sure how that would help if the evidence of her guilt was compelling enough. He should cut his losses now. Call the PPD, have them pick her up and hold her overnight. They could transport her to AC in the morning and the most he would have to do was give his testimony, if it even went that far.

So why was he hesitating? Simply put, he didn't think she was lying. There was nothing in her actions, words or expressions that suggested she was playing a game. No physical signs that her amnesia was anything but real.

If he was being played, then it was because she was a master. And if he was being played by a master, he intended to beat her at her own game. Greg had been wrong once, but since then he'd rededicated himself to perfection.

But if he wasn't being played, then the woman who just taught Chuck how to eat pasta with a spoon might need his help.

He wasn't sure what was worse. Keeping her with him so he could study her, or keeping her with him because he wanted to be some kind of hero. Greg didn't do hero. Not anymore.

Speaking of heroes, an antihero type came to mind. Someone who might be able to unravel the mystery of Eliza Dunning's past. Interesting that Dunning wasn't an Italian name after his original assumptions about her and her presumed connection to D'Amato. Of course it would be stereotypical to assume that anyone affiliated with the mob had to be of Italian heritage. The organization was so much more inclusive these days. All they cared about now was having hardened criminals willing to do bad things. Greg knew enough about D'Amato to know even he wasn't fully Italian. His mother had been Puerto Rican.

Greg hit his contact list and tapped a name. He waited until Mark answered.

"Yo."

"I need a favor."

"Awesome. I've been waiting for this moment."

"Why?"

"Ever since you helped JoJo deal with her past I feel like I've owed you. I hate owing people."

"Wouldn't it be JoJo who owes me since she was the one I helped?"

"She already paid you back today by vouching for your character. Which, had I known, I would have advised her against, if only to make it more difficult for you. I can only assume you're calling about the same woman? We've been waiting to hear this story. Anyway, JoJo's debt is my debt, too. It's a married kind of a thing you wouldn't understand."

"Oh, really. And you've been married for what, three weeks?"

"Three amazing weeks…hey, is that it? Are you ready to follow in my footsteps? Do you need me to do a background check on your Match.com date?"

"I so wish I had called JoJo right now."

"She would have told me, anyway. Fess up. What's going on?"

"I need you to find anything you can about an Eliza Dunning and Hector D'Amato."

"I know D'Amato by reputation. He owns The Grande in Atlantic City. Rumors are he's connected."

"Was connected. He's dead."

"Holy shit. Are you telling me the woman staying with you is involved?"

"Up to her eyeballs. Eliza Dunning. Everything you can find out about her, her past and any connection she had to D'Amato, as fast as you can get it to me."

"Do I need to be worried about you and Chuck being alone with a woman who may potentially be dangerous?"

"Do you really think Chuck and I can't handle a woman?"

"Is she hot?"

Freaking Mark. He should have called JoJo.

"Your hesitation assures me she is. Which means that Chuck definitely can't handle her. You, maybe not, depending on how much she needs you. Does she need you, Greg? Because you strike me as the type to be helpless against a woman in need."

Greg had to swallow his first answer for something less inflammatory.

"It doesn't matter if she does or not," Greg said, trying to sound blasé when he felt anything but. "I'm not in the business of helping people anymore, remember? Hardened cynic, lie detector. That's all I'm good for these days."

"Yeah, I wish I could believe that—I would be less worried about you and the damsel in distress. I'll get to work. I trust you and Chuck can hold it together for...how long?"

"She has to go in for questioning tomorrow. ACPD wants to talk to her."

"You going with her?"

"Probably not." Definitely not. But he didn't want

Mark to know that the idea of returning to Atlantic City sent him into a near panic.

"Do you care enough to make sure she has a lawyer?"

Greg winced. "Hell, I would care enough about you having a lawyer if you were going to be questioned by the ACPD. They're not exactly warm and fuzzy with murder suspects down there."

"Can you blame them?" Mark asked. "How would you like to be a cop in a city of vice? You should call Elaine." Mark disconnected the call and Greg considered his advice. He was already there.

Elaine was going to be his next call. Elaine Saunders worked for the Tyler Group on a contractual basis, helping out when Ben needed legal assistance. However, she also ran an independent practice for criminal cases. With the money she made working for Ben, she could afford to take only the cases that struck her fancy.

Elaine was a crusader who believed more in fighting for justice for the innocent, than making sure the guilty had access to legal representation. If she looked at this case on the surface, he couldn't see her jumping on it. The amnesia would make her skeptical.

That was the problem with amnesia. It was an easy thing to lie about, because it couldn't be medically determined, so no one ever believed it was real.

Greg attributed it to the fact that at some point in everyone's life they had consumed too much alcohol, done something stupid and then lied about remembering it when questioned. Hell, he'd spent four years in college avoiding girls who wanted more than one-night stands with his patented, "Oh wow, did we hook up last night? I totally blacked out."

Which made him an ass back then, but he certainly wasn't alone in the crime of faking a blackout.

Amnesia, however, was slightly more complicated to pull off than a blackout. Greg telling Elaine he didn't see any physical signs that Eliza was lying might intrigue her. That he was going to ask her to take on the case as a personal favor would seal the deal.

The people who worked for the Tyler Group were an eclectic bunch. Together they had lots of talent in lots of different areas. But they all had one thing in common. At some point in each of their lives they had fallen on hard times and Ben, the leader of their group, had been there to pick them up. It created a bond among them. They all knew where they had been and how hard they had worked to crawl back up from the bottom.

Greg hit his contact list again and found Elaine's name. After a few rings her voicemail came on. After the beep he gave a brief synopsis of the situation and asked about her schedule for tomorrow. He finished with a request to call him back as soon as possible, but given that it was Sunday night he wouldn't blame her if he didn't hear from her until morning.

The ACPD was going to have to wait then. Eliza wasn't going anywhere without Elaine by her side.

Chuck wasn't going to be pleased about it, either. Elaine might possibly be the one woman on the planet Chuck didn't have on his list to seduce. At least not anymore.

A couple of months ago Greg had consulted on a case for Elaine. She'd come by to review notes with him and Chuck had made some feeble attempts at hitting on her, until she put him firmly in his place. Greg remembered being amused by their interaction. Then something happened. Chuck did the completely unpredictable thing and started treating her as a person he wanted to get to know, not someone he wanted to have sex with and forget about.

Greg knew that Chuck didn't believe he could wow a woman physically, but he did believe he could wow women with his mental prowess. The come-ons, the one-liners, were designed to showcase his cleverness.

With Elaine he'd been different though. With Elaine he'd been…himself. Greg thought they made a good match.

Then one night, Chuck came back to their place drunk. Greg knew he'd planned to meet Elaine that night but when he asked about her, Chuck had nearly bitten his head off. He'd been mad at the world and had refused to talk about it. Since then, Chuck and Elaine had been at each other's throats.

Greg had tried to find out later what happened, as Elaine was someone who Greg needed to work with occasionally. But for someone who typically held nothing back, Chuck was surprisingly closemouthed about whatever had gone down between them.

He would have to get over it. Elaine was the best and Greg needed her.

He walked out of his bedroom to find Chuck and Eliza—no, Jane. He needed to think of her as Jane, at least for tonight. The two of them were washing dishes at the sink. Jane washing, Chuck drying. Jane laughing, Chuck flirting.

A piece of aluminum foil had been placed on top of Greg's plate to keep it warm. Since he doubted Chuck even knew they had aluminum foil in the pantry, Greg knew who had put it there.

"Hey, sorry about that. Another contract I'm working on."

Jane turned around and smiled. Her long hair, now dry, shifted along her shoulders when she moved. It was pretty the way it did that. "I hope it's okay that we went ahead and ate without you. Chuck didn't want to wait and I didn't want him to eat alone. I can sit with you, though, if you'd like. Chuck says there's ice cream."

"There will be ice cream," Chuck corrected her. "I'm going to run out and get some."

"You're going out to get ice cream? It's after eight on a Sunday. Really?"

Chuck shrugged, evading Greg's eyes. "What? I'll find someplace open. A man needs ice cream every once in a while. You said you liked chocolate, right?"

"I think so," Jane answered. "It sort of hit me that chocolate ice cream would be amazing. But you should get whatever you want."

"No, no. Chocolate is my favorite, too."

"What a coincidence," Greg drawled.

Chuck didn't bother to respond and darted out of the apartment like he was on a mission for the government. Greg sat down to finish his dinner, peeling back the foil and watching as the steam rose up into his face. It was a nice thing to do, keep his dinner warm. Something a mobster's mistress would have done? Did mobsters have nice mistresses?

"I hope Chuck isn't pestering you. He's really fairly harmless."

"I like him," she said, sitting at the table, her hands wrapped around a damp dishcloth. "He's so…open. Out there. You know what I mean."

Out there was a pretty good way to describe him.

"I don't think I'm like that."

Greg pinned her with his gaze. "You remember something?"

"No. It's just, when Chuck was talking and making all these silly memory jokes, I had a sense that I wished I could be more like him. More open with people. Which made me think I'm not."

Her expression grew serious as she turned her thoughts inward. She looked exactly like a woman trying hard to recall something. As if she could squint out the memory through her eyeballs.

"Then you got a craving for chocolate ice cream," he said trying to distract her.

"I did." She smiled. "It sounded like a good idea."

"I'm sure it will be. No doubt Chuck will scour the land to find you the finest chocolate ice cream there is. Besides being out there, he's also been known to go over the top."

She smiled again and it did funny things to him. Made *him* feel guilty for lying to *her*. Which was ridiculous.

"You'll take me to the doctor's tomorrow, then?"

"I will." Maybe. If there was time, after Chuck took her to Atlantic City. If she wasn't in jail by then.

"I'm really hoping I'll go to sleep tonight and tomorrow I'll wake up and this will all be over. Like it will all come back to me in the night."

"It might."

He could see that she hoped he was right and another dagger shot to his heart. She seemed so damn sincere. Clear pale blue eyes on pale skin with pale hair. She could have been a damned fairy princess.

Instead she was D'Amato's piece.

"Look, you're probably exhausted."

"I am. But Chuck went to get the ice cream…."

"My understanding is that it comes frozen and will last until tomorrow. Listen, why don't you take my bedroom. I changed the sheets while you were in the shower. If you're right and all you need is a good night's sleep, you won't get that on the couch. Too soft."

"Oh, I couldn't take your bed. The couch is fine."

"No, this way is better. It will be quieter, too. You really need to rest."

She looked at him, assessing him as she had at the hospital earlier that day. He could actually see her coming to a conclusion.

"Your friend was right. Your woman friend. You're a good person, Greg." She put her hand on his forearm and squeezed for a second. Then she got up and made her way back to his bedroom, softly closing the door behind her.

"No, Eliza," he said quietly to an empty room. "I'm not."

CHAPTER FOUR

"Wake up! Please, Greg. Wake up!"

He was sprawled on a couch she could see was too small for him. He had one arm flung over his eyes and a blanket that covered him only from chest to thighs. His feet were naked and for some reason she found it disturbingly intimate.

He was twisting now, moaning, and the forces of sleep fought against her relentless attack.

"Please wake up." She hated the desperation in her voice. Hated the panic that was threatening to overwhelm her, but she had to leave this place. She had to find out where she came from.

Finally he lowered his arm and blinked open his eyes. After taking a moment to understand that he was on the couch and a strange woman was standing over him shaking his arm, recognition dawned on his face.

Along with suspicion.

"What's the matter?"

"We have to leave. You have to help me look for where I live. I think New Jersey makes more sense. The city doesn't feel right. It's too noisy. I think if I lived in Philadelphia I would be used to the noise but I'm not. Maybe closer to the shore. I know it sounds crazy, but I was lying in bed and I thought what if I have a dog. It will be hungry and trapped inside."

Greg slowly pulled himself into a sitting position. "Hang on. What time is it?"

"Almost five in the morning. Please, I know it's a lot to ask but I have to try."

He rubbed his hands vigorously over his face and finally looked at her. Really looked at her.

"You want to drive around South Jersey looking for the place you live, without having any idea of where that actually is, because you think you might have a dog?"

"I don't know if I have a dog." She got up from where she'd been kneeling and began pacing in front of the couch. She pulled on her fingers and listened to her knuckles crack, then dropped her hands to her sides immediately, having a sense she wasn't supposed to do that.

Young ladies don't crack their knuckles.

Greg was right. Manners were important to her. Someone had given her a sense of what was proper and what wasn't. She could feel it.

"If you don't know, then why are you so upset?"

"Because what if I do? I might have left not knowing I was going to be away a whole day. It could be hungry or thirsty. Trapped in a house with no access to food or water."

Greg blinked. "Let me get this straight. You're worried you might have a dog but not worried you might have a husband who doesn't know where you are?"

"A husband can feed himself and pour his own drink. He might be scared, but he won't be helpless or vulnerable."

"What about a kid?"

"I wouldn't have left a child alone. Someone would be watching it."

He nodded. "Then I take it you're not a cat person."

"I love all animals!" That felt right. It wasn't a memory but it was a sense she had. Of who she was. She would take that as a sign that she was getting better but it wasn't fast enough. "Cats are more independent. A dog needs to be walked and fed every day. Please. I know it sounds crazy. If we drive around I'm sure it will come back to me. I know I'll remember."

He reached out while she was pacing and grabbed her wrist. With a yank he pulled her down onto the couch next to him. It was warm where he had stretched over it and she felt the side of his body pressed against her arm. She shivered.

"Listen to me, you're panicking again."

She was. She could feel it coming on. Her heart started to race and her lungs tightened. Deep breaths, deep breaths. "I feel out of control."

"That's perfectly natural. In this situation you are out of control."

She shook her head. "I don't like it. I don't like feeling this way."

"Who does?"

She looked at him then and there was a calmness about him. She sensed that he'd seen people in her state before and it didn't rattle him.

"Keep breathing," he ordered. "Tell me quick, gut reaction. You like big dogs or small dogs?"

"Big dogs. They make me feel safe."

He nodded. "Okay, if you have a dog, especially a big one, that would mean you probably live in a house. Someplace with a backyard so he could run around."

"I hope so. Big dogs need space." She clutched her chest as she was gripped by an overwhelming feeling of sadness. She wanted to cry but she had no reason for it.

"Well, if you live in a house, then I bet you have neighbors. And if you live in a neighborhood, I'm guessing you know everyone on the street because you would be out walking the dog. A neighbor who knows you and your dog might see that you didn't come home last night and might hear your dog barking. Maybe this neighbor would have a spare key. To collect your mail when you go on vacation, or let the dog out when you're not there. I'm sure if there is a dog, everything will be fine."

Her breathing calmed as he spoke and when she looked at him, she could at least believe he was being sincere and not patronizing.

"I woke up and realized I still didn't have my memory and I flipped out a little. I'm sorry I woke you."

"You should be sorry. I am *not* a morning person."

She smiled. "You were a little hard to wake up."

He smiled back. "Just be grateful you weren't trying to wake Chuck. He's worse than I am and he flails."

"I thought I would be better." Her voice cracked and she hated how completely broken she sounded.

He bumped her shoulder with his. "Can I make an observation?"

"You're asking me? If I recall last night, and I do at least remember that, you've already made several."

"Did it upset you?"

She shook her head. "I was ready to cling to anything you told me. Hoping it might trigger something. You can't know how this feels. It's like an emptiness. I want to say I've never felt anything like it before but…"

"But what?"

"I feel lost," she said, dropping her head. Shame, deep shame, replaced the sadness she'd previously been feeling. "I feel like it's not the first time, either. Like I've been here before. In this mental place.

Only I don't know when or why. I only know I hate it. What was your observation?"

"That. What you just did. Dropping your head, covering your face with your hair. You're going through this major thing right now where you don't know who or what you are. You should be angry this happened to you. You should be scared shitless. Instead I feel as if you're…embarrassed."

Embarrassment. Shame's weaker twin. He was right. She needed to get over these feelings and start thinking about a plan of action. "I'm sorry I woke you. I should let you get back to sleep."

"Yeah, that's not going to happen now. How about I make us some coffee?"

"Okay. I don't think I could sleep now, either. How soon do you think we can call the doctor at Thomas Jefferson to see about scheduling an appointment? I'm hoping I can walk or take the Speedline to get there. Then I won't have to be a burden on you."

"You call it the Speedline," Greg noted as he stood. "Not the subway. You're definitely a Jersey girl."

He snatched up his T-shirt which reminded her that he was half-naked. Half-naked with a lean sculpted chest, covered in the same dark hair that stuck out messily on his head. She looked away as he dressed and padded over to the kitchen on the bare feet that had startled her earlier. He scooped out some ground coffee and put it in a filter.

She wasn't sure why but she considered his non-answer somewhat ominous. "You don't think I'll be able to get an appointment today. Is that it? Are you worried I'll be stuck here longer? You know I was thinking, if you could lend me some money... Ugh, this is so awful. I know you don't know me, but I swear I would pay you back. Before I washed it I looked at the label on my dress and I looked it up online on your computer upstairs. It's fairly pricey. You said yourself you think I come from a wealthy family. I promise I would repay you. I think five hundred dollars would be enough to last me a week. I would have to be back to normal by then."

"It's not that..."

"Two hundred. I don't really need that much to eat. Then I wouldn't be so dependent on you." She laughed humorlessly at herself. No, she'd just be in debt to him. She might as well have offered him sex for money. At least then there would be something in it for him.

If he was even attracted to her. Why she was wondering about that was completely beyond her.

"It's not the money and I'm not worried about you being here for a few more days. I didn't answer your question about the doctor because I'm not sure what your schedule is going to be like today."

She snorted. "My schedule? Unless you know something I don't, I think my schedule is going to consist of sitting on this couch trying desperately to remember something."

He folded his arms across his chest and she could see his expression was serious. "I'm afraid I do know something you don't. The sheriff called last night. I didn't want to upset you, but you're going to need to talk to some detectives in the ACPD this morning."

Her heart thumped hard in her chest. "Why?"

"I don't want to alarm you…but there's been a murder."

"I DO KNOW SOMETHING you don't."

"I don't want to alarm you."

It had been seven hours since he'd said that to her. He'd only mentioned the murder. As if it was just an inconsequential detail.

"There's been a murder. You need to go in for questioning. I shouldn't have told you that much but…well, I guess I did."

It was all he'd given her. Not the rest of it. Not the most important part. Not even her name.

He wouldn't make the trip to Atlantic City. Which was fine with her. She didn't need him anymore. Now that she knew who she was.

"Ms. Dunning? Do you understand what I've told you?"

She stared at the detective sitting across from her and nodded her head.

Her name was Eliza Dunning, but she went by

Liza. She was an accountant. She was on the payroll of The Grande Casino. She was also known to be a close personal—there had been a subtle emphasis on that word—friend of Hector D'Amato's.

Hector D'Amato was dead. Shot and killed with a bullet to his face.

Liza looked down at her lap. She'd had to turn in her dress to the police as evidence. Her attorney agreed. Liza confessed to washing it, wanting them to understand that it hadn't been an intentional attempt to hide evidence. The ACPD already had the original piece the Brigantine sheriff had taken and they didn't seem concerned with the compromised evidence.

Now she was in a pair of too-big sweatpants and an Atlantic City P.D. T-shirt but she felt more comfortable in this than she would have if she'd still been wearing Greg's clothes. At least the sweats and T-shirt were honest.

Liza turned to her attorney who was sitting calmly next to her at the table. Chuck had introduced her to Elaine Saunders and told her she'd be representing her during the questioning. They had picked her up at her office on the way to Atlantic City. Elaine worked on the other side of the Ben Franklin Bridge in New Jersey.

Just her and Chuck and Elaine. Because Greg apparently didn't go to Atlantic City. Ever.

She'd listened with half an ear during the drive

down while Elaine—a short woman dressed in a severe, professional suit, with an odd pairing of shoes—traded barbs with Chuck the whole way.

Elaine criticized Chuck's clothing, his driving, his goatee. Liza might have felt sorry for him if Chuck hadn't fired back regarding Elaine's makeup, hair and clunky silver loafers.

Then Elaine had dismissed him altogether and called Greg. She'd listened intently to what he was saying on the other end before ending the call with a "Got it. I'll call you after we finish."

At the time Liza had thought how thoughtful it was that Greg had arranged a lawyer for her.

He lied to you. He knew who you were last night and didn't tell you. Why?

"Ms. Dunning?"

"Yes."

"You understand everything I've said?"

"Yes. I understand what you said, but it doesn't mean I remember anything. I don't know why I was at the casino so late Saturday night or on the highway the next morning. I don't know whose blood it was. I don't remember anything before hearing the sound of a squad car pulling up next to me on the side of the road. Do you understand that?"

The detective, a large black man with kind eyes, sat back as if reassessing her. Abruptly, the kindness vanished from his eyes and they reminded her of Greg's, how they had looked the first time he questioned her.

"You don't remember visiting with D'Amato that night?"

"No."

"You don't remember that you worked as an accountant for his casino?"

"No."

"You don't remember the man who was rumored to be your lover?"

"No."

"Detective, do we really need to go any further?" Elaine interjected. "My client has explained to you she has a medical condition. A condition which she would very much like to have treated. You can sit here all day asking her questions she doesn't have the answers to, or we can seek the treatment she needs."

The detective's scowl was menacing, but Liza saw that Elaine wasn't intimidated in the least.

"Because we both know you're not going to charge her."

"I've got a dead guy, witnesses who place your client at the scene—"

"You mean her place of business. You have witnesses who saw my client at work."

"Late Saturday night?"

Elaine shrugged. "Casino hours. It's open 24/7. The fact that there are witnesses around the place proves that. Who knows what her normal business hours are."

"Then, hours later, she's picked up on a highway not far from here covered in blood."

"Strange. As is her current *medical* condition. But you don't have a witness to the crime, you don't have a weapon, you can do a gun residue check…"

"I'm guessing since she was covered in blood she's probably taken a shower since yesterday."

Elaine smiled without humor. "What you have is a circumstantial, albeit strange, case. Let me take her to a doctor. Let's see what he can tell us about her condition first."

The detective pointed to Liza. "You don't leave the area."

"No, sir. But…is there any way… Does anyone have my address? Where I live? I would like to go home, if that's possible."

The detective left the interrogation room and came back with a sheet of paper and a large oversize handbag that Liza suddenly knew was hers. He pushed it forward on the table that stretched between them.

"You left it in your office at the casino."

She took it and hugged it to her. It felt like a lifeline, something she actually recognized. One more piece of her puzzle. She was tempted to empty the contents right there and then and study everything inside, but she didn't want to do that in front of the detective. Not that she could be sure he hadn't already thoroughly searched it.

He passed her the piece of paper with her address, although she could have just checked her driver's license. Reading the sheet, she discovered she lived in a small upper-middle-class historical town not forty minutes west of Atlantic City. How did she know that? How did she know the town, but not remember that she lived there?

"Jog any memories?"

She shook her head. "Not really. I know the town was founded in 1692. I know there's an exclusive country club a lot of people belong to. I don't know why I know either of those two things. I can't picture what my house looks like from the outside, or any of the rooms inside."

There was nothing but facts and emptiness. No memories at all. She turned to Elaine. "Please, will you take me home?"

Elaine gave her a hard look, and the skepticism she'd seen in Greg's face that first day was there, too. Then, suddenly it was gone and she was reaching out to pat Liza's hand rather awkwardly.

"It's going to be okay."

Liza didn't see how. She was found covered in blood hours after a man she was supposed to know had been shot. She agreed more with the detective than she did her own lawyer. What were the odds that she wasn't somehow involved in his shooting?

Slim. Maybe zero. But she knew she wasn't the one who killed him. She wouldn't have killed anyone. All she had was her gut reaction to what the detective said when he told her about Hector being shot in the face and that reaction said it wasn't her.

Chuck was waiting for them in the lobby. Together, the three of them left the building and didn't linger on streets that weren't really safe even in the middle of the afternoon. The difference between life in the casinos and life on the streets of AC was vast. Several of the casinos had even gone so far as to build passages both above and below ground so if a person wanted to hop from hotel to hotel in an attempt to change their luck, they never had to venture outside.

As soon as they were in the car, Chuck handed Elaine his phone. "He's waiting for your call. Thinks it was taking too long."

"I have him in my phone," Elaine said as she hit a few buttons. "You should take the Black Horse Pike, it's more direct."

"And slower than mud. I'm taking the AC Expressway."

Elaine huffed. "Why do I have the feeling if I had said to take the AC Expressway you would have taken the Black Horse Pike?"

Chuck considered that. "Probably because I would have. Why do you feel the need to determine which route the driver is going to take when you are, in fact, the passenger?"

"Because having been your passenger more times than I would like to remember I know from experience you have a lousy sense of direction."

Chuck was about to fire back when Elaine stopped him with a raised finger.

"Greg, it's me. Hey, we're done. I'm taking her home first. Yes. No. I don't know…that's the best that I can give you. But I can tell you it's a lot more than when you told me the situation this morning. She's very convincing…"

Liza clenched her teeth, feeling a burst of rage surfacing. She wanted to hit her fists against the seat in front of her to remind Elaine that she was there. But she didn't. Instead, she simply said, "I'm sitting behind you in the backseat. It's not polite to talk about people in front of them like that."

Her attorney thought she was convincing. Liza didn't imagine that was a good sign because it began with the premise that Liza was trying to convince someone of something when all she was doing was experiencing what was happening to her.

Just because Greg had decided Elaine could represent her didn't mean Liza had to retain her as her lawyer. There were other lawyers. Maybe other ones she knew personally. Maybe when she saw the town where she lived and her house, it would be the thing she needed to bring her life back. Once that happened she could function again.

"He wants to talk to you."

Liza stared at the phone. She thought about simply refusing. He'd helped her, yes. But then he'd withheld information from her. It felt like a betrayal. She didn't owe him anything as a result.

Then she changed her mind, her anger still dictating her actions.

She wanted to tell him she didn't care if he believed her or not. She wanted to tell him not telling someone what her name was when she'd forgotten it was the cruelest thing she could imagine. She wanted to tell him he could take his doubt and his judgmental eyes and go jump off a bridge.

She took the phone. "Why didn't you tell me?"

There was a pause on the other end of the line. "I was instructed not to. The police wanted to be able to see your reaction firsthand. I shouldn't have even told you about the murder, but I didn't want you to be completely blindsided."

"Screw you. This is my life you're playing with."

"Hey, I'm the one who helped you, remember?"

"Yes. It's very easy to remember every detail when your whole life as you know it consists of a little more than twenty-four hours. You knew who I was, you knew my name and you didn't tell me."

"Eliza. Wake up. You're a murder suspect. Do you get that?"

She was an amnesiac, she was not stupid. "It's not Eliza. It's Liza. And, yes, I get it. What I don't get is why you care."

Liza ended the call and handed the phone through the seats to Elaine.

"I appreciate you representing me for my interrogation but I'll no longer be needing your services. You can send me a bill for your time this morning."

Elaine turned around in the front seat and looked at her with a frown. "You don't want to do that, honey. I'm the best. I get why you're ticked at Greg, but, honestly, he didn't have a choice."

"He could have told me my name. He could have given me that much."

"Maybe," Chuck said. "But if he had, would you have been satisfied with that? Listen to Elaine. You need help. Serious help. And she's right about being the best."

Elaine's head snapped toward Chuck. "Did you just compliment me?"

"Hell, no. I save compliments for two things. My mother's cooking because I want more of it and sex because I want more of that, too. Telling Jane…Liza, I mean, that you're a good attorney is a fact. You wouldn't be part of the Tyler Group if you weren't."

"I'm taking it as a compliment, anyway. And reminding you that you're talented enough that you could be working for the Tyler Group, too."

"What and give up the squirrels?" Chuck shook

his head, clearly exasperated. "That is so like you. First, I tell you it's not a compliment but you can't accept that because everything has to be your way. Second, you think it's okay to tell me I'm wasting my talent on squirrels."

"Because (a) you are wasting your talent on squirrels, and (b) my way more often than not *is* right."

"Please," Liza interjected. Their fighting was giving her a headache. "Thank you both. I'll consider what you said, but I would really like to find someone who believes me. I understand why you all don't, but I would rather be alone than have to look at another person who wonders if I'm just a talented actress."

Elaine turned and studied her again. Liza turned her head away and stared out the window instead.

"I don't think you're an actress."

Liza met her stare directly. "Thank you."

"I do, however, think you know something about Hector D'Amato's death."

So did Liza. She knew she didn't kill him. She trusted that much. But what if she'd somehow inadvertently caused his death?

Because as much as she didn't want people looking at her and believing her to be an actress, she really didn't want people thinking she was a murderer instead.

CHAPTER FIVE

THE SUN STARTING TO SET behind him, Greg stood at the end of the stone walkway and looked at where Eliza Dunning lived. The house seemed very normal. A ranch-style house, and probably the smallest one on the block of fairly large colonials, it should have stood out like a sore thumb, but there was a stately elegance to the brick house.

It looked solid, too. Like he could huff and puff and never blow it down.

Only he wasn't the wolf. Greg never played the part of the wolf. He was the good guy in those stories. Or at least he used to be before he gave all that up and turned to a life of gambling instead.

Now that he'd given that up, too, he wasn't sure what he was anymore. Neither hero, nor villain. Maybe interested observer?

That was as good a reason as any to be standing in front of Liza's front door. He was merely *curious* about the woman who claimed to have no memory. A story that crazily enough was now even more credible after talking to Mark, who had dug up some interesting information about her.

Apparently, this wasn't the first time Eliza Dunning had lost her memory.

He rang the doorbell and waited.

The door opened slowly, which meant she'd already identified who was on the other side of it. She had good reason to be cautious.

"What are you doing here?" Her suspicion was evident, but beyond that he sensed hurt. As though he'd disappointed her. Which was pretty much his specialty these days.

"I came to talk."

"Not apologize?"

He looked down at his feet. "You hung up on me."

"You didn't tell me my name!"

Greg lifted his head. "Look, I know you're upset with me but we are talking about murder. I was told by the sheriff not to tell you anything, so I didn't."

"I know what we're *talking* about. I'm living it. Your part is done, isn't it? I mean, the police hired you to consult and you did. So, like I said, what are you doing here?"

Curiosity. It had to be the only reason he was there. It couldn't be because he wanted to help. Or offer her friendship. He'd purposefully made his world small and he wanted to keep it that way.

Since he didn't think she would appreciate being the object of his curiosity, he decided to play his ace. "I have more information about your past. JoJo, who you spoke with yesterday, is a detective. She and her husband have their own firm. I hate to admit it, but Mark is a master when it comes to gathering information other people overlook."

"Overlook?"

"Can't find."

She tilted her head. "You mean don't have access to."

Greg smiled. She was in the middle of a mental crisis, but it wasn't impacting her acuity. "I don't ask too many questions about how he comes across the information he does. He found quite a bit on you. You might want to hear about it unless you've remembered…"

A tight shake of her head told him all he needed to know. He imagined her walking through her front door, hoping it would trigger everything only to realize that it hadn't. She would feel like a stranger standing in someone else's space.

If she was telling the truth.

She stepped back from the door and let him inside. He was struck at once by the home's aesthetic. The foyer opened up to a room filled with comfortable furniture in soft pastels covered with bright pillows and afghans. Nothing overtly cute or immature but certainly a room designed for a woman.

If she was Hector's lover, which he had his suspicions about, then it was doubtful the man was living here with her. A man living in this house would feel like an alien creature on foreign soil. Not uncomfortable, necessarily, just out of his element.

"Can I get you something to drink? Despite not remembering, I was able to figure out where all my glasses and plates were. It's the craziest thing, but I considered where I might want things in certain cabinets and that's where I found them."

"So you and your old self think alike."

"I guess. I don't remember this room, but I like it. It makes me feel…"

"Protected?"

"I was going to say snug. Why do you think I crave protection?"

"You knew Hector D'Amato and many people believed he was a dangerous guy."

She closed her eyes as if struggling again to find some wisp of a memory. "I guess I did. I mean I had to. I worked for him. I hope I didn't know he was into anything illegal. I don't feel like that would be something I could turn my back on."

Greg followed her through a dining room and into a large spacious kitchen. For a ranch house it was surprisingly large and spread out. The kitchen resembled the other room in that it was filled with colorful vases on top of all the cabinetry. The ceramic floor tile had pink and purple hues. Pretty. That's the word that struck him. Everything in her home was pretty without feeling like he was standing in a bad version of a doll house.

"I have iced tea."

"Sure."

Greg sat down at a white circular table surrounded by what looked like antique wrought iron chairs. Liza put a glass filled with tea and ice and a slice of lemon in front of him. The perfect hostess. The lemon slice was even balanced on the rim of the glass.

She poured her own glass and sat down across from him. She was wearing denim capris and a blue T-shirt that made her look accessible in spite of her beauty. He hadn't really let himself think about her in those terms, but in the afternoon sunlight with her hair falling down her back and her figure in clothes that actually fit her, she was stunning.

Do not get sucked in by this woman.

The order came from the practical side of his brain. He was fairly certain he had the wherewithal to make sure that side stayed in control. Fairly certain.

"So, no dog?"

She appeared confused for a moment, but then must have remembered their conversation earlier that morning. She shook her head. "Nope. I found a picture, though. In my bedroom, on my dressing table, there were several pictures. One was my arm around an old black Lab. I'm wondering…maybe he died. I felt sad looking at the picture. Then I felt this horrible guilt that I couldn't remember his name."

"You need to give yourself a break. You have to stop thinking every time you turn a corner that it's all going to come rushing back."

"That's exactly what I think! I can't stay like this. Not in this vacuum."

Greg frowned and thought about what he had come to tell her. It wasn't good news and might unsettle her more, but he was coming to the realization that he needed to make a decision. He either needed to believe her and treat her accordingly or concede that she was lying.

As a former psychologist, he used to always believe in people, always gave them the benefit of the doubt. He thought he had crushed that side of himself. Buried it under his cynicism. But now he knew it still lingered. Buried, but not dead.

Greg wanted to believe her.

"You said you have more information."

He nodded and took a sip of his tea to postpone the inevitable. "What did they tell you at the police station?"

"You know what they told me."

"Humor me."

"My name is Eliza Dunning. I work as an accountant for The Grande. I knew Hector D'Amato, possibly intimately…"

He noticed the smallest shiver, as if she'd suddenly felt a chill.

"I know that he was shot and killed late Saturday

night or early Sunday morning, I guess. That I was there for some reason."

Greg nodded. It could be they hadn't put all the pieces together. Eventually they would. They would learn what Mark had already told him. In the context of the case, he wasn't sure if the information helped or hurt. He imagined each side could use it either way.

"They didn't mention your father?"

"No."

He could see her face go white. "Family! I didn't think. I should call my family. I must have someone. Maybe a brother or sister. My parents…"

"Your parents are dead."

"How do you know that?"

"Because I read the article that reported their deaths."

Greg watched her reaction and felt like a man kicking a puppy. A helpless puppy who was expecting a pat on the head instead of pain. He wondered why the police hadn't told her who her parents were. They had to know; the name and the connection to D'Amato was too obvious. Maybe they thought it worked against their scorned-lover theory.

"Your father was Arthur Dunning and your mother was Louisa. They were shot and killed when you were eight years old. You were their only child."

Shot and killed in their home. At the dinner table. When the police arrived they found Liza huddled under the table in a state of shock—and she had no memory of what had happened.

"Why?"

"Your father was in the mafia."

"My father." She gulped.

"I'm sorry."

She stood then and walked over to the sink, poured her untouched tea down the drain and then held on to the counter as if it was her only support. "I don't know how to process this."

"I wish I could sugarcoat it but I can't."

"In the pictures…" Liza left the room and Greg got up to follow her. Off the living room was a hallway that led to two bedrooms and what looked to be a home office. The largest bedroom was in the back of the house. Greg hesitated before stepping over the threshold. A man didn't just walk into the bedroom of a woman if he wasn't sleeping with her.

But she was right there near her low dresser holding a picture in her hand. She showed it to him, and in essence invited him inside her room, inside her space.

"I figured they were my parents. But the photo did look dated and I didn't have anything more recent." He could see that her blond hair came from her mother. But she had her father's eyes.

She picked up another picture. "Who is the woman? Is this my grandmother?"

Greg looked at the older dark haired woman with

the big smile and her arms wrapped around what looked to be a ten- or eleven-year-old Liza. "No. I'm guessing it was Hector's grandmother, on his father's side. That's who you lived with after the shooting. Hector D'Amato was your legal guardian and he took you to the woman who raised him, his grandmother."

She made an awful face. "And I was having sex with him? The man who was my guardian?"

"That's speculation, not fact. It could be the reason you had a personal relationship with him was because he was your guardian. It's not common knowledge. Obviously the police weren't aware of it or they would have said something. My friend had to dig deep to find the connection. The woman who raised you, Maria Angelucci, had divorced and remarried. The fact that D'Amato hadn't made it public knowledge that he was your guardian was maybe his way of keeping you safe. You obviously must have been close for people to think you were his mistress."

She set the picture down. "Is that the worst of it?"

"No."

She closed her eyes. "Tell me."

"Maybe you should come back to the living room and we can sit down…"

"Tell me. Now."

Greg shoved his hands in his pockets. "At seventeen something happened to you. You spent almost a month in the hospital. After that you spent another six months at a private mental-health facility about an hour outside the city."

Her head dropped and he waited to see what her reaction would be. After a moment she lifted her head. "You're saying I'm crazy?"

"I'm—I used to be—a psychologist. I don't say anybody is crazy. I'm saying you were ill."

Her expression changed and she looked at him with near desperation. "Then you believe me now, right? I mean I'm obviously not the most stable person. Of course something happened and—pop—there I went again. So I'm weak or weak-minded, but I'm not a liar. Tell me you believe that I'm not a liar."

This was it, he figured. It was time now to make that decision. Believe her and treat her accordingly or don't believe her and cut his ties.

He hoped like hell he was making the right call because he could already feel himself slipping. He was becoming invested in her. In her life, her condition. Too late now.

"I believe you."

He could see the relief overcome her. She took a few steps back and plopped down on the bed. "Okay. Okay. You believe me and I'm not crazy. Then I need you to believe this, too...I know I can't remember what happened but I don't *feel* like the kind of person who could kill someone. I mean, I had to be there, right? I knew him, he was shot, I was covered in blood. I had to be there, but I don't think I did it. Would you believe that, too?"

"I think it's more important that your lawyer believes that."

"No. It isn't. I need *you* to believe me."

Her urgency made Greg uncomfortable. He didn't want to be needed by anyone. That wasn't his role anymore. But he could see he was basically offering his support like food to a starving animal. Of course she would take it, of course she would hold on to him. The weight of the responsibility made his own breathing tight.

"Why me?" he asked gruffly. It was more a question for the universe than for her.

Still, she answered. "Because right now you're the only person in the world who knows me. Who really knows me. Which I guess makes you my friend and I would really like to have a friend right now who believes what I'm saying. I didn't kill another person. I couldn't have. Okay?"

Friend. There was that word he liked to avoid. With everyone but Chuck. Because friends needed each other for things and he really didn't want to be needed.

Then he opened his mouth and the word *okay* slipped out. Shit.

"Okay," she repeated. He watched her take slow deep breaths and figured it was probably a technique some therapist had given her to use when she was a teenager. Greg had asked Mark if he knew what her condition was, but Mark had only been able to learn about the hospital stay, not about her particular diagnosis. The information he ferreted out about her stay at the mental-health facility was a total violation of her private health information, but Greg had implicitly given Mark permission to bend the rules.

Still, a month-long stay in a hospital before moving on to treatment? It suggested that there was a physical component to her condition in addition to the mental component. Maybe she'd been recovering from something she had done to herself?

A failed suicide attempt might put someone in the hospital for a period of time. Greg considered himself something of an expert in suicide. It was why he wasn't a psychologist anymore.

"Why was D'Amato my legal guardian? What was the connection between him and my father?"

"He worked for your father. There were a few articles on Dunning where D'Amato's face could be seen in the background of a picture. Maybe he was a bodyguard. Maybe he was his second-in-command. They must have been close for your father to trust him with his only daughter."

She nodded. He didn't need to expand on that. Now that she understood her father was part of the mafia, it was a good bet that Hector was involved, as well. Which meant she was working for a man she knew to be a criminal.

She was working for the man who had a hand in raising her.

"Is that everything?"

She was waiting for the next blow. "If it matters, I don't think you have a weak mind."

She gave a brief laugh. "I can't remember anything right now and you just told me I spent six months in a mental-health facility."

"When you were a teenager."

"What difference does it make? I'm not right."

He sat on the bed next to her and took her hand. He figured it was what a friend would do and she had officially declared him to be her only friend so he figured he was on the hook. He forced himself to breathe through the constriction in his own chest.

"You were sick then—you're sick now. It's not about right and wrong. Trust me, Liza. I know."

She looked at him and smiled, and then she squeezed his hand. "Thank you."

He thought she was stunning before, but now she nearly took his breath away.

Warning! Danger! Getting sucked in...commencing now!

Then his mind went to a completely different kind of sucking and he had to shake his head. Had he seriously been thinking about kissing her?

"You called me by my name. It sounded good. It sounded familiar."

"Liza, what you're experiencing is hysterical amnesia brought on by what had to be a traumatic event. Maybe not even so unusual considering your history. With some time and rest and being around familiar surroundings the most likely thing is that you will regain your memory."

Her smile faded. "Yes, but when I do, am I going to find out I was working for a criminal and I was somehow connected to his murder?"

Since the answer was yes, Greg didn't have much else to offer her. Or maybe he did. Maybe sitting there on the bed, holding her hand, was all she really needed. That's when he realized what he'd done. He'd officially let himself be *needed*.

The worst part about that was despite the tightness in his chest, it felt really good.

CHAPTER SIX

ELAINE POUNDED ON THE LOFT door harder than necessary, impatient for it to open. She winced when Chuck opened the door instead of Greg.

He obviously saw her wince and made a face in return to let her know he wasn't any more pleased to see her. The childish nature of these gestures was not lost on her. Elaine often felt like the teenage version of herself when she was around Chuck.

Why couldn't she be normal around him for once? Every time she saw him since *it* had happened, she felt awkward and uncomfortable in her own skin. He would immediately pick up on her vibe and be just as awkward, which invariably led to them slinging insults at each other. Which would lead anyone who spent any time around them to assume that they hated each other.

Only she didn't hate him. It had just taken her a while to figure that out.

"Yes?"

"I need to talk to Greg. I know who Eliza Dunning is."

Chuck swung open the door, which she imagined

was the only invitation she was going to get from him, and she stepped inside, shutting the door behind her. He was walking toward the kitchen and she followed.

"Day, dollar and all that, sweetie pie. He knows everything already."

"About who her father was and her parents' murder?"

"Yep. Mark tracked down her information."

Then Greg knew everything because Mark didn't leave any information on the floor. Which meant he knew about her previous stay in a mental-health facility. As Liza's lawyer, she'd been able to access personal information fairly easily. The hospital administrative assistant had probably divulged too much information, but Elaine wasn't going to complain. Having others provide information about Eliza Dunning was necessary when Liza couldn't provide it herself.

"She tried to kill herself once," Elaine muttered. "I'm not sure if that lends itself to her being capable of violence and committing a murder, or to being truthful about the amnesia."

Chuck popped the top on a can of Coca-Cola. "It could mean both."

"Where are they?"

"He went to her place. To lay the whole story out for her. Figured it was going to come out anyway if the police were investigating her. I haven't heard from him. Guess she's taking the news pretty hard."

She watched him tip his head back and drink the soda in a series of slugs that moved his Adam's apple in a way that for some unknown reason she found sexy. There was nothing sexy about Chuck. Not his red hair, not his faded freckles, not his short lean body that was about the size of hers.

Nothing except his brain and his Adam's apple.

Which was now to her the sexiest thing imaginable. Ugh!

"You're not going to offer me something to drink?" she asked, pointing out his rudeness only because she was irritated with herself.

"We don't have any *diet* soda."

And they were off. She was about to open her mouth to retaliate when it hit her. She didn't want to do this anymore.

"When are we going to get past this?"

His eyebrows nearly hit his scalp. "I don't know—"

"Bullshit. You know exactly what I'm talking about. You asked me out, and I thought you were kidding so I gave you a crappy answer."

Her answer hadn't been crappy. It had been gutting.

Right. Like I would ever go out with someone like you.

Because she'd thought he'd been teasing her. Because she'd thought he was doing what Chuck always did, which was flirt with every woman in sight. Chuck was Chuck. Perennially on the prowl, and it used to really piss her off. Because he could never be serious about anything. Not women, not even his work. What the hell was she supposed to think when he blurted the question at the bar where they were hanging out after he'd had a few beers.

It wasn't until she saw the expression in his eyes, saw the humor that was always part of his natural expression fade, that she realized he hadn't been kidding.

He'd actually wanted to take her out and she had totally blown him off.

She hadn't seen him look at her with that humor in his expression since. It was only after it was gone that she realized how much she missed it. It was only after Chuck was gone, that she realized how much she missed him.

"Elaine, if you think I care about that anymore—"

"If you don't, then why are you always so mean to me?"

That made him flinch. "Hey, I'm not the one who winced like she'd been slapped when you saw who answered the door. You give as good as you get, lady, so don't give me that 'mean' crap. We're mean to each other because we don't like each other. No big deal."

"It is a big deal. Greg and I do a lot of work together so there are times you and I will be in the same space. Like now. Only now I'm standing here in my skinny jeans thinking about how I look fat instead of focusing on what steps we're going to take to deal with Eliza and her case."

He shrugged. "Sorry."

"If you could just forget what I said back then."

"Sweetie pie, it was forgotten the next minute. I've moved on. Maybe you need you to, as well."

She hated it when he called her sweetie pie. She hated it because it's what he called every girl he met. The girl at the coffeehouse, the girl who took his movie ticket at the theater. *Sweetie pie* was his way of making her sound unimportant. Just another random woman whom he'd happened to bump into along the road of life.

"Fine. Whatever. Have Greg call me when he gets back. Like I said, we need to think about where we go from here."

"Will do."

She looked at him then, to see if her statement had done anything to change the status of their relationship, but his eyes were lifeless and unfunny, so she knew she hadn't.

She walked back to the door and he didn't even bother to follow her out. She thought about slamming it behind her. She thought about creating a sound as loud as what she felt inside, but she didn't want to give him the satisfaction. So instead she closed it quietly behind her and when it was shut she leaned against it and sighed.

"I think I screwed up," she whispered to an empty hallway because she could never say it to him. "I think maybe I do like you, only I blew it and now I'm really sorry."

LIZA WOKE THE NEXT MORNING and waited. Waited to remember her tenth birthday, or her high school graduation or memories she had of being in the hospital when she was a teenager.

Nothing. Still it was different today. Different because she knew her name and she knew who she was even if she didn't remember any of it.

Different because she knew someone in this world now believed her.

Then she heard a noise coming from another part of her house and tensed. In a flash she remembered how the evening had ended last night. Greg had stayed with her, distracted her, and then he'd gone out for pizza and brought back a six pack of beer. They had eaten and drank. Liza realized she didn't really care for beer. They talked mostly about him. Since she didn't have much to offer, he spent time rattling off story after story. He told her first about his family.

His parents, now retired to Florida, were older, his mom having gotten pregnant with him sixteen years after having his sister. In some ways, he told her, it was like being an only child while in others, it was like having three parents in his life. All of whom pressured him to live up to his potential.

She watched his face grow sad, then. As if he was disappointed in himself. When she wanted to ask him about that, he quickly changed the subject to his sister's kids and her husband who had moved them to Ohio for his job.

Then Greg talked about his job. The work he did for the Tyler Group, an organization that she concluded was filled with really smart people who solved other people's problems.

Lord knew she was putting her faith in Elaine to solve her very big problem. After his third beer, they both decided he shouldn't drive all the way back to the city and so she put fresh sheets on the bed in the guest room and he graciously accepted her offer to stay the night.

She remembered going back to her room and closing the door and having the strangest sensation overcome her. As if she'd never known what it was like to have someone stay with her in this house. As if his presence was an anomaly.

Cautiously, she got out of bed. She brushed her teeth and hair and washed her face and stared at the image in the mirror. Still a stranger. An instinct made her open the cabinet. How stupid of her not to have already checked the cabinet in her bathroom. The place where she would put her most private things. But the cabinet was empty except for a full jar of prescription pills. She looked at the label and frowned. The expiration date was over ten years old.

Why did I keep pills for ten years that I never took?

Like every other question she had asked herself, there was no answer. Throwing on a T-shirt and jeans, she stuffed the pills in her pocket. She didn't know if she wanted to show Greg or not. She didn't know what they meant, but when she checked in with her gut, it warned her not of trouble, but of danger.

Which was ridiculous because pills couldn't be dangerous unless you took them. She didn't bother with socks because her feet weren't cold and when she made her way to the kitchen she could see he hadn't bothered either.

His feet were bare again. What was her obsession with his feet anyway? Oh God, what if she had some crazy foot fetish? The thought made her giggle, which she decided probably meant that men's feet were not her secret sexual turn-on.

Still, he was standing in her kitchen measuring out coffee in the same jeans and T-shirt he'd worn last night, his hair mussed and his feet naked, and she was overcome with a gut-level attraction.

She wanted to walk up to him and put her hands around his middle and rest her cheek against his back and have faith that he was strong enough to make everything all right for her. That he was strong enough to carry both their weight.

The image disgusted her. She shouldn't need anyone to make everything all right for her. She should do it herself. Rely on herself. She didn't need anyone's help. Not anymore.

That was a memory. A sense that she'd let people take care of her before and she didn't like it.

"Hey," he said, without turning around. He must have sensed her presence, not that she'd been deliberately quiet, and her floor did squeak in places.

"I noticed the light blinking on your phone. It probably means you have a message."

She knew that. Only when she lifted her phone, she realized she didn't have the passcode to access it. One more reminder of everything that she'd lost. No wonder she felt the urge to let him take care of it all for her. But she had to fight it. She knew that, too.

He turned to her and was staring at her. "What?"

"I remembered a feeling of being taken care of. Pampered, I think. I didn't like it. I mean, I don't like it now either. I wish I didn't need your help."

"Okay," he said slowly. "Only I think you realize that you do need help, which is a good thing. Anything else?"

Yes, I want to kiss you.

Liza immediately shut that thought down. She was grateful to him for believing her, for helping her when she needed it. That was all. Of course she would be attracted to her rescuer. Only that persistent thought that someone had tried to rescue her before and she hadn't wanted it, still remained.

She decided she couldn't give herself too much grief over her attraction. He *was,* technically speaking, handsome. Tall and lean, but not skinny, with dark hair and brown eyes. She remembered thinking his eyes were mean before. Now she found them comforting.

"Would it be too much pampering if I made you coffee?"

"No, that's an obligation, I would think. First up should make the coffee. Let me see what I have in the way of breakfast."

She found eggs in the refrigerator and some spinach that had seen better days but was still fresh enough to add to an omelet.

"It's weird—it feels like I've been gone so long because I can't remember when I was last here, but my refrigerator is filled and everything seems to be pretty fresh, as if I had only gone grocery shopping a few days ago."

"You probably did, and it might help you to go back to the grocery store again. See if you have some plastic bags tucked away in a cabinet or drawer. That will tell you where you shop. Then go there and see if walking the aisles brings back any memories. The mundane routine of chores, those things you do over and over again, might be the first things that come back to you."

Liza nodded as she cracked the eggs into a bowl, added a splash of milk and started to stir. Then she heated up a pan with a bit of oil and added the spinach. Instinctively, she reached above the stove to open a cabinet filled with various spices and seasonings neatly arranged in alphabetical order.

She could feel Greg coming up behind her, standing close enough that she felt his presence without him actually touching her.

"Alphabetical order? You like things orderly. Could speak to your wanting to have control over everything in your life."

"I do," she answered instinctively.

"You think or you know?"

"I know," she said, feeling more certain. "Control is a big thing for me—I know that." She turned to him. "It's coming back, isn't it? I mean, I thought it would happen sooner, but it will happen. I can feel it. I know I can cook. I know these eggs are going to taste good when I'm done."

"Bonus for me." He smiled. Then he placed his hands on her shoulders and her whole body went warm. She hoped she wasn't blushing. "Listen, it will happen. You have to relax and let it come to you."

She wiggled a bit and he dropped his hands. She hated to be rude, because he was only trying to be comforting, but she didn't feel comfortable with him touching her. Not because of her attraction, either. She had a vague sensation that touch of any kind was foreign to her. It made sense if the mere touch of his hands was enough to make her blush.

He looked at her and she could tell she was being assessed. She didn't like that, either. It made her feel as if she was some kind of experiment to him. A case study instead of a woman.

He took a step back. "I'll pour the coffee while you finish the eggs. Cream and sugar?"

"Yes," she answered. Because she knew that's what she liked in her coffee. She reached for the salt and garlic salt because she knew that would enhance the flavor of the spinach in the omelet.

After deftly pouring the eggs and incorporating the spinach she flipped the omelet and then slid it onto a plate where she added whole wheat toast that had popped. She set the plate down in front of him with a sense of satisfaction because the toast was perfectly brown and the eggs perfectly done.

She set about making her own dish and when she joined him, she could see he had powered through most of his breakfast, which told her it must taste as good as it looked. She sipped her coffee and watched him, smiling a bit at the grunting noises he made as he piled on one last bite of egg on his toast.

After he swallowed he looked up and made a

strange, almost boyish, face, as if he was embarrassed to have been caught.

"You were right. You can cook. That was really good."

"I can see that."

"I don't usually fuss with breakfast. Mostly just eat cereal. Chuck keeps the cabinets stocked with what I'm pretty sure are made-with-sugar-only cereals that he can't seem to get enough of. I eat it, but I hate myself after."

"How long have you lived together?"

"A little over a year."

"Why? I mean, it seems like a really nice place. If you can afford that, you could probably both afford to live on your own somewhere else."

Greg leaned back in his chair and crossed his arms over his chest.

"You don't want to talk about it," she said. "That's fine."

He looked at her. "You figured that from my body language?"

"You tensed up and crossed your arms, which could be construed as a defensive gesture. It wasn't exactly hard to tell."

"You would be surprised what people see and what they don't." He sighed as if coming to some internal conclusion. "Over a year ago I got into trouble."

He paused as if waiting for her to ask what kind of

trouble. She wanted to. She wanted to know in what way this man had failed or made a mistake. But it was selfish. She only cared because she thought it might make her feel better about her own situation and that wasn't reason enough to pry into his life.

"Chuck helped me out. And he's been helping me out since. Lately I've been thinking that it's time to move on. We get along all right and having a roommate does help financially but I have this fear that we're going to grow into these two old curmudgeonly bachelors if we don't shake things up."

"Plus I imagine it must be hard with girlfriends… bringing them back to your place."

"I think Chuck considers it a badge of honor to showcase his conquests." Greg smiled.

"I meant you, too."

Was that obvious? Had she just asked him if he had a girlfriend? Liza glanced down at her omelet and focused on using her fork to break off a perfect, square bite.

"Yeah." His obvious sarcasm caught her attention and she looked up to see him smirking. "That hasn't really been an issue for me, either. I've spent the past year trying to get my shit straight. Not to mention I ended an engagement. That probably deserved a little mourning before moving on."

"You were engaged?"

He nodded.

"What happened?" This time she had no qualms about prying.

"I told you. I had some trouble."

"And she left you?" Suddenly, she was angry at this unknown woman for no good reason. She didn't know what the trouble was, but surely someone as close as a fiancée should have stuck it out with him.

"She had every right to. I was a mess."

"Well thank goodness you didn't marry her."

"Why do you say that? You don't even know her. I was the problem, not her."

Liza shook her head even as she unleashed her fury on the defenseless omelet. "No, I know you don't leave because of trouble. Everyone has trouble in their lives, everyone has bad times. If you can't stick it out through the bad times then you shouldn't get to have the good times, too. She left you when you needed her."

"I wouldn't let her help me. I didn't want it."

"Then she should have tried harder."

GREG SAT AND WATCHED HER molest her eggs with a fury he knew was on his behalf. He smiled a little sadly. He always blamed himself for the breakup with Irene. Certainly, he held the lion's share of the blame. Irene had tried to get him to stop gambling. She'd tried to get him to seek help. He wouldn't listen. She never even really understood what sent him on the path in the first place. So of course she had every right to leave.

However, in hindsight, he could look back on what happened between them and realize that not only hadn't he cared enough to stop for her, but she hadn't cared enough to stick it out. Liza was probably right. He remembered thinking at the time he proposed… *Is she the one?*

It didn't occur to him until much more recently that he shouldn't have still been asking that question. He should have known. Because he'd proposed in the spring and she wanted a big splashy wedding, they had planned to wait a year and get married the following spring. Then Tommy died and it upended his world. To the point that he hadn't been able to find his equilibrium. Irene could no longer stand to watch what he was doing to himself and she left before she had ordered the flowers or the cake and, thankfully, before she had mailed out the invitations.

"What about you?" he asked.

"What about me?"

"Do you feel as if there might be someone in your life? Maybe you found some pictures?"

She shook her head as if she was instantly rejecting the idea. "There's no one. I'm sure of it."

"How can you be sure of it?"

He watched her while she tried to think of an answer. Eventually, she shrugged. "I just know there isn't."

"You're lying." Wow. It felt good to see it. Her body language screamed it. She couldn't meet his eyes—he was sure if she did he would see a slight dilation. He'd decided yesterday that he believed her and he found it comforting to have that reinforced. He knew when she was lying. He could see she was doing it now. Which meant she wasn't unreadable.

"Do you always call people out when they're lying?"

He considered that. "No, I never do. People have reasons for it. But I do tuck away the knowledge that they have lied. It helps me understand them better and it lets me know that the information they chose to provide isn't accurate."

She nodded. "I don't think I have a boyfriend because last night when I went to bed I thought it was an odd thing to have someone in the house with me. It gave me the sense I'm used to being on my own."

"Okay."

"Also when you put your hands on my shoulders before…"

"You didn't like it. It made you uncomfortable. I could see that."

"It felt weird. Like I wasn't used to being touched. I think…I hope…if I had boyfriend he would want to touch me and I would like it."

"If you had a boyfriend, he would want to touch you all the time."

Her eyes widened and he thought about what he

said. Yeah, that might have been slightly inappropriate. Especially on the heels of the thoughts he'd had about her last night. About kissing her. He squirmed in his chair and then got up and took his plate to the sink.

Where in the hell had that comment come from?

He wouldn't even let himself answer the question. This woman was a patient. Even though he didn't have a practice anymore, it was how he was choosing to look at this relationship. It was why he felt compelled to help her. Why, when he sensed that she needed someone to stay with her last night, he'd purposefully had a third beer because he knew it would provide her with an excuse to offer him the invitation. He knew she would be worried about him driving. It was a sense he had about who she was as a person.

She was going through a psychological trauma and while he was no longer a psychologist he knew he had the skill set to help her. That was all it would be. Once he concluded that she no longer needed his help, he would leave her be.

"You know I was thinking," she said as she joined him at the sink. He shifted ever so slightly away from her lest they brush up against each other. "About what you said earlier. About me wanting to be in control."

"You said that about yourself. That it was important."

"Given my history that makes sense right? I was

institutionalized. That's about as out of control as you can get. It occurred to me that if I was there for a period of time I would have had doctors or counselors. People who know what I went through, who also know about my recovery. I want to talk to them. I want them to tell me what I was like back then. Then maybe I can figure out why this is happening to me now."

Greg agreed. He wanted to talk to them, too, and he knew he couldn't do it without her permission.

"What about the specialist you were going to see. The one at Thomas Jefferson?"

She shook her head and her hair cascaded over her shoulders in a way that shouldn't have fascinated him. "Don't you think it makes more sense to find the doctors that treated me before? They'll know my history."

"Okay. So what's the plan?"

She took in a deep breath and he could see her battling some demon that had taken up space inside her head. She reached into her pocket and pulled out a bottle of pills and handed them to him.

"I found these. In my medicine cabinet."

Greg looked at the prescription and let out a soft whistle.

"What?"

He didn't want to tell her. Instinctively, he knew it would only upset her. But he'd already lied to her once and doing so again didn't feel right. "Liza, these

are some serious drugs. Not mild antidepressants…
these drugs, they would make you forget who you
are."

She shivered. "The cap is still sealed so I guess
it's a good thing I never took them."

"Yes, but why did you keep them?"

"I don't know. But I think I have to find out. Based
on the date, I was prescribed these pills when I was
seventeen by a Dr. Verdi. I think I need to find him.
Greg, you have to take me back to that hospital."

CHAPTER SEVEN

"I can't believe it. You came! I didn't think you would."

An older gentleman who actually looked vaguely familiar to Liza stood in the doorway of his office as if he'd been struck by a Taser and couldn't move. Greg and Liza had given their names to his assistant hoping for a moment of his time between appointments, but once the woman said Liza's name into the phone, the door had opened only seconds later.

Liza approached him cautiously. "Dr. Verdi, thank you for seeing us on such short notice."

She shook his hand, and he held it for a second too long for her comfort. That simple gesture made her feel trapped, as if she couldn't breathe. When she tugged a bit, he let her go and allowed them to walk past him into his office. It was a spacious room with an impressively large desk and high-quality artistic prints on every wall.

The depression business seemed to be paying well for him. Dr. Verdi wasn't only a licensed psychiatrist, he was also the owner and operator of the facility.

Liza wished the room would have seemed familiar to her, but nothing triggered a direct memory. Not the large-scale prints or the French doors that lead out to a courtyard where she could see staff and patients milling about. No, nothing sparked a flashback to when she'd been there, although her overall feeling of unease grew. Grew, until it was big, so consuming that she had to fight the need to run away. Only her need to have answers kept her there.

"Please have a seat. There isn't anything I wouldn't do for you. You know that, Eliza. I can't believe you're really here. Is this because of Hector? I heard what happened and I've actually been trying to locate you. I called the casino a few times, but they said you haven't been at work."

Liza blinked. She'd come here thinking she hadn't been here or seen this doctor since she'd been seventeen. She must have been wrong.

"Why would you do that?" Greg asked. He must have been equally confused.

The doctor seemed startled by Greg's question. "I'm sorry. Eliza, who is your…friend?"

"Oh, sorry…" Liza said as she took one of the guest chairs, realizing how rude she'd been to not introduce him. She blamed it on her current state of agitation. She'd started feeling uneasy when they'd driven through the gates of the hospital. The feeling had been compounded when she shook the doctor's hand.

"Greg Chalmers," Greg introduced himself as

he shook the man's hand before taking a seat next to Liza.

The doctor's eyes narrowed. "Why does that name sound familiar to me?"

"I used to be a practicing psychologist. I wrote a number of papers in journals I'm sure you've read."

"Of course, Chalmers. All the business about the physiology of lying."

Greg's lips quirked. "I take it you aren't a believer."

"Sorry, no. Not that I doubt the physical impact of lying. I just doubt another person's ability to detect such minor physical changes. I'm sure it's a fun idea, though, for movies and TV shows and whatnot."

Liza turned to Greg. She'd heard the condescension in the doctor's voice, and she was sure Greg had, too.

"I believe I heard you had given up your practice. Obviously, you have, by your saying you *used* to be a psychologist. A shame," the doctor lamented. "So many people need the help of a good therapist. But that begs the question, if you've given it up, then what are you doing here with Eliza?"

Liza took the opportunity to refocus the doctor's attention. "I was hoping you could help me with some insights into my care here." Liza took the pills out of her purse and put them on his desk. "You prescribed these. It's your name on the label."

The doctor took the bottle and nodded. "I did. You

needed them back then. If you remember, you were very distraught. Maybe if you had taken them—"

"I didn't." Liza stopped him. Her instincts were screaming she was right. Why couldn't she remember, though? She was tired of relying on her feelings. She wanted her damn memories back to prove to her she wasn't this person. "I mean, I don't think I did need them. I think that's why I didn't take them."

Dr. Verdi looked at her with an expression that clearly indicated he was the doctor in the room. She ignored that. He didn't feel like an agent of good to her.

"Did you work with me directly?" she asked.

He appeared confused and of course he should. Only Liza wasn't sure she was ready to tell him everything yet.

"Yes. We spent many hours in therapy together. You had your other counselors, of course, but we were quite a team. I never like to say I'm responsible for someone's recovery. In the end the patient does all the work, but I liked to think I gave you a helping hand when you needed it. You decided you were ready to leave this place, and I agreed."

"But Greg said these pills are serious medication."

"Yes, they are. I didn't realize you weren't taking them back then. The fact that you were able to overcome your anxiety without them shows me how well therapy was working for you."

Liza looked to Greg, searching for his help. He

seemed to understand because he asked the question she needed answered.

"I was hoping you could explain her condition to me. From your perspective, of course."

The doctor made a face and Liza could see he didn't like the idea.

"Eliza, is this man treating you?"

"No."

"Yes," Greg said over her. "Unofficially, of course. But yes."

Liza looked at Greg again. She didn't know how she felt about what he just said, but she couldn't think about it now. She'd come here for answers. She wanted them quickly, so she could leave just as quickly. "Please feel free to share everything with him."

The doctor sat back and Liza could see the suspicion in his face, but he touched his fingers together and nodded. "All right. What do you want to know?"

"Let's start with why she was admitted."

"Eliza hasn't told you that herself?"

"Of course she has. But again, I would like to hear it from your perspective. As clinically detailed as possible."

The man sighed as if reluctant to speak. "Eliza was admitted after a drug overdose that nearly killed her. After spending several weeks in the hospital recovering physically, Hector and I agreed she needed additional care and placed her here to recover emotionally."

Liza tried to control her breathing but she could feel a rush of panic overwhelm her.

Kill herself? Drug overdose? It didn't seem possible. It didn't feel right.

"Deep breaths, Eliza," Dr. Verdi said. "You remember."

She didn't like that. It was an instinctive reaction that told her not to listen to him, even though he was giving her sound advice.

"Do you know how she came by the pills?"

"Yes, they were prescribed to her. Eliza took the death of her adopted grandmother very hard."

"Nonna," Liza interjected. "That's what I called her. She was Nonna to me."

"Yes. Well, after her passing you were quite distraught. You were prescribed antidepressants and things seemed to spiral from there. I blame this on the fact that you weren't properly treated after the trauma you suffered in early childhood. Hector and I had many arguments about that."

Liza closed her eyes and the memory hit her like a ton of bricks. She was huddled under the table in a large dining room. Her knees pushed up to her chin, her arms circling her body as the blood that was leaking out of her father and mother formed a river and made its way toward her.

Please don't let it touch me. Please don't let it touch me.

"*What should we do with the kid?*"

"*Leave her.*"

"*What if she made us?*"

"*She's a kid. No one is going to listen to her. Besides, the retribution will be too much if we take her out, too.*"

"*So we're going to leave her here.*"

"*The housekeeper will come in the morning. She'll find her.*"

Liza opened her eyes and, though she couldn't remember grocery shopping last week, she could remember the conversation the two men who murdered her parents had while she'd sat huddled under the table. She hadn't moved the whole night, only a few inches to avoid the blood seeping into the carpet. The housekeeper found her there the next morning, her pants soaked with pee because she hadn't even gotten up to go to the bathroom.

She remembered being embarrassed by that. Because she was a big girl and big girls didn't wet their pants.

"His approach to what happened to you was to try and block the event out for you. He thought if he could make it go away then it wouldn't affect you, but obviously he was wrong. He didn't think you actually remembered...."

"I remember," Liza said dully. Her only memory and it was that one. A river of blood.

"You do?" Greg asked sharply.

She turned to Greg, nodding. "I just had a flashback from that night. It's not the memory I wished I had."

"I don't understand what you mean, Eliza." The doctor asked her, "What memory do you wish you had?"

All the rest of them, she thought. "What happened to me after I left here?"

"Eliza, please. Tell me what this is about. Why are you here with this man? Are you suffering again? I knew you would have this type of reaction after I heard about Hector. It's why I wanted to reach you. To hopefully find you before your behavior started to spiral again. You don't handle these types of stresses well."

There was no getting around it. If she was going to get the answers she wanted, the most expedient way was to tell him the truth. "I guess you could say there has been an effect. I've had… I've…had an episode."

Dr. Verdi stood and came around his desk to stand in front of her. He took her hand again, and that sense of being trapped returned. The gesture seemed overly familiar of him, but she supposed he had treated her for some time. Maybe they were still close. He knew she worked at the casino. What else did he know about her? Maybe she was supposed to trust him.

"Tell me."

"I've lost my memory."

The doctor turned to Greg and the small nod of his head confirmed Liza's statement.

"Of course. A condition of psychogenic amnesia. Given your past history with depression and your previous reaction to death, coupled with your godfather's violent murder, certainly that could trigger such a reaction."

A murder she didn't know if she had a part in. "You could say that."

Dr. Verdi stood. "Well then, it only makes sense. You have no memory yet you came back here. To me. Your instincts were correct. This is where you need to be."

"I came here hoping to find some answers," Liza said, not understanding where he was going.

"No, Eliza, you came back to get help. And you were right to do so. We need to admit you now."

GREG WATCHED ALL THE COLOR drain out of her face. It had him wondering if she might actually faint.

"No," she whispered.

Again the doctor took her hand, as though he needed to be connected to her to make his case. Greg had to fight the instinct to take her other hand and jerk her out of the doctor's reach. Which truly wasn't like him at all. He'd never before exhibited any caveman urges, but around Liza they seemed to be right there. Just waiting for someone or something to threaten her, so he could jump in and protect her.

When she pulled her hand free of the doctor's, he knew she was capable of handling the situation herself. Of course she was. But it still didn't stop him from wanting to pick her up and carry her out of this place.

"It's for the best. Who knows better how to treat you than I do? You belong here with me now."

She shook her head, violently this time. "No."

Greg got the message loud and clear. She wanted out of there and she wanted out of there now. Maybe it wasn't appropriate to carry her out like his caveman self was telling him to do, but he certainly could expedite their departure by getting her the answers she needed so they could leave.

"Dr. Verdi, we're not staying. We're trying to help put the pieces of her life back together. Anything you could tell us about this time in her life, her treatment…that's what we need to know. That's all we need."

The doctor looked indignant. "But she needs me. I mean this institution. Everyone here helping her. Eliza, we saved you the first time. We can do it again."

She shook her head and Greg watched as she pulled her arms around herself. It was as if she was trying to hide in plain sight. Again he fought his instincts because this time he wanted to pull those arms away from her body and put them around him instead, where he could shield her with his strength.

"We'll take care of you, Eliza. Like we did last time."

Her head snapped up. "I don't *want* to be taken care of. I can take care of myself. My memory will come back, it's already starting to. It would help, however, if I had some understanding of the events that brought me here and what happened to me after I left."

Dr. Verdi backed away and returned to sit behind his desk. Greg could see it was a ploy, backing off to give her the appearance he wasn't threatening her, when Greg sensed that all the doctor really wanted to do was pounce on her. If the doctor did pounce, he would be surprised when he realized he would have to go through Greg to get to her.

"As I said, you were brought in to deal with your depression and to recover emotionally. My understanding is that after you left here you were sent to a private school in upstate New York."

Another piece of the puzzle they could track down. Where Liza went to school, and then college. If he could lay out the path her life took, then it stood to reason that memories of that path would start to surface. Unfortunately that path also included the presence of her godfather and ultimately led to his death.

"How would you characterize her relationship with D'Amato?" Greg asked.

Immediately, the doctor's expression changed from concern to annoyance. He hesitated for a moment before choosing his words. "Hector and I didn't get along especially well. He was constantly questioning my methods and, as I said, in my opinion his lack of attention to your situation as a child was nearly criminal, given the damage that event had on your psyche."

Greg didn't care about Verdi's relationship with D'Amato. "That's not really what I asked. I'm curious how he was with Liza. How she was with him?"

The doctor's face pinched up as if he'd tasted something sour. "She adored him, of course. Always so polite and respectful. A perfect godchild. And he doted on her, too. He was always bragging about you. How well you were doing in math, that you graduated high school with top honors."

"D'Amato kept you up to date about her life? Even after she left this place?"

"Yes."

"Is that usual?" Greg wanted to know. "To follow up on patients who leave here."

"Of course. We're more than a mental-health facility. We care about everyone who comes through these doors. It's why I'm certain we can do for Eliza what no one else can. I can help her recover."

Greg studied the man's face, his eyes, the slight twitch of his lips. He registered every physical element about the man and reached a definitive conclusion. The same conclusion Liza had already come to.

"No, you can't."

Greg heard the resolve in her tone. He also liked the fact that she was no longer hugging herself and had put her arms on the chair rests instead. He knew she had done it deliberately. A sign of her strength in the face of what he could see was great fear. Hell, her whole effort to come back to this place was nothing but a sign of true courage. It made him more than like her. It made him admire her.

But now she was done having to be strong.

"I think we've gotten everything we came for." Greg stood and offered a hand to Liza. She grasped it as if it was a life preserver.

"If you're thinking your memory will simply come back to you, Eliza, that could be naive. Considering your past history and somewhat fragile mental condition…I think you're wrong to leave now. Mr. Chalmers, I think as someone who used to practice, you're being irresponsible for encouraging her decision to leave."

Greg shrugged. "Doesn't really matter what I think. Liza's a grown woman and she can make the decision for herself. Do you want to stay?"

"No," she said again. Standing next to Greg, she let his hand go. "Thank you for your time."

"Maybe you should at least leave your home number with me. Then I can follow up with you directly in a few weeks. See how you're doing."

"Sorry, Dr. Verdi," she said. "I've forgotten that, too."

Greg forced himself not to smile as he followed Liza out of the office. They didn't speak until they had left the main building and were in the car.

"Please get me out of here as quickly as possible."

"No problem. You want to tell me what's going on?"

She laughed humorlessly. "I don't know. I just know I haven't felt well since we drove through these gates and I know I'll breathe easier when we leave."

"Makes sense."

"It does?"

Greg put the car into reverse and backed out of the parking spot. "Yep. You have every reason to feel suspicious about the good doctor."

"Why do you say that?"

"Because I know he was lying."

GREG PULLED UP INTO LIZA'S driveway and turned the engine off. She hadn't said much since they left the facility. She also hadn't responded to his assertion that Dr. Verdi hadn't been completely honest. Which meant she already sensed that the doctor was lying or that something else was weighing on her mind.

Greg was guessing it was the latter and he had a pretty good idea of what it was. Liza should have been the biggest walking mystery he'd ever encountered given her condition, but instead he found himself being able to read her like an open book.

A book he particularly liked. Maybe too much. When they had been in Verdi's office, he hadn't been thinking about her like a psychologist, but instead like a possessive boyfriend. Greg needed to get his shit under control. He'd known this woman only three days, but it was as if she was changing him.

"You want to talk about it?"

She looked at him and he waited patiently for her to get the words out.

"Did you hear what he said? I have a *fragile* mental condition. Translation—a weak mind."

"Is that what you think about yourself?"

She didn't look at him when she spoke. "It's not a question of thinking it. It's a fact. I can't remember who I was, so I have to rely on what other people are telling me. I was depressed, suicidal. The fact that I'm in this situation in the first place pretty much backs that up. Something happened to me and my whole mind is gone. Poof! Pathetic."

"It's likely that what happened to you was you were involved in a violent…"

Greg's voice trailed off as the significance of his

thoughts caught up to him. She'd been covered in Hector's blood!

"Holy hell. How could I not think of this?"

"What?" Liza asked.

Without answering her he pulled out his cell and called Elaine.

She answered on the second ring and Greg didn't bother with the preliminaries.

"She was covered in Hector's blood!"

"What?" Elaine asked, trying to catch up. "We already know that."

"We both know she didn't kill Hector, but she was splattered in blood. If she wasn't the one to pull the trigger…"

"Then someone else did and she had to be standing close enough to see him."

Greg grimaced, his heart starting to race while the possibilities ran through his mind. "She can't remember the killer, but he or she doesn't know that. Which makes her a witness."

"You don't know that. If she was truly a witness, why wouldn't the killer have shot her, too?"

The undeniable pang to Greg's chest startled him. Why didn't that happen? Why wasn't she dead next to D'Amato? Why couldn't his only knowledge of the case be from some sordid story he read in the newspaper? Casino Owner Gunned Down. Female Witness Also Shot.

He could feel Liza's eyes on him, knew he was

probably scaring her to death, but he couldn't bring himself to look at her yet, couldn't let her see the fear in his own eyes until he found a way to control it.

She wasn't dead. She was alive. He had to keep repeating that to himself. Then he had to ignore the feeling in his gut that was telling him that was so vitally important.

Greg rang off a number of possibilities to Elaine's question. "He could have been interrupted. She could have fought him. Too many scenarios to know."

For a moment, Elaine said nothing. Then finally, "What do you want to do?"

Greg finally looked at Liza who wasn't looking at him any longer but was staring straight ahead. The tightness of her jaw signaled that she understood the ramifications of what they were saying.

"I don't know yet. But phone the AC detective. I want to make sure we're being updated. I also want to make sure he understands what it could mean if she wasn't a killer but a witness instead."

"Got it."

Greg ended the call.

"You think I'm in danger?"

"Maybe." Yes, he did. He did and it was making his hands tremble. "Until you get your memory back, it's all speculation. But I don't think you should take any chances. I think the safest thing would be for you to pack a bag and come back to my place."

"No," she said, shaking her head. Then she got

out of the car. He followed and hurried to enter the house in front of her so he could check for bad guys. He was certain there was some formal procedure for this, but he simply bounced through each room, determining that it was empty.

By the time he returned to the kitchen, she was standing there with her arms crossed over her body.

"I have a security system," she muttered.

"Which was off."

She laughed humorlessly. "Yeah, well I couldn't remember the code to that either."

"Pack a bag, Liza. Come…back with me." Greg swallowed the word *home*. *Home* wasn't a word he used when he talked about the loft he shared with Chuck. It was his place. His apartment. The loft. *Home* screamed a permanence he didn't feel about the place.

But he'd thought it. He'd thought the word *home*. In reference to her. Which was a little messed up.

"No."

Greg hadn't realized she'd refused him until he looked at her and saw the expression on her face.

"You're going to be stubborn. Why? To what end? If you were there when D'Amato was killed and you didn't kill him, you do understand someone else did."

"Yes. I'm not an idiot."

"I don't think you are, so why would you stay here? If whoever killed D'Amato learns who you are, which it wasn't hard for the police to do, then he could find you here. Staying with me is safer."

"So you want to protect me? Shelter me? Maybe I should have stayed in the hospital with Dr. Verdi then."

Greg shoved his hands into his jeans pockets. "Hey, I'm not him. That guy…well, I'm not going to lie…it felt like he was a little obsessed with you. I'm guessing you felt that, too."

"I know how I felt being there. Suffocated. When he said I needed to go back…" She shuddered.

"It was the first lie I caught him in. About his level of concern for you. He doesn't care about all of his patients the same, the way he indicated. You're special to him for some reason."

"Because apparently I'm a walking poster child for 'please, someone save me.'"

"It could be that he had the hots for you."

Liza's eyes narrowed.

Greg didn't relent. "Seriously, you're beautiful. He could be a pervert who wanted into your pants."

"I was seventeen when I was there!"

Greg shook his head sadly. "I hate to reeducate you on how scummy men can be."

"Well, that's sick. I don't want to be there, but I also don't want to leave here. This place is familiar to me now."

"Listen, I get that you have this hang-up about being seen as weak."

"Not 'seen as,' I am weak. The only way to change that is to stop letting people take care of me and do it myself."

Greg was getting annoyed. "By facing danger for no reason?"

"I don't plan to be the stupid girl in the horror movie who wanders down to the basement alone. I'm going to call the security company and reset my password. I will make sure the house is secure. I can be safe."

"To prove a point."

"To take back my life."

Greg walked up to her, his hands circling her arms above the elbows where she still had them crossed in front of her. He squeezed gently to make the point without hurting her.

"Needing help doesn't mean you're weak."

She remained unconvinced.

"Listen, you think I live with Chuck because as a grown man what I really want is a roommate? Shit, no. I live with Chuck because he keeps me on the wagon."

A noise escaped her. "You drink?"

He could see the softness in her eyes as if her first thought was to comfort rather than to judge.

"No, I gambled. I gamble," he grudgingly admitted.

"That's the trouble you told me about."

Greg nodded.

"Atlantic City," she said. "That's why you wouldn't go with me to see the police."

Again, he gave a tight nod. He didn't want to think about the other reasons he couldn't go to AC. "I try to avoid temptation. I live with Chuck because he watches my back. He also looks for signs I might be jonesing for a gambling fix. He distracts me until it passes. He *helps* me. It doesn't make me weak. It makes me smart for using what tools I need to help kick this thing."

"Why do you think—"

A noise came from below the house. Barely loud enough to hear. A creaking sound. Like a weak step. Greg held his hand up to stop Liza's question so he could listen for it…oh, hell.

The basement. He forgot to check the basement.

Now who was the stupid character in the horror movie?

CHAPTER EIGHT

GREG GRABBED LIZA'S HAND and bolted for the door.

"What…"

It wasn't a second later that he heard the thud of something hitting the wall behind them as they sprinted outside and back to his car. Not a loud gunshot, which meant a silencer. The man had come to kill.

"Oh my God, Greg!"

He didn't react to Liza's screaming. He simply focused on each task. Get out of the house, get away from the person with the gun. Keep her safe.

"In the car now." He threw himself behind the wheel as Liza was tumbling into the passenger side.

Keys out of his pocket he steadied his hand and started the ignition, putting them into Reverse as another sound made Liza scream.

Again not reacting to her shriek, he hit the gas and barreled out of the driveway in Reverse. Only when he turned the wheel hard and shifted into Drive did he see a masked figure running away from the house then hopping the fence that was out back. Then he was gone.

Not in pursuit of them.

Greg wasn't taking any chances. His heart racing a million miles an hour, he drove away from Liza's house, the only thought in his head to put as much space between them and the killer as possible. If the killer was running away, he was driving in the opposite direction.

It was a few moments later, as he drove them toward the Ben Franklin Bridge, which would take them into the city, that he saw the small round hole in the center of his windshield.

"Holy shit," he cursed as he pulled over on the street. He followed what he imagined would be the path of the bullet—right between the two of them—and he could see a small hole in the backseat of his Porsche.

Liza was staring at it, too.

"You okay?" Greg asked. He checked her body up and down but saw no traces of blood. Two shots and they had survived both.

"Yes," she confirmed.

"Coming back to my place now?"

She nodded. Then after a beat she asked, "That was the person who killed Hector?"

"Most likely."

"Greg, I'm scared."

It was at this point that he probably should have told her everything was going to be okay. Only as they drove over the bridge with the bullet hole in the windshield, he thought he really didn't want to lie to her.

THE POLICE OFFICER STOOD IN Liza's kitchen with an irritated expression on his face. Elaine wasn't surprised. She had a particular habit of irritating the police. Mostly because she was never completely sure they were going to do what she asked them to. So she found herself repeating her requests often.

"I'll touch base with the detective in AC, but you do understand this could have been a simple break-in."

"A break-in? By a man carrying a gun with a silencer?"

"You don't know that he had a silencer. Your friend was running for his life. He says he heard a thud, but maybe that's how his brain processed what was happening. Happens all the time—people don't hear things correctly when they're freaking out."

Elaine rolled her eyes. She wasn't going to get into why Greg wasn't the type to panic and not accurately hear a gunshot. "Okay. What about the security system flag on the front lawn," Elaine pointed out. "Who breaks in to a house with an alarm?"

The officer snorted. "Yeah, because alarms always work. The system wasn't even armed. Plus you said the house had been empty for a day. Someone casing the neighborhood might have noticed."

"All I'm asking you to do is consider the connection."

"And I told you I *would*. All I'm saying is that we need to keep all options open. Also, I'm going to need to interview the witnesses."

Greg had called the local police, but only once he'd gotten Liza tucked away. He'd explained the events over the phone but apparently that wasn't going to be enough.

"I'll let you know when we can make that happen. As you can imagine the homeowner is in shock right now. My friend is trying to calm her down."

"Sure thing. But make it soon."

"Thank you, Officer." Elaine shook hands with the cop who started clearing out his team.

A team that consisted of two other cops dusting for prints and digging a bullet out of a wall. Greg would have to turn his car in as evidence. Elaine didn't get the sense that Liza's small town hosted a robust police department. All she could ask was that they didn't dismiss the connection to the D'Amato case.

Which she imagined was why Greg called her immediately after he called the police to report the shooting. Greg must have also told Chuck what he asked her to do, because Chuck had been waiting for her outside her condo when she was getting ready to leave for Liza's house. She hadn't questioned his presence and simply accepted the offer of a ride. Intellectually, she knew the man who had shot Greg and Liza was gone, but it still made her slightly nervous to be there alone while she waited for the police to arrive.

Had Chuck been worried about her? The idea that he still liked her enough to worry about her brought a warm feeling to her middle. Maybe whatever chance they might have had wasn't completely gone.

Then, as if he'd been able to read her mind and wanted to assure her that he had no personal concern for her, he explained that Greg had asked him to pick up some of Liza's stuff. Greg thought Liza was still a little too rattled to go back to the house.

Right. Of course. Chuck was helping Liza, not her.

Elaine didn't bother to respond. After their last conversation she wasn't really sure what to say anymore. She got his message loud and clear. He wouldn't be doing this if Greg hadn't asked.

Then he had completely upended every thought in her head.

"Besides, Greg shouldn't have told you to come by yourself," Chuck had said as he got behind the wheel of his hardtop jeep.

Elaine naturally balked, as any strong independent woman would. "It's not like there's any danger. The shooter's gone and the cops will be there."

"It's the point," he'd mumbled. "What if the guy comes back and is watching the place? He'll have seen you."

Elaine thought to point out that he will have seen Chuck, too. But she stopped herself because she

thought he might actually be trying to be chivalrous and she didn't want to ruin it. If he was worried about her, then that had to mean something.
Didn't it?

Now they were alone in the house and he was
holding up a small overnight bag that didn't look
as if it would hold enough if Liza was going to be
at Greg's for an extended stay. Given the underly-
ing fear Elaine had heard in Greg's voice when he
called her, she didn't imagine that Liza was going
anywhere for a while.

Which was a different sort of problem. Elaine
wasn't exactly sure who Greg was to Liza. He
seemed to have embraced the role of her hero pretty
quickly. No doubt he felt guilty about not considering the potential danger she was in, but then again
nobody had thought of it.

Elaine felt her own twinge of guilt. No one thought
Liza was in danger because no one had believed her,
really. Not completely. Greg had obviously made up
his mind on that score. The question was did he believe her because he was convinced of her innocence
or did the fact that she was a beautiful woman have
anything to do with it? What if Greg was letting this
become personal?

He wasn't a practicing psychologist so it wasn't
as if his involvement would compromise his ethics.
But it still begged the question as to what he was

doing with her. Helping her, clearly. Protecting her. Believing her.

Falling for her?

Elaine hoped not. Even if Liza wasn't his patient, she was still a person of interest in a murder investigation. Was Liza playing him? Elaine didn't think so, but she couldn't be naive to the possibilities. Liza was obviously involved with D'Amato's business. No one could say for sure that D'Amato was clean. What if Liza wasn't, either? Maybe her claim of amnesia was fake and this was all part of an elaborate plan. Her ultimate goal was to have the world's greatest human lie detector determine she wasn't lying.

"You should really go through this. I have no idea what to pack."

Elaine took the bag from him and emptied the contents. Three pairs of jeans, one shirt, no bra and two thongs.

Elaine held up a lace pink undergarment with an expression that said "really?"

"What?" Chuck said defensively. "I reached into her drawer without looking and that's what I pulled out."

Elaine arched her eyebrows even higher. She was a pro when it came to eyebrow communication. It had derailed more than one witness taking the stand.

"Okay, I looked a little," he admitted.

"I won't bother to explain why that's creepy on so many different levels. I will, however, tell you that when a woman is suffering from psychological trauma and has been shot at by an unknown perpetrator the last thing she wants to wear is a thong."

Chuck smirked. "You're sure you're not jealous because you don't own any?"

Elaine swallowed her outraged response, which was of course a contradiction. No woman admitted to not owning thongs in front of a man she hoped to sleep with. However, she was too smart to fall for such bait.

"You seriously think I'm going to tell you what's in my underwear drawer?" Which was a little smug considering she almost had.

"Hey, all I know is a woman who wears shoes like you do is probably not walking around in stuff like this."

Elaine looked down at her clunky clogs. They were a vibrant orange that matched nothing and she loved them. So of course he hated them.

"I'll pack her stuff," she said, stuffing the thong back into the bag and trying not to be hurt that he thought she was a girl who didn't like pretty panties. "I noticed a laptop on a desk in one of the guest rooms. You're supposed to know computers, right?"

Another smirk. Elaine braced herself for some snarky response, but it was as if he didn't even care enough to come up with one. Instead, he left her while she went back to find Liza some comfortable

underwear and wondered yet again why it seemed
that she and Chuck weren't capable of having a normal conversation.

CHUCK FOUND WHAT HE ASSUMED served as Liza's
home office in one of the bedrooms. He opened the
lid of the laptop and powered it up.

"You're supposed to know computers, right?" he
repeated in a high falsetto, wondering why he let her
get to him every time.

What she said the other day at his place about
how they needed to grow up and stop being mean to
each other rattled him. While intellectually he knew
his behavior was childish and he probably needed
to give her a break, the truth was, inside he still...

He still hurt. She'd been the first woman in a long
time that he'd actually liked. Not had the hots for.
Not just wanted to get into his bed. But liked. After
his initial attempt to flirt with her, which she saw
right through, he backed off. He figured she and
Greg worked together sometimes, which meant she
would be coming around the loft, so he put her more
into the friend column. She'd been herself with him
and he'd been himself with her.

Then he found himself looking forward to her visits. Which he suspected weren't always about whatever she and Greg were working on. It felt as if she'd
come to spend time with him. After a couple of
weeks he'd started to really like her. Then he'd found

himself thinking about her romantically. He'd never had that happen to him before, gotten to know someone first before he wanted to sleep with her. Wanted to talk to someone first, then get her into bed.

He remembered texting her to meet him at the bar around the corner from her place. He'd been so nervous about actually asking her out on a formal date that he'd had more beers than he should have. By the time she got there, he was halfway to drunk. Then he'd blurted that they should go out.

And she'd hammered him.

He supposed he couldn't be mad at her about that either. He hadn't exactly given her a reason to think she was special to him. As far as she could tell he asked out every woman he met under the age of twenty-five.

Chuck had learned at an early age that his advantage with women was in the statistics. He wasn't the hottest, the most athletic or the coolest guy in school. Certainly not the richest. His defining attributes were his brain and his lack of fear when it came to rejection.

He figured out that by running the numbers and asking out as many women as he could, his likelihood of getting a positive response from someone grew considerably.

Elaine probably figured she was just another number. Even though she hadn't been. It was the way she recoiled at his proposition, though. As if going out on a date with him was equivalent to getting a boil lanced.

It hurt not because he hadn't been rejected in similar fashion by other women who considered themselves outside of his league. No, it hurt because he'd believed…he'd sort of hoped…she liked him, too.

Before he asked her out, the snarky comments they exchanged had been of the teasing variety. Before she slammed the date door in his face, she would laugh at his jokes. Before he ruined everything by wanting to take things to the next level, she'd been the best part of his day any day he saw her.

Now all she did was make him feel uncomfortable, which made him spiteful, which made him nasty. He didn't like himself very much when he was with her and that really sucked. Because before, when he used to hang out with her, he'd felt like a king.

Hell, he even liked her shoes. Her ugly, ridiculous shoes because they were reflective of Elaine being Elaine and not giving a shit what anyone thought of her.

Except she seemed to care what he thought because every time he stabbed her in the heart he could see the pain in her eyes. It satisfied him, because it meant she was hurting like he hurt.

What an a-hole that made him.

Shaking off the guilt, he tried to refocus. The laptop prompted him for a password, which he quickly bypassed by reverting to the operating system and coding a quick program to circumvent it. Computers were so ridiculous with their meager attempts to keep people out. Unfortunately, getting around the password was too easy and not enough to distract him from thinking of Elaine.

She would absolutely bust a gut if she knew how often he thought about her. He recalled what she said the other day. That maybe they could move past this. Maybe if he stopped being so mean and she stopped yapping his ear off all the time, telling him what to do, they could at least get back to what they were before. Friends.

He was an adult despite his displeasure at being one. Adults came with hang-ups and issues and real-life shit. Not that he'd had much more fun growing up as a scrawny kid from the wrong side of town, but at least then he'd only had one focus, which was to find a way out. Maybe that was why he liked the games so much. They provided him with the money he wanted while making it possible to avoid grown-up realities. Only, he was closer to thirty now than he was to twenty, so there was no getting away from owning his adult self.

He could maybe sit down and talk with her honestly. Tell her he'd really liked her and that was why he had asked her out, not because she was someone on his list to check off. Then he would listen while she looked at him with sad eyes and told him he was "sweet" and "nice" but she didn't think of him like that.

Which he already knew. So why bother?

Yeah, Chuck didn't see having a heart-to-heart with Elaine anytime soon. With a shrug, he let the disappointment roll off his back. Complete computer access available to him, he checked out the folders and started rummaging around in a way that made him feel worse than he felt about sticking his hand in Liza's underwear drawer. Computers said a lot about a person, Chuck always felt. How they organized things, what they chose to keep versus what they chose to delete. Where they went on the internet.

All sacred stuff. He found a folder marked The Grande and clicked on it. There was a list of files identified with date stamps, all encrypted. Chuck considered shutting the computer down at that point. He could take it back to the loft and let Liza herself show them what was on it.

Although it was doubtful she would remember any of her passwords. Still, it was snooping. Not that there couldn't be a perfectly good reason why, as an accountant for The Grande, she might have had needed to bring work home. The fact that the files were encrypted meant she was at least some-what conscientious about security. Still, a casino's books potentially on her home computer?

It didn't sound on the up-and-up.

After a few moments of hesitation he decided that

it was probably best if he checked out the files first. If there was nothing on them, that would only help Liza's case that she was innocent in all of this.

Otherwise, Greg needed to know who he had brought home. That was crazy, too. Never once since Chuck had known him had Greg been the type to bring home strays. If anything he'd been the opposite. Reserved, definitely closed off from people. Not unfriendly, just isolated maybe.

So the fact that he was treating Liza differently meant something. Chuck wasn't sure he knew what, but it made his decision easier. Anything they could find out about Eliza Dunning now was better than finding out something they didn't want to know later.

After he coded another program he was able to decrypt the files without the assigned password. When he started going through each one, it became perfectly clear to him why D'Amato might have been killed.

And worse, why Liza might have been the one to do it.

"Elaine!" Chuck called down the hallway.

"What?"

"You're going to want to see this."

Elaine came up behind him and looked over his shoulder. "So you could hack it."

Her doubt annoyed him. "Seriously? Do you not

get that I've made millions coding apps? Hacking computers is amateur hour."

She scowled at him. "If you're that good, then I would think you'd want to do something more worthwhile than writing silly games."

"Are you really going to start that again? I told you. The squirrels pay."

"Not everything is about money."

"It is when you've been poor."

He could see he'd startled her. Like a light slap across her face that she didn't know how to process.

"Can we focus on what's important here?"

Elaine seemed to shake herself back to awareness. "Fine. What am I looking at?"

He could feel her leaning over his shoulder to look at the screen. For a brief second he thought he felt her boob brush against him but she quickly pulled away.

"I don't get it. Looks like a bunch of spreadsheets to me."

"Yep," he said, studying the numbers and doing the math quickly in his head. Looking at various boxes she was highlighting. "Spreadsheets showing that someone was embezzling a whole lot of money from The Grande."

"Uh-oh." Elaine groaned.

"Really? That's the best you can do?"

"How about 'oh, shit.'"

Chuck nodded. "Now that is more like it."

"How do you think Greg will take the news?"

"That depends," Chuck hedged.

"On what?"

"On what's really going down between him and Liza."

CHAPTER NINE

LIZA TOOK THE CUP OF tea from Greg. She was seated on the couch and he'd taken the added precaution of throwing a blanket over her legs, even though it was a disgustingly humid September day outside. Eventually, fall would find them, but not today.

She pushed it off her. "I'm not in shock if that's what you're worried about."

She didn't know how she felt, but surprisingly she didn't feel out of control. If she had to label what she was feeling right now, she would call it... anger. Someone had shot at them! Fired actual bullets. Not just at her, but at Greg. Greg, who only wanted to help.

"You don't know what you are right now. Relax and drink your tea."

"I know what I am," she snapped.

"Okay."

Now he was placating her and she hated that, too. More, she hated this feeling that everything around her was happening to her and completely beyond her control. As if she was a passenger on a crazy dangerous ride. A ride where people shot at other people.

"Tell me what you're thinking."

She glanced up at him as he came to join her on the couch. "I think that sounded suspiciously like it was Dr. Chalmers asking me that question."

"Can't really call me that anymore. Also, I would prefer if you didn't use the word *doctor* in relation to this."

He waved his finger back and forth in front of them. She wasn't sure what that meant, either. But strangely she liked it. It made her feel as if they were connected in some way, although that didn't sound very rational.

They had only known each other for a few days. And what was the thing that had brought them together? That's right, she could barely recall who she was.

Now she was back at his place with him when she'd tried to be strong and stand on her own two feet. Worse, she felt glad for it. Glad to be sitting only a foot away from him. Glad that he made that motion with his hand as if to suggest there was some something between them. Glad that he'd been the one to find her when she'd been so lost.

"You told Dr. Verdi you were my doctor," she reminded him. She remembered not liking it, too. God, had that been this morning? It felt like a million hours ago.

"I lied."

"But if you were a doctor and you were treating me…"

"I'm not," he said. "I'm only helping you. There's a difference."

"You're telling me there is a difference between treating me and helping me?"

"Yes," he nodded firmly. "If I'm treating you, it comes with all kinds of strings. Confidences and promises and ethical considerations that need to be observed. If I'm helping you, I'm under none of those obligations."

"And that makes you feel better?"

"Yes. It does."

"Why?"

He smiled. "Now you sound suspiciously like a psychologist."

"I'm trying to understand you."

Greg stood and plunked his mug of tea down on the coffee table. "There isn't anything you need to understand. I'm doing what any person would do. Nothing heroic, just being a Good Samaritan and helping someone in need."

"Please don't use that word. I hate that word."

She didn't have to elaborate on which word she hated. "I told you before that getting help, *needing* help, isn't a weakness. It can be a strength."

"It doesn't feel that way when you're always on the other side," Liza said. It made sense why he would think it was a strength. His whole life had been about helping people who needed him. "Tell me why you stopped practicing."

"No."

She blinked. It was as if a steel wall had come down between them. Liza decided to climb over it. "Was it because of the gambling?"

"Yes."

She thought he answered too quickly. "I don't believe you."

"Then you would be correct. It seems counterintuitive that a person responding quickly to a question would be lying, but if the person had already determined not to tell the truth then a quick response could be indicative of deceit."

She wouldn't be dazzled by his little show. "So you admit you lied."

"No, I'm explaining I have no intention of telling you the truth."

Liza huffed. "That's it, then. I tell you everything, rely on you for everything, but you can't even tell me something as basic about yourself as why you stopped practicing."

He took his mug to the sink, speaking over his shoulder. "Look, it's not some great mystery. I don't like to talk about it."

"Does Chuck know?"

"No. This was before I joined the Tyler Group. Before I met him."

Liza didn't bother with any more questions. It

wasn't an interrogation and he didn't have to confide anything to her. Like he said, he was helping her. There was nothing she could offer him in return, really. Except maybe a sympathetic ear. A person he could tell his secrets to. If he didn't want that, she couldn't force it on him. She only knew it would make her feel less lopsided about...them.

Which brought her back to the silly idea that there was a "them." Which of course there wasn't. Pestering him for answers regarding something he didn't want to talk about, only to make her feel better, was kind of selfish.

Maybe he understood that. Except she was surprised when he sat next to her on the sofa again, a little closer this time. He stared at his hands, which he had clutched together in front of him, and wouldn't look at her.

"It's not like it's really that shocking or...I don't know what. Like I said, I don't like to talk about it."

She didn't think that was entirely true, either. People didn't want to talk about things that were uncomfortable to them. Which meant whatever it was, was something that still haunted Greg. It didn't have to be shocking to be significant. At least to him.

"Okay," she said, letting him off the hook. After all, he didn't owe her anything. Which was particularly frustrating because she owed him so much. Including her life.

He looked at her then, assessing her, and then

sighed. A long, deep sigh as if he'd opened up a door inside him that had been closed for a very long time and some old musty air had blown out of it.

"About three years ago I had a patient named Tommy. He was seventeen, depressed and being treated by a psychiatrist who had prescribed various medications. His parents weren't very happy with his progress and I could tell they weren't fans of the drugs-can-cure-everything approach."

"What about you? Where do you stand on drugs?"

"I think drugs can do miracles. I think they can also create false hope. If the reason for the depression is a result of a chemical imbalance then yes, drugs can provide relief. If there are other factors involved, drugs aren't the magic bullet some make them out to be. 'I'm sad, here's a pill,' doesn't always equal happiness."

Liza nodded. Dr. Verdi had told her she'd been on prescription medication prior to being admitted. Given that she ended up in the hospital anyway, drugs clearly hadn't cured her depression. The reminder that she had taken those drugs, abused those drugs, didn't sit well. It made sense that it was disturbing to her to think about her suicide attempt, but that wasn't what was bothering her. She felt as if there was some niggling thought in the back of her mind that wanted to get out, something that would tell her about her suicide attempt. Then Greg was talking again, and she turned her focus back to him.

"Anyway, Tommy started seeing me and his parents thought there was improvement. You have to understand, when you consider my research into the science of lying, it makes bullshitting me seem stupid. The more honest patients are in therapy, the more progress they tend to make. It's what made me really good at my job."

"Sounds reasonable."

"Tommy talked to me every week. I would ask how he felt, and the answer was always the same… better. I remember thinking what a smart guy I was. Here I had taken this kid and done what the meds couldn't do. I was the best psychologist in the world. Better than drugs. So full of myself and my skills. Right up until Tommy hung himself."

She gasped and reached for his hand. She squeezed it gently, and he let her.

"We'd had a session the day before it happened. Last thing I asked him was how he felt. This time he said good, really good. He was lying through his teeth and I didn't even pick up on it a little."

Liza held on tight. "Was he the only patient you ever lost?"

"No. But he was the only one I lost to hubris. I had grown so comfortable with the idea that I knew every sign, that no one could fool me, that I stopped relying on other indicators. Other signals. His parents had told me he had stopped taking his meds, but

I thought that was a good sign. Since I was making so much damn progress."

"So that's why you stopped working? Stopped treating all your patients?"

He played with her fingers, squeezing them in between his. "No, not right away. But I made it my personal mission that no one was ever going to lie to me again. Next time I would catch it. Next time I would know. I started playing poker. Poker is a game about…"

"Bluffing. Yes, I get it." It was so clear to her. Greg was supposed to be the guy who saved the day. The hero. Not the villain. When Tommy killed himself, he showed Greg a weakness in his armor. A weakness that Greg obviously had to correct. No matter what the cost.

"You became so immersed in that world, you lost your other one."

"Lost everything. Not money—that I had no problem raking in—but everything else. My practice, my fiancée. Then something happened in AC where you could say I hit rock bottom. Ben Tyler, who formed the Tyler Group, heard about me and gave me an opportunity to do something else with my skills. It's how I met Chuck. He was still working for this tech company who I was helping to negotiate a merger for. I don't even know how it happened that we started talking. I wasn't talking to most people back then. I was too…*ashamed,* I guess, is the best word. He didn't seem to care, though. He latched on to me and took me on as some kind of project. Gave me a place to stay, has kept me gambling-clean for a year now. So that's it. That's my story."

"I'm sorry it happened. But I'm glad you told me."

"Are you?" he asked her. "It wasn't hard for you to hear about Tommy after what you learned today?"

She shook her head as a feeling of certainty sprinkled over her like a rain shower. Filling her with knowledge about herself that wasn't a guess. That thing in the back of her mind that had wanted to come out was suddenly there in front of her.

"No, because I didn't try to kill myself."

Greg blinked as if he hadn't heard her correctly. "What?"

It was so clear. As though she could see something that had only been in shadow before.

"I didn't," she said with confidence, her voice rising. "I remember now. I didn't try to kill myself. I don't know what happened that night. The doctors weren't sure either. They said it could have been a reaction to a combination of drugs, or the combination of prescriptions drugs and alcohol. I had been out with my boyfriend. I was upset and had a few beers, but that was it. Just a few beers—I wasn't much of a drinker. The next thing I knew I was in an ambulance. Then everything spiraled out of control. After my grandmother died and I was so sad, no one would believe me that I didn't mean to harm myself. Instead they put me in a hospital and treated me like…"

"Like you were crazy," Greg muttered.

"Yes," she screeched, feeling all the outrage she'd felt back then and couldn't express for fear it would make her situation even worse. "Like I was this delicate piece of china waiting to splinter into pieces. But I told them, the doctors, Hector, I told them I hadn't done it to myself. I didn't want to die!"

Liza got off the couch, a sense of urgency chasing her. "Why can't anyone freaking believe me? What is it about me that screams liar? I'm not a liar!"

Greg, too, was off the couch and walking toward her as if to settle her again. But she didn't want to be settled. She wanted to vent her anger. Over what happened then and what happened in AC and what happened at her house today.

"I'm sick of this, Greg. I'm sick of being mistaken for some victim. I want this to end. I want all of it to end."

"It will. Once we find out who was in your house today. Once you get your memory back."

His tone was gentle and reassuring. She didn't want gentle and reassuring. She didn't want a lecture by Dr. Chalmers on how everything was going to be okay when clearly it wasn't. Her parents were dead, her grandmother dead, her godfather dead. She was lost and in trouble. Real effing trouble. Someone wanted to kill her, for Pete's sake.

She wanted to feel something different. She wanted to be the person controlling her fate. She wanted…

Taking two determined strides toward him, she lifted her arms around his neck. "This," she whispered against his lips. "This is what I want."

Her lips came down on his mouth and suddenly she was lost again.

GREG FELT THE IMPACT OF HER mouth on his instantly. It was like a soft, warm, delicious piece of fruit he hadn't realized he'd been hungry for. Thoughts about who she was and why he shouldn't be doing this registered like an echo, as if said from far away. Only this mattered. The physical. The connection between them.

Her hands were in his hair and he could feel the scrape of nails along the back of his neck. It was so completely arousing he nearly groaned. He wrapped his arms around her and with one hand he lifted her enough to fit her center to his erection, which had flared out of control as soon as she'd touched him. In his life he'd never been this turned on, this fast, by a simple kiss.

There was nothing simple about Liza.

He knew that. Knew that there was something combustible between them that despite the circumstances neither of them could control.

He tugged at her bottom lip. He pushed his tongue

into her mouth. She sucked on him and he was lost to the sensation of her surrounding him. She was tall. It was something he knew, but never understood what it meant about how she would fit him. What it would be like not to have to bend his knees to shrink himself, or bend his back to align their mouths. Instead she was there, like a missing puzzle piece that simply fit into all the edges and angles of his body.

He squeezed her ass and heard her whimper. Then she was pushing her tongue into his mouth and the wonderful sensation of it was like nothing he'd ever known. He took her feet off the ground and, with a few steps, carried her back toward the couch. Then he laid her down on her back, her white-blond hair spread out over the pillows.

Like an amazing feast that had been set out before him. And he wanted to eat it. No, not eat. Devour it.

She was trying to bring him down against her body. He rested his knee on the couch next to her thigh and reached down to the button on his jeans. In his mind, he was already there. Could already see himself plunging inside her, fast and steady, her body rocking to his thrusts as she took his cock deep. The consuming need to be inside her was maddening. It made his fingers shake as he undid the first button and he had the very real fear that he might embarrass himself and come in his jeans because he was that desperate to have her.

"Greg, please. I need you…now."

It was like a cold slap to the face. Jumping off the couch, he staggered until he was a few steps away from her, nearly tripping and falling to the floor in the process. His cock throbbed and his balls ached and he clung to the pain of it.

"What the hell was that?" he shouted. She had made him lose control. Instantly, with only a kiss. He was supposed to be helping her, and instead he'd been about to take her on his couch. "Ugh!" Greg was angry at himself and suddenly angry at her. This was her fault. She'd started it by throwing herself at him. How the hell was a man supposed to fight that? "What the hell were you thinking?"

She sat up on the couch looking stunned. As if he'd slapped her. Which apparently he had, at least verbally.

"I…"

He shook his head, not needing to hear an excuse. She didn't have one to give him, anyway. What he wasn't about to do was acknowledge that he'd thought about doing that since the first moment he'd seen her. But she couldn't know that.

She could never know what thoughts had run through his mind in that first moment he'd seen her with her bloody dress and her sad, lost eyes, crying out to him to help her. Yeah, hell of a Good Samaritan he was. The ugly truth was that he'd seen her in that room and, shit…he'd wanted her. Wanted to pick her brain, wanted to prove she was lying. But beyond all that, he'd had a very real, visceral reaction to her.

Oh God, is that why she's here? Is that why I took her home? Is this all about sex?

Greg started to pace, his hands returning to his jeans to fasten the one button he'd managed to undo. His fingers were still shaking.

Focus. He needed to detach himself and think about the situation logically. It wasn't the biggest deal. He was a man and he was a psychologist. He was used to compartmentalizing his life. In the past, if he'd found a patient physically attractive, he used his mental discipline to turn off that reaction completely.

Never once in his years of practicing had he ever crossed the line. Had he ever wanted to cross the line. It didn't matter if the woman was drop-dead gorgeous, or cute like the girl next door, or so completely wonderful that any man who met her would want her. As soon as she walked through his office door, he accepted any reaction that he might have to her as a man, and then simply turned it off. Like a faucet. A faucet that never leaked.

Until Liza. It was what made him so angry. He hadn't turned anything off when it came to her. And he'd tried. He'd had the thought about kissing her and then backed away from it. When she'd walked into the kitchen that morning and he'd seen the sunlight reflecting off her hair, he had to fight the pull of attraction.

He'd tried calling her his patient. Only it didn't work. Then, when they had been sitting in Verdi's office, his reaction to the way the doctor had talked about her had been too extreme. As if she was his possession. Liza didn't know that Greg would never have let her stay in that hospital, that he would never have left her with Verdi. That the choice to leave really hadn't been hers.

All of it had been right there. So close to the surface, but as long as he'd avoided it, he could tell himself it wasn't really happening. That the feelings itching at him weren't really there. Not really.

He could see now that he'd been lying to himself. Him of all people. He never lied to himself!

She'd done that to him. How pathetic.

Finally after a few moments of silence, she must have felt she needed to say something.

"I'm sorry," she whispered. "I really don't know what… It's probably the shock, right?"

Greg could have kissed her again. What a perfectly reasonable excuse. After the day she'd had. First their meeting with Verdi, then being attacked in her home. She'd also had some significant breakthroughs in her memory. Remembering the death of her parents and a time when everyone thought she had attempted suicide, but actually hadn't. Of course she'd reached out to him for some comfort.

He wished he wasn't so damn good at what he did. It would have been such an easy thing to believe.

But he could see it in her face. She was lying.

Which meant she wanted to kiss him again, too. Wanted him. Period. Given his lightning-fast reaction to her, she had to know the feeling was mutual. He'd had her on her back in seconds.

The situation was flipping impossible.

"Liza…you're my.…"

She shook her head. "I'm not your patient. Don't say that. Say that you don't feel the same way, but don't use that as an excuse."

Greg closed his eyes and summoned his willpower. He said aloud the thing he knew to be true. "You are going through a ton of shit. Taking advantage of you now would make me a monster."

Wanting her the way he did made him sort of a monster already but he couldn't help his feelings.

She laughed awkwardly, clutching her hands in her lap. "Uh, I think you have that backward. I was the one taking advantage of you."

He thought about telling her the truth, of letting her know that he'd been thinking of doing the same since he'd first met her. But it would only make things worse. It was hard enough for him to control himself. If she knew how easy that control could be broken, she might be tempted to try again.

"I'm not sure what to say," he said.

Standing, she held out her hands. "Don't say anything then. I'm not sure I get what happened, either. Let's forget it, okay? It's been a long day and I'm tired. Do you mind if I…"

He was completely hosed. Because the only words in his mouth right now were would she please sleep in his bed naked. Would she please let him join her.

"Yeah," he managed to choke out. "Sure. You go ahead to bed." Now, before he couldn't stop himself from touching her again.

"Yes. Sleep might help clear my head."

"Good idea."

She started to walk by him and it was comical how she kept her eyes on him as if he might pounce any second. Or as if she might. What the hell were they going to do?

The door to the loft opened and startled them both.

"Yo, Greg! You are not going to believe this."

Chuck was holding a laptop above his head and Elaine was right behind him shutting the door and looking decidedly unpleased.

Liza shifted where she stood and Greg could see that she checked herself in case something was out of place. But no, her shirt was still tucked into her jeans. He hadn't gotten that far yet. Her clothes were fine. Even her hair had fallen back into place. The only problem was her lips. Her red, slightly swollen lips. Her bottom lip, in particular, where he'd bitten down a little too hard with his teeth.

It had been delicious.

"Oh Greg," Elaine said, not looking at him, but at Liza. "What did you do?"

"What?" Chuck asked, clearly oblivious.

"Elaine, it's not what you…"

"That's my laptop," Liza interrupted, pointing to what was in Chuck's hand. "Why do you have it?"

Chuck's face shut down as suspicion hardened his expression. "Worried about what I found on it, Liza?"

Greg looked at Liza and, if it was possible, she had grown paler. Or maybe she was returning to her natural skin shade. When he'd kissed her she'd flushed an amazing pink.

"Chuck, enough with the drama. What are you doing with her computer?"

"Sure you don't want to tell him, Liza?"

She shook her head. "I can't… I mean, I don't…"

"Remember?" Chuck filled in for her. "You say that a lot. Pretty convenient, isn't it?"

"Chuck!"

Chuck looked at him. "Sorry man, I know you think she's telling the truth, but I don't buy it anymore."

It felt as if Greg had swallowed a stone and he could feel it sinking all the way to the pit of his stomach. "What did you find on the computer?"

"It seems someone has been stealing money from The Grande. I'll give you one guess who my prime suspect is."

Chuck was looking at Greg when he asked the question, but it was Liza who answered.

"Me," she said stiltedly, as though she was trying to pull another memory out. "My records, they show the embezzlement. I kept them on my computer."

That was when Greg knew things between them had gotten a whole lot more complicated. Because as far as he could tell, she was telling the truth.

CHAPTER TEN

"Liza, go to bed."

She shook her head. It was right there in front of her. A spreadsheet of numbers that she could see clearly in her mind. An account called Expenditure Funding. There was something not right with it. Was that a memory?

"Can I see what you found?" she asked Chuck, ignoring Greg's soft command. She would have liked to ignore Greg for the rest of her life but she had a feeling that wasn't going to be an option.

What the hell was that? What were you thinking?

It was quite obvious she hadn't been thinking of anything. She'd been angry, and the only thing to penetrate the haze of fury was the idea that she wanted to kiss him. She'd wanted him to kiss her back. It had seemed an honest and real emotion in her world which had become totally surreal.

"Sure. But don't touch anything."

It's my laptop.

The thought bubbled up, but she suppressed it. Chuck no longer believed her, if he had ever believed her to begin with. If she started getting snippy with him, with all of them, they might decide to send her back to her place. Alone.

Where the man in the mask had been hiding in her basement.

Chuck opened the laptop and didn't bother to ask her if she remembered her password. He simply by-passed the security as he must have done before and then opened the files that proved his theory of embezzlement.

Liza walked forward with her arms wrapped around her middle so there would be no concern that she would touch any of the keys. She studied the numbers on the screen and they were familiar. The spreadsheet was the way she remembered it. The columns lined up in a way that made sense to her, which told her that she had created this spreadsheet herself.

Then there was another sheet with an account that didn't seem right. It hit the same discordant note in her brain that told her it was off. Another tab detailed payment transactions to a vendor that she knew, somehow just knew, wasn't an actual vendor. The payments were always even and always in increments of ten thousand.

It was so familiar, she felt tears fill her eyes.

Liza could feel the warmth of Greg's breath against her neck. She didn't need this distraction. Even though she had created it.

What had she been thinking?

The answer was horribly clear. When he'd laid her on the couch and reached to undo his jeans she'd been thinking *yes, please*.

Because it would feel good? Because it would make her forget her situation?

Those answers didn't seem like good reasons to get intimately involved with a man.

Because she liked him? Because she felt like a better version of herself when she was with him? Because it felt like he cared and she liked the way that made her feel?

Maybe those were better reasons but her actions were still flat-out stupid. She already hated feeling needy. Asking him for sex was adding another layer of dependence.

Except in some ways she didn't feel dependent. Maybe that was attributable to him. He didn't make her feel as if she owed him anything. He didn't make her feel as if she was an obligation he had to fulfill. She had a deep sense that she'd been in that position before and she hadn't liked it.

"I don't know what I'm looking at," Greg mumbled.

"See this company," Chuck said, pointing to the screen. "I checked. It's a shell. So here's my theory. D'Amato found out you were cooking the books. He confronted you. You plugged him. Then, because of your past history, you faked the amnesia thing to set up being declared mentally unfit to stand trial or some shit like that."

Liza backed up a few steps, watching everyone as they turned to look at her. It shouldn't have hurt that Greg wouldn't meet her eyes, but it did.

She shrugged. "I can't refute what you're saying. I can only tell you I'm not faking it. But I won't lie either. Those numbers do look familiar. I feel like…"

"What?" Greg urged her. "Go with it. What are your instincts telling you?"

"That I knew about the embezzlement. That I brought those files home for a reason."

"Greg, come on," Chuck said, sounding aggravated. "How far are you going to let her take this? It's a perfect play, too, because right now she's not lying to you. If she was the one cooking the books then of course she knew about the embezzlement."

Greg stuffed his hands into his jeans.

"He's not exactly wrong, Greg," Elaine agreed.

Liza tried not to be hurt. It wasn't as if Elaine was a friend. But she was supposed to be her lawyer. Her advocate.

Elaine looked from Liza to Greg. "I'm sorry. It's getting really hard to put all the facts together and not come to the same conclusion. D'Amato was shot, you were seen at the casino that night, you were found covered in blood and now you have possession of account statements that show money being paid out from the casino to some shell company. That's motive."

Yes, it was. For a killer. Liza was very good at math and Elaine was right. Everything added up. She only knew that they were wrong. She didn't remember it, but she knew it deep inside. She would not have pulled a gun on anyone. Would not have shot anyone in the face. She couldn't have.

"I guess I'll need a new lawyer then. Let me get my things. Then I'll call a cab."

"You're not going anywhere." Greg stopped her. "Except to bed."

"Greg, please. I'm so tired and I don't want to be here anymore. I know what you all think of me. I don't even blame you for it. But I don't want to be here with you."

Chuck closed the laptop. "Another excellent ploy. We let you leave now and you take off for good, which puts Greg on the hook with the authorities."

"I wouldn't do that," Liza said. "I want to know what happened more than anyone. Running isn't going to help that."

Chuck shrugged. "Sure, if we believed you."

"Chuck," Greg snapped. "Let it go. Elaine, someone was in her house today. Someone shot at her. I was there when it happened. There is no getting around that."

Elaine nodded as if she understood where Greg was leading her. "Okay, if we do believe her..."

"I'm standing here," Liza shouted. "Don't talk about me in front of me. Don't do that!"

"Sorry," Elaine muttered, speaking to her now. "Okay, if we believe you, we could probably come up with a scenario where you discovered the embezzlement. Maybe you went to Hector to let him know. Maybe the actual thief shot him in front of you, and then went to your place to recover the laptop, hide his tracks and kill the only witness to his crime. It's another theory."

"Oh great," Chuck exclaimed. "I didn't know it was story hour. How about this? D'Amato was stealing the money himself. Was so grief-stricken that he killed himself in front of Liza over here. Then his ghost came back to steal the laptop."

Greg walked over to Liza. "Go to bed. You're exhausted and we're not going to solve this tonight. The best thing that can happen is for you to get your memory back. For that you need rest."

Fatigue weighed on her. It seemed ironic to her, but right now all she wanted to do was lie down and forget the whole day.

Maybe not Greg's kisses. Those she would allow her brain to hold on to. Maybe she shouldn't have taken them, but they were hers now and she didn't want to let them go.

"Okay. I'm really sorry."

"For what?"

Right. There wasn't anything that had happened

to her that she could have changed. Except for kissing him, and that was the one thing she didn't want to change. So she had nothing to apologize for.

She smiled. This, she thought, was why she liked him. Because when she was with him she felt stronger, not weaker. She was pretty sure he was the only man in her life who had ever made her feel that way.

"Nothing," she said boldly. "I'm not sorry for anything."

He cupped her face and brushed his thumb over her cheek. "There's my girl. Now sleep."

GREG WATCHED HER WALK TO his bedroom and waited until the door was shut. After a minute he could hear the water running in his bathroom and figured she was taking a shower. Good, he thought. It would help her sleep.

Then he turned on Chuck. "What the hell is your problem?"

"My problem? Dude, this is not my problem. This is your problem. You don't want to see what's right in front of you." Chuck tossed the laptop on the couch as if proving his point that the evidence was there in front of him.

"I told you already. I believe her. All you have to do is spend time with her to know she's not the sort of person who would do any of the things you're suggesting." Greg ran his hand through his hair as he considered what he'd said. If he was acting on his instinct rather than facts then it was because he was getting to know her as a person. He was starting to care.

Not the way he cared about his patients in the past. What he was feeling for Liza, beyond the sexual desire, was something different. It was freaking the hell out of him, too.

"Unless she's playing you! Did you ever consider that? I know, I know. You're the great almighty lie detector. The unfeeling coldhearted analyst who sees through everyone. Greg, you think you're infallible."

"I don't," he said. He knew better than to ever think that again. "I'm only telling you I believe her. That wasn't some damn ghost in her house today."

"It could be someone she hired. This could all be a setup."

"Tell me, Greg," Elaine interjected. "Who initiated the kiss?"

Chuck's eyes nearly popped out of his face. "Kiss? What kiss?"

Greg looked at Elaine and saw that she knew the truth. He also saw the question in her eyes that she wasn't asking. If he was being played then adding sex to the mix would only further compromise his objectivity. If Liza had set about to systematically create a story out of nothing but fabrications and half truths, while relying on the fact that he, an expert in being able to determine when someone was lying, would fall for it, then sex would be a logical play on her part.

Beautiful woman. Helpless victim. Needs protection. What man wouldn't fall for it? Especially someone whose nature was to offer help to those in need. It was why he'd become a psychologist in the first place.

"I did. I kissed her. It was nothing. A reaction, I think, to everything that's happened. Don't worry about it."

It didn't feel good. Lying. But if he told Chuck and Elaine that Liza had kissed him it would only add to their negative opinion of her and he needed their help.

He needed someone else besides him to believe Liza. He couldn't say why but Greg felt certain that her life depended on it.

Elaine shrugged. "I don't want to judge, but I think it's not going to help the situation. You being involved with her...like that."

Chuck wasn't so circumspect. "Really? You think the two of them making out will mess with his head if she turns out to be a freaking killer?"

"Chuck!" This time it was both Elaine and Greg who snapped his name.

Chuck held up his hands. "Look, whatever you guys want to do. I'm just the sidekick, right? The good friend who's had your back for a year, but now

Princess Memory shows up with her long blond hair and her blank mind and suddenly I'm the bad guy."

"You're not the bad guy, Chuck." Greg sighed. "I just don't think she killed D'Amato. Why can't you trust me and what I do, if not her?"

Chuck shook his head. "I'm trying to help you see reason, man."

"I appreciate it. But we're in this thing now. So let's see it through. We know now that someone was stealing money."

"No," Elaine corrected him. "We know someone was altering the books. The physical money would need to be traced."

"Fine. Someone was altering the books. We know Liza knew it because the files were on her computer. We know someone broke into her home. Ostensibly to take her out, if she was a witness to D'Amato's killing. The man was masked, armed with a silencer, so I think the intent was to kill. But at the very least he was probably also there to take back the evidence of the embezzlement. If we go on the assumption that she's innocent…"

"You know what they say about *assuming*," Chuck sang.

"Got it, Chuck. We know where you stand. If you're wrong and I'm right, then where would we start?"

"*We* shouldn't start anywhere," Elaine said. "We

should turn what we know over to the ACPD and let them deal with it."

Greg shook his head. "If we turn over her laptop to the ACPD, they'll arrest her."

"Right," Chuck agreed.

Greg ignored him. "We need to find out more about D'Amato. Who did he work with? Who would be bold enough to steal from him and think they could get away with it?"

"Or maybe they knew they couldn't get away with it, which is why he's dead," Elaine concluded. "From the reports I've read about the man, I can't imagine D'Amato allowing anyone who stole from him to live."

Greg nodded. "Then it's a plan. We're going to need to go to the casino. Talk to people there. See if anyone else had a reason or motive for stealing from him. If Liza can get access to her work computer, maybe more things will start to make sense to her. She is starting to remember. Bits and pieces, but it's coming back."

"Wait a minute." Chuck stopped him. "*You're* going to the casino? I don't think so."

He wasn't happy about it, either, but Greg didn't see a choice. Although, as soon as the thought formed in his head, he could feel the sweat break out along his brow.

No, he told himself, he could control this reaction. He could handle the physical panic. He could keep his shit together long enough to do what he had to do. Someone wanted Liza dead. That had to take precedence over his fear of being anywhere near Atlantic City.

"I can't ask you to do it," he told Chuck, as the thought of driving into the city, being there, nearly made him gag. Greg took a deep breath. "Not when I know how you feel about her."

How the hell was he going to make this happen? He was standing in his loft, nowhere near a car even and already he was shaking.

"That's my point!" Chuck shouted, helping to distract Greg from his own meltdown. "I don't *feel* anything for her. I'm looking at what's in front of me and drawing some conclusions. You've been different since she crashed our party. At first I thought maybe it was a good thing. It was nice to see you engaged for once. Like you actually cared. I mean, you're into her. I get it. She's hot."

"You think she's hot?" Elaine asked. "Really? I mean, do you see her as your type?"

Chuck shook his head. "No way. Too tall for my type."

"I thought so," Elaine muttered. "I didn't really see you going for the tall, willowy kind…"

Greg closed his eyes. "Can we focus here?"

Chuck folded his arms. "Look, you need to understand that you're treating her different than you do other people. Will you accept that?"

Did he have a choice? Chuck had lived with him for the past year. If anyone was going to call him out on his behavior it would be his damn roommate. So yes, he was treating Liza differently than other people.

Because he wanted to rescue her. Because his latent hero complex, which he'd suppressed after Tommy killed himself, was suddenly roaring back to life.

Because she was hot. The mental image of her on the couch, her hair spread out, her legs open to him, her body welcoming him... Yes, she was hot. Yes, he wanted her. That was why he was treating her differently.

"I accept that she's different. For me. I also get why that's a problem for you two. But I don't accept that it's fundamentally compromised my objectivity or that it's made my highly trained skill to determine when people are lying suddenly irrelevant."

Chuck nodded as if he'd won a small victory. "Fine. Then I guess I have to trust you. Elaine and I will go to AC. We'll take Princess Memory with us and see what we can find out. Then you have to trust our opinion when we tell you what we learn."

Greg nodded. The sheer relief of having been saved from making that trip was palpable. He'd treated many people with phobias over the course of his career. But he hadn't known that he'd never truly understood what those fears did to a person's insides. It had felt as if he'd been sweating from every pore of his body. "Okay." He swallowed. "I...I really appreciate it."

"You know I would do anything for you, man."

Yes, he did. It was the lesson he'd been trying to teach Liza. Because you needed someone, depended on them, didn't automatically make you weak. Sometimes that bond made you stronger.

Chuck and Elaine agreed on a time to meet and then Elaine left. Chuck said good-night and Greg found himself alone on the couch. Where only an hour ago he'd been kissing Liza. He swung his legs up and settled into what he knew would only be an attempt at sleep. His brain was too wired to allow him to rest. He grunted when his feet hung over the edge.

He wanted to be in his bed. No, check that. He wanted to be in his bed with her.

Holding her, kissing her, coming inside her. That kiss had rocked him. It was why he'd reacted so sharply. She must have thought...hell, he didn't know what she thought. Maybe that he was some hypersensitive virgin. Or worse, gay. After all, he did live with another guy.

Although he was pretty sure his facial expression read hungry horn dog when he'd been staring down at her. It was certainly how he felt. He couldn't remember the last time he'd felt that intense need.

The drive not just to have sex, but to be inside another person.

Yes, there had been a few women since Tommy's death, since he and Irene split, but that had been nothing more than relieving a little pressure. Scratching an itch. Nothing that touched him inside. Nothing that made him go back for seconds.

If he'd followed through with Liza, he knew it would have been different from those other experiences. He definitely would have wanted more.

Was it because maybe he was finally accepting what happened to Tommy and he was ready to start trusting people again? The fact that he'd told her the story at all seemed significant, when he'd told no one before. Or was she the first person, the first woman, in a long time who hadn't yet tried to lie to him? Not really. Not seriously. Only when she tried to protect herself and then when he pushed her, she confessed immediately.

Unless Chuck was right and all of it was one big lie and he was being played for the biggest fool imaginable.

Please, Liza, he thought as he closed his eyes and tried to stop asking himself a thousand questions he didn't have the answers for. *Please, don't be a liar.*

CHAPTER ELEVEN

"PEOPLE LIKE HER. She has a way about her."

Elaine watched as Liza approached an older woman sitting behind a desk outside of D'Amato's casino office. Up on this floor it was a startling quiet compared to the raucous activity on the game floor, where lights flashed and machines rang and people cheered with joy and groaned in horror as they won and lost money. Sometimes fortunes. Personally, Elaine never did understand the appeal of it.

Chuck folded his arms across his chest in a defensive pose. "Didn't people like Ted Bundy?"

"Seriously? You're going to go there."

"If she's lying effectively enough to fool Greg then she's in all likelihood a sociopath."

Elaine watched as the older woman burst into tears and hugged Liza. Then Liza tried to comfort her by rubbing her back. Elaine and Chuck kept a discreet distance, but they could hear Liza crooning to the woman and telling her it would be okay.

"Yeah, she looks pretty dangerous if you ask me. What with all the comforting and calming."

"Don't judge a book by its cover, sweetie pie."

"Ha!" Elaine snorted. "That coming from you? All you care about is the cover."

"What the hell is that supposed to mean?"

Elaine snapped her mouth closed. She didn't want to fight with Chuck. Like any good lawyer, she had laid her case on the table. He knew now that she hated it when they said mean things to each other and he knew she was sorry about what she said when he asked her out. If they were going to return to the friendship they had previously, then it was going to be up to her to be the grown-up in the room.

Of course he didn't know the part about her realizing too late that she actually had feelings for him. No, that part she kept hidden because she could only imagine how gleefully he would reject her if he ever found out. Maybe that wasn't the picture of maturity, but Elaine only had so much in her.

But she had to wonder, if she did tell him how she felt, would his rejection be based on spite? A revenge rejection? Or would he reject her because she'd been right all along and he'd asked her out only to check her off his master list of women he wanted to screw, but who really didn't mean anything to him? Ugh. Why did this stuff always have to be so hard?

"Nothing. Forget I said anything."

He scrunched up his face, no doubt deciding if she wasn't going to tell him what she meant, then he would figure it out himself. "What? Is it because of the girls I date? I happen to like *attractive* ones."

Don't go there, don't go there.

She really didn't have a choice. "Emphasis on the word *girls*. When was the last time you dated someone over twenty-three?"

"I'm only twenty-nine. Any woman in her twenties is perfectly acceptable. Now when I hit thirty it changes. But then I'll go by the standard rule of man-to-woman dating-age restrictions."

Elaine knew they were supposed to be focusing on Liza, observing how she interacted with the people who she used to work with. Trying to get a real sense if she was playing with them or being truthful. But there was no way she was going to let that one go.

"I'm sorry? The standard rule of man-to-woman dating-age restrictions? You sound like you pulled that from the Constitution. Trust me, I've actually read the Constitution and that's not in there."

"It's in the unwritten Constitution, sweetie pie."

"Please stop calling me sweetie pie," Elaine said between clenched teeth. She told herself he only did it to get under her skin, but damn it, it worked.

"Right. Sorry, *Elaine*. Anyway, the dating-age restrictions go like this—you take half your age and then add seven. That's as young as you can go. So when I'm thirty I can still date women as young as twenty-two, but twenty-one is off-limits."

Elaine shook her head. "That is the most ridiculous thing I've ever heard." She did not care, she did *not,* that he made her feel as old as dirt when she was only thirty-one.

"It's fact. Personally, I don't like cutting off any women. You never know where you're going to strike gold. But a rule is a rule. I don't want to seem creepy, you know what I mean."

"Then I assume the same goes for me. I've always preferred the company of older men, but maybe I should give the twenty-two-year-olds a try, as well."

"Not in those shoes."

Elaine looked down at her chunky variation on patent black Mary Janes. Were they weird? Maybe. She preferred to think of them as eye-catching.

"I get it," she said. "You hate my shoes."

He snorted. "Those shoes were how I knew you grew up in some fancy neighborhood, probably went to all the best schools."

Elaine frowned. She did, but she'd never tell him that. "How would you tell that from my shoes?"

"Because only someone very confident in their style could pull off those shoes. Confident because even though the clothes and the shoes don't match, they were expensive so it doesn't matter."

She thought about what he said about how money was important to him because he'd grown up poor. "Is that why you hate them so much?" It made her sad to think there was yet another barrier between them.

He looked at her oddly as if he had to swallow

what he'd wanted to say. Instead, he distracted her completely with a different question.

"When was the last time you went out on a date?"

Right. They had been talking about him dating everyone. How long had it been for her? God, she couldn't remember. Two years maybe? Not that she would admit that. Looking back on it, she remembered thinking how nice it was to have a guy friend. Chuck was someone she could hang out with without having to deal with all the man-woman drama that she was never particularly good at, anyway.

They went to movies together, ate burgers together, had drinks together. All totally innocent. Good old Chuck. There for her when she wanted company. How stupid of her not to realize she'd been falling for him the whole time. She certainly hadn't been seeing anyone else. Definitely hadn't been sleeping with anyone.

Then he'd asked her out and she remembered thinking she was not about to be one of Chuck's numerous conquests. It wasn't about her pride, either. It was about being hurt by the idea that he would think so little of her as to treat her like he did every other woman he asked out.

She thought being his friend made her different. Then when she saw his reaction, she realized maybe she was different to him. Only it was too late.

She hated those words. "Too late" was, in her opinion, the saddest expression in the world.

"Holy cow! You can't even remember when your last date was. Sweetie pie, I hate to say it, but that is a little pathetic."

Elaine felt a surge of anger overtake her. How dare he! She turned on him and pressed her finger in his chest. "It was last Tuesday. He was tall." Because she knew that would hit him directly in his short man's solar plexus. "And the sex was amazing!"

She took satisfaction in the twinge of pain she saw on his face, but quickly realized she might have raised her voice a tad too high for that last part. Liza and D'Amato's secretary stared at her. Then Liza said something to the woman and the woman nodded.

Liza came over to them, hope radiating from her expression. "That's Jeanine. I remembered her name. I didn't even have to think about it, it just came back. She was Hector's secretary. She said I called Hector that Saturday and he had her make an appointment for us that Sunday morning. Which was strange because I didn't work Sundays."

"Not strange if you made an appointment so you could whack him. You know, with the gun in your purse."

Elaine wanted to hit Chuck on the arm for his insensitivity, but given the blow she'd already dealt him, she figured he'd endured enough punishment.

"But I didn't whack him then, did I?" she said sarcastically.

"No, instead you showed up that night," Elaine pointed out. "Why, if you were meeting with him the next day?"

Liza shook her head. "I don't know. Although I do know I didn't have my purse. I had left it in my office here. Remember? The police gave it back to me when they questioned me."

Elaine understood where she was going. She was trying to make the case that unless she was packing heat under her dress there would have been nowhere for her to conceal the weapon. Chuck only shrugged.

"What next, then?"

"I asked Jeanine who was running things now. She seemed surprised by my question. It's probably something I would have known. But she said Freddy Ortiz is now the acting CEO. I think we should talk to him. She said he's on a call now, but if we wait a few moments she can get us in. She said he's been anxious to find me."

Elaine agreed. "Don't say anything about the accounts though."

"He needs to know. Whether it was me or not, he should at least know. Whoever it is is now stealing from him, too."

"No," Chuck said. "Elaine is right. If it wasn't you, then it was someone else. A person who might have had a motive to steal from Hector then kill him, might be the person who had the most to benefit from his death. Which it sounds in this case like it would be Freddy."

Liza twisted her hands together. "What am I supposed to say, then?"

"The truth. That you don't remember anything." Chuck laughed humorlessly. "You're good at that, right?"

LIZA SAW THE MAN BEHIND the desk stand up. He made a sound that she wasn't sure was an expression of relief that she was all right or show of surprise that she was there. Then she felt his big muscled arms go around her, squeezing her. Holding her.

Only she didn't know who he was. Not even a little bit.

Damn. She'd been so sure when she remembered Jeanine's name that it had been a major breakthrough. That any second it was all going to come flooding back, including the day she'd gone looking for Hector. Had apparently followed him as he left the building.

"We were so worried for you. You left your purse here so we couldn't get you on your cell. I've left I don't know how many messages for you at home, but you didn't return any of my calls."

Liza thought to the blinking light on her phone. She hadn't known what her access code was to hear the messages.

"Then your car has been parked in the garage these past few days. I didn't know what to think."

Her car, Liza thought. Of course. She had found car keys when she eventually emptied out the contents of her purse, but she hadn't thought about where she would have left it. Of course it was at the casino. She would have driven there that night to meet with Hector. And she had her keys with her. When Chuck and Elaine had packed some of her things, they had included her handbag.

"Then the police came, asking all these questions about you. About your relationship with Hector. Honestly, Liza, I didn't know what to tell them. I don't understand how any of this could have happened."

Of course the police had been there, had questioned the people Hector worked with. It was how she'd gotten her purse back, after all. Intellectually, she knew that, but with so much happening to her it was as if she'd almost forgotten about their existence.

The Atlantic City detectives were, however, very real. For the first time she felt a looming presence over her shoulder. Like a bomb that was counting down to the final seconds, waiting to explode.

She was under suspicion of murder. It seemed so completely surreal. How did she explain to the police that she felt innocent?

"Who are these people?" Freddy asked, interrupting her thoughts.

Liza followed his gaze over his shoulder. "That's Elaine Saunders, she's my lawyer, and that's…her assistant, Chuck."

Chuck made a face, but she ignored him. Instead, she focused on Freddy, who was frowning. He was a handsome man. Brown skin, which his Latin last name suggested, bald head that didn't look natural, which he must prefer cleanly shaven. He didn't look completely at home in his suit, but he didn't look like a killer, either.

"Why didn't you come find us? Where have you been all this time? Hector would be furious with me if he knew how I failed to protect you."

Liza looked over her shoulder. Elaine gave her a slight nod, but Chuck's expression was inscrutable. She had to stop worrying what he thought about her. She also had to stop wishing Greg was there with her.

She was a grown woman. She would deal with this on her own. "The truth is…I don't remember."

"Don't remember what?"

"Don't remember anything really. Except Jeanine's name. And some other things from my past."

Last night as she slept, she wasn't sure if it was a dream or a nightmare, but images of when she was in the hospital as a teenager came back to her. She could see the white room where she'd recovered. Could remember feeling how thin the hospital gown was and how exposed it made her feel. There was someone in the room, someone she felt she should recognize, but he stayed out of focus.

The only person she could see was Hector, whose face she now fully remembered.

When she looked up at him from the hospital bed, she could see the disappointment in his face. Or was it guilt? Guilt because he thought he was to blame. It didn't matter. In the dream she told him she hadn't done it on purpose. He hadn't believed her.

She remembered feeling so trapped. As though she was stuck behind a glass wall and she was shouting and crying out for help, but no one could hear her. Or no one would listen.

It was her first glimpse into her actual relationship with Hector. They weren't close. They couldn't have been. At least not emotionally. Because if he'd loved her, he would have believed her. When she tried to think about how she felt about him, she understood only the role he served as her guardian.

Then why had she come to work for him? There would have been an obligation. He'd sent her away to a private school. Paid for her education. Maybe she felt she owed him.

"You're saying you don't remember me? At all?"

Liza shook her head. "I'm sorry. I don't."

"Are you certain? I mean, of course you are. You wouldn't lie about something like that. I don't know what to say. How did it happen?"

Freddy was asking about her condition. He'd circled back around his desk and offered seats to the three of them. Liza sat down and looked around the office hoping it would spark another memory, but nothing came.

"I'm sorry. This room must seem unfamiliar to you now. I had all of the pictures removed. They were too difficult to look at. But I have them in his apartment, if you want them. The one of you and Hector at your college graduation is an especially good one. He was so proud of you that day."

"How long have I been working here? Since college?"

Freddy chuckled and shook his head. "No, no. Hector used to moan and groan about it all the time. But you were stubborn. You wanted to make it on your own. You worked for one of those massive accounting firms in Philadelphia. I always forget—"

"McKay and Fitz." Another name that popped out. Yes, Liza thought. She used to work for McKay and Fitz. She hadn't come here after college. She'd found a job on her own. The idea pleased her.

"That's the one. No, you've only been here, well, actually working here for a little over eight months. You were always around, though. Hector insisted you make time to have dinner with him once a week. Sometimes when he was busy, he'd have me order something for the two of you to be delivered here to his office. I don't know what he said to eventually get you to change your mind, but I can tell he was very pleased to have you under his roof again."

Under his roof. "Hector lived here?"

"Yes. Oh, I'm sorry. That's what I meant about the apartment. It's the penthouse, of course. You often had dinner with him up there as well."

Liza looked at the man she didn't recognize. He seemed guileless but it felt as if there was a subtle suggestion he was making about her and Hector. One she instinctively knew not to be true.

Hector D'Amato had never been her lover.

"I guess I should explain why I've come. Obviously, I was hoping that being here might trigger all of my memory to come back...."

"But it hasn't," Freddy said, looking as if he felt sorry for her.

"No. I was also hoping to get some answers. About Hector and who might, well, who might have wanted to hurt him. Murder him like that."

Freddy raised his hands, palms up, as if to suggest he had no ideas. "I don't know. I told the police the same thing. As far as I knew, Hector didn't have any enemies, any criminal ones. There were always rumors about him, because of his past connections. The truth, though, is that Hector was a man committed to keeping this business clean. After what happened to your father...sorry."

Liza shook her head. "No, it's fine. I know what he was."

"Anyway, after what happened to your father, Hector wanted to get out of the racket. Make this a legitimate business. I'm trying real hard to figure out why someone might have wanted to kill him. Unless…"

"Unless?" Elaine prompted.

Freddy looked down at his hands. "Unless it was… personal."

Liza nodded. She had a sense where Freddy was taking them. She wanted to know exactly where she stood with everyone. If they were all against her, then so be it.

"Personal," Liza repeated, feeling something ominous in the word. "You mean like a lovers' quarrel or something like that?"

Freddy nodded.

"Do you know if there was a woman in his life? A girlfriend?"

Freddy didn't look at her when he answered, "Liza, you were the only woman in Hector D'Amato's life."

AFTER LEAVING FREDDY'S office they made their way to the parking garage for casino employees and Liza found that she was the owner of a very nice, very practical white Ford. She loved it on sight. A car meant freedom. A car meant she could go where she wanted, whenever she wanted, without needing someone else's help to get there.

She no longer had to rely on people who inherently didn't trust her. It was going to make her plans for returning home easier to execute. She immediately told Chuck and Elaine that she would drive herself. As she drove, she realized Chuck and Elaine were following her, which she figured was to be expected. Liza pulled into her driveway, and when she got out of her car, they were pulling in behind her.

The jig was up. It was time to let them know she wasn't going back with them to Philadelphia. She walked over to Chuck and Elaine, who were already shaking their heads as they got out of the car.

"Oh, no," Chuck said. "You can't be thinking about staying. Greg is not going to like that."

Only at this point, she didn't care what Greg thought. She'd spent all day wishing he'd been with her, but he hadn't been. She had to handle the situation on her own and she'd done it. She wasn't angry with him; she understood why he couldn't be there. But after another day of enduring suspicion and innuendos, she decided she was done with everyone. She was tired of being surrounded by people who were constantly judging her. It didn't mean she didn't understand the risk.

"I called the local police earlier this morning and asked them to do regular drive-bys. I also called the security company and reset my password so I can secure the place once I'm inside. I'm not planning on going anywhere. I plan to take every precaution."

"Every precaution." Elaine snorted. "Does that include wearing body armor?"

"I know the logical assumption is that the person who was here yesterday is somehow tied to D'Amato's murder, but what if he isn't? What if it was just an opportunistic criminal who found an empty, unprotected house?"

"Most opportunistic housebreakers don't shoot at the people who catch them. With silencers. They run from them," Elaine reminded her.

Liza didn't want to think about that. She was scared, certainly, but she wasn't stupid. She also really wanted to stay in her own house. "Listen, I do appreciate everything you've done for me. But I can't stay with you. I can't spend another day being looked at like I'm a… I won't do it. If something happens, then it's on me."

Chuck half laughed at that. "Yeah, right. Like Greg will understand that."

"Then convince him you're right. That I'm a sociopath who has been lying to him this whole time. That should make everybody feel better."

Liza turned her back on them and walked up the front steps to her house. She pulled her keys out of her bag, but when she tried to put the key in the lock, it wouldn't slide in. Then she heard Chuck jogging up behind her.

"Hey, wait. At least let me check out the place first."

The door opened, then, from the inside Greg stepped forward. "That's okay, Chuck. I got it from here."

"How did you…" Liza's voice trailed off as she looked at her keys.

"I called the locksmith. Had him put more secure locks on the front and back doors." Greg handed her the set of keys. "I didn't keep a copy for myself."

Liza took the keys and frowned. "This is where I tell you, you had no right."

"This is where I say you're right. But I had a gut feeling you wouldn't come back to the loft and I wanted the peace of mind that you were as secure as I could make you."

Liza looked around for his Porsche, wondering how she'd missed it.

Greg motioned to the dark sedan across the street. "Rental. While you were in AC I went down to the county police station to give my account of the incident yesterday. They impounded my car for evidence."

"They haven't called me…" She had no idea what the protocol was for being shot at. She only knew, given that one set of cops wanted to arrest her, she was probably better off avoiding all of them.

"I explained your situation. You'll make an appointment when you're ready. There's nothing you can tell them that I haven't already."

Chuck started to back down the walkway. "Okay, if you're cool, we're leaving. See you around, then?"

"Yeah," Greg said over Liza's shoulder. "Later."

Liza didn't bother to wave goodbye. It felt petulant, but she had to stop thinking about Chuck like she had the first time she met him. That he was a good guy who wanted to help her out. He wasn't that person anymore.

He thought she was a sociopath who embezzled from the casino, probably slept with Hector to keep her job and then killed him when he discovered the missing money. As for Elaine, Liza didn't know what she thought, but after she sat there and listened to Freddy's veiled innuendos about her and Hector, it probably made sense to start thinking about finding a new lawyer. One she could trust completely.

On top of everything, she had Greg intervening in her life in a way that made her believe he cared. Only she didn't know what to think about him, either. He confused her, and the truth was she was tired of that, as well. She wanted to be free from all of this, even if for just an hour.

"Are you going to leave?"

"I was hoping you would tell me about what happened in AC."

Right. Because he hadn't been there with her. While she couldn't be angry at him for not being with her, she was still hurt by it. It had felt like abandonment. Selfish, but true.

That he was here now should have made up for it, but she was tired of the roller coaster of emotions when it came to him. She wasn't getting off the ride yet it seemed.

"Fine. I'll tell you everything."

She stepped inside and took the key from Greg, locking them both inside. Then she walked over to the alarm panel in the small foyer and pressed the code to arm it to make sure it worked.

Dropping her purse onto the floor, she made her way through the living room and into the kitchen. She wanted a drink. Whether it was memory or instinct, she opened the short cabinet over the sink. A half-full bottle of good bourbon sat there, as if waiting for her.

Hector's drink of choice. She'd bought the bottle for him. She was certain of it. When he came to visit, he always liked to talk over a drink.

Taking it down, she poured some into a glass then added ice as the fumes from the bottle assaulted her nostrils.

"Based on your nonresponse, I take it things didn't go well."

Liza shook her head and offered the bottle to him. He took it and poured his own glass.

"A little decadent, drinking in the middle of the afternoon, but I certainly wouldn't want you to do it alone. Tell me what happened."

Liza took a sip and felt the sting of the alcohol on

her tongue as it blazed a trail down her throat. She wasn't sure if it would solve anything, but she liked the feeling it gave her. As if she could do what she wanted, when she wanted. Such a bad girl drinking in the afternoon.

"I remembered Hector's secretary's name. Jeanine. It came to me just like that."

"That's good."

"I guess." She set the glass down on the counter and crossed her arms over her chest. "Then we met the man who has taken over for Hector. His number two, I guess. Freddy Ortiz. I didn't remember him, but he obviously knew me." Liza pointed to the blinking light on the wall phone behind Greg. "That must be his message because he said he called me. Only I can't remember the damn password to retrieve it. I need to call the phone company."

"You can do that later. What did he tell you that has you so upset?"

"He implied that Hector and I were lovers. He's not the first. You told me there were rumors about us. He said that he couldn't think of any criminal element that might have wanted Hector dead. That Hector had done everything he could to run a clean business, unlike my treacherous father. Which meant whatever the motive was for killing him had to be personal. He couldn't look at me when he said this, of course."

"Do you think it's true? About you and Hector?"

"I know it's not!" Liza shouted. She wanted to scream. She wanted to claw at something. She felt so damn trapped. Trapped by circumstances that were out of her control. By a brain that wouldn't function the way it should and give her the information she needed to prove herself innocent. "What does it matter? What does any of it matter? My lawyer thinks I'm guilty, the people who knew Hector think I'm guilty. Any minute the police are going to come and formally charge me and I can't stop them because I can't tell them what happened."

"You seem agitated," Greg said softly. "You need to calm down."

"Stop that! Stop using your calm, reasonable voice with me. I hate that voice. You said so yourself—I'm not your patient. I don't know if you believe me or not, Greg. Here is the thing—I don't care anymore. I don't give a shit about who thinks what. I just want everyone to go away and leave me alone."

Greg took another sip. "Are you done?"

Liza clenched her teeth. "No. I feel like I want to hit something."

Greg set his glass on the table and walked toward her. He took her glass from the hand that was clutching it so hard she thought she could actually break it.

He smiled. "You want to hit something, huh? I think I have an idea."

CHAPTER TWELVE

"YOU BROUGHT ME TO A batting cage?"

Greg contained his smile at Liza's horrified expression. "You said you wanted to hit something."

She looked at him as if he was slightly crazy, and possibly he was. He thought after some really intense days, she needed a break.

A couple of hours where she wasn't suffering from a traumatic condition. Where she wasn't surrounded by people who thought she was lying. Here, at a park, with a bunch of moms and dads and their kids swinging bats, this was normal. She needed normal for a few hours. After her outburst, he told her to change into something comfortable for outside. She'd come back in a pair of shorts and a white sleeveless top. A plain, simple outfit. Still, it messed with his willpower.

He knew he didn't think of her as a patient anymore; that option was gone. But he wanted to not think of her as a lover. His solution was to try and consider her a friend. Only a friend probably shouldn't want to rip off her shirt and pull down her shorts so he could see her naked.

Get a grip.

When he headed to her place earlier he'd been considering a movie, but when she said she wanted to hit something, the cages popped into his head. After Tommy killed himself, on days when Greg couldn't get out of his own way, the physical satisfaction of swinging hard at something and making physical contact helped to take him out of his brain.

If only he'd gotten addicted to that instead of gambling.

He knew what it was like to need a break from his life and he knew that after last night Liza would never come back to the loft. Not after Chuck made his feelings so evident. Greg didn't blame Chuck. The evidence against her was strong. Greg also didn't blame Liza. He wished he could be a better man for both of them. One wanted him to see reason. One wanted him to have faith.

He was a failure to both of them.

However, Greg decided that one of them needed him more. So he spent the day after leaving the police station thinking first about what might distract Liza and then about what he could do to make her house safer because he was too much of a pansy to accompany her to Atlantic City. Because he really, really didn't want to think about the reasons he couldn't man up and join her.

So he'd bought some deadbolts and called a locksmith and that made him feel better. Manlier, which was completely and utterly silly, but no one ever accused men of not being silly.

Now he'd brought her to this park and while she was not smiling she wasn't frowning as intensely, either. "I don't know if I can even hit a ball. I don't think I'm very athletic."

"You're in shape." She was in amazing shape. He'd felt that shape up close and personal so he knew for certain it was near perfect. Small, soft breasts, flat belly, firm little ass... But he wasn't going to let himself notice that because she was his friend.

Willpower. That's all it is. Willpower not to gamble. Willpower not to want her.

"You must do something to stay fit," he said.

She looked down at her feet as if another memory was surfacing. "I run, I think. Not like marathons or anything. I think I do that to compensate for sitting at my job all day."

"Another memory?"

She nodded. "It's going to come back. I can feel that now."

"Then all of this has a finite time frame. You should hold on to that. In the meantime, what's happening to you needs to be set aside. You're a normal woman out with me and we're going to try and hit some balls. Most likely you will swing and miss and I will laugh at you and that will be fun, too."

"You know, you're asking someone who is already suffering from a brain issue to step into a batting cage where hard balls will be hurled at me at high speeds. You're sure this isn't a variation of the theory that if I get hit in the head, my memory will come back?"

It was working already. That was a joke. Greg was certain of it.

"Nope. Just want to give you a chance to hit something and give me a chance to laugh at you."

He opened the car door and got out, pleased when she followed him. They picked up two bats and batting helmets and Greg stepped into one of the cages with a few rolls of quarters he'd traded a twenty in for.

Clouds were breaking up the sun, which helped to offset the sticky heat of late summer. They were outside, about to play around and he hoped they got a couple of laughs out of the day.

In another universe it might have been a date.

"Okay, what do I do?"

Greg opened the cage and watched as she stepped inside with trepidation. Memory or no, he could tell she wasn't comfortable in the cage, which could mean this was her first time doing anything like this.

A batting virgin. His first.

"Okay, stand sideways and turn your face toward the pitcher." He watched her pick a side and realized she was a lefty. He got behind her and put his hands on her hips.

"You want to keep your hips steady."

His hands rested on either side of her hips, and even though he had purposefully left room between their bodies he still felt the impact of touching her to his very toes. Shaking it off, he continued. "You want to spread your legs a little farther apart to give you balance."

Under his hands he could feel the tension in her body, as well. He wasn't trying to be deliberately seductive. But he also had to admit he liked the way she reacted to him. Especially when he knew she didn't want to react to him at all. Or wouldn't after the way he rejected her the night before. Not wanting to push his luck, he decided verbal instruction would be better. He stepped away from her and then leaned on the back of the cage.

"Now swing a few times."

She raised the bat over her shoulder, and then brought it down across her body. It was hopeless.

"Maybe I should have taken you golfing instead."

"Maybe I need something tall and unmoving to hit. If you want to move a little closer…"

Another joke. Progress. Greg dumped a quarter into the machine and hit the slow button, sorry there wasn't a superslow option.

"Okay, now keep your eye on the ball and let it rip."

She was about two seconds and two feet off from hitting the first ball. And the second. But as she got used to the speed and the eye level of the ball, which was the same every time, eventually she started to make some contact. Finally, with one solid whack, she sailed a ball back over the pitching machine and into the netting behind it.

"I did it! Did you see that? That was, like, so far."

Greg didn't imagine the ball would have cleared the second baseman on a baseball diamond but she was pleased and that was what this day was all about.

Pleasing Liza. No, he quickly changed his mind. Not pleasing her, distracting her. Taking her mind off what was happening so that maybe her brain might rest. If it got the rest it needed, it might heal. Getting those memories back was going to be crucial in her defense if the police felt they had enough evidence to convict her. Greg thought it felt like the quiet before the storm. The detectives weren't around, they weren't asking direct questions of her, but they were still out there doing their job. Building their case.

Or hopefully *not* building their case.

"My turn."

Liza happily backed off the base pad and let him take his turn.

She leaned against the wire cage and he tried not to feel too self conscious as she watched him.

How long had it been since he cared about what a woman thought? Too long, that much was a given. Too bad the woman he most wanted to impress right now should be off-limits to him.

Not taking any chances, he set the speed to medium and let a few balls go by him before he started to swing.

Like it had in the past, the feel of the bat making contact with the ball sent a jolt through his body. It was intoxicating.

"Oh my, you can really hit it!"

Not really. He was only at medium speed but he smiled anyway.

"I used to come here a lot…when I was battling my demons."

"Did you win those battles?"

"No," he confessed. "I only kept the demons at bay for a while. Eventually they came roaring back and I found other weapons to fight them with."

She wasn't looking at him, just staring out to some point on the horizon. "Gambling was one of those weapons?"

"As effective as a bazooka. Of course, it came with its own price."

"Now you've won that battle, too. You conquered your demons and your crutch."

Greg swung at the last ball and sent it sailing. Then he pushed the bat head down into the dirt. "I don't know if I deserve that kind of credit."

"I think you do."

Her face was so honest and open. So in awe of his victory that it almost hurt.

Greg shook his head. "I couldn't stomach the idea of being in Atlantic City. Even though I knew you wanted me there with you. That's not victory over my crutch. It's simply…managing it."

"I was fine. I know you want to be my hero…"

"I don't," Greg denied. "I'm nobody's hero."

She laughed at that. "Hate to break it to you, but you might as well be wearing a cape. Sad to say, I've been happy to let you take the role, too. I think… I feel like that's happened to me a lot. Like there was always someone there stepping in to make my problems go away. Likely Hector, mostly. It's why I was happy to know that I hadn't worked for him my whole career. That I was on my own at McKay and Fitz."

Greg knew the accounting firm. "Why do you think you left?"

Liza shrugged. He hadn't wanted to ruin the afternoon by making her think about her situation, but this was something he could easily fix.

He pulled his phone out of his back pocket and looked up McKay and Fitz. He found a number for the office and called it. It was the middle of the afternoon, during the work week, there should be no issue getting someone on the phone. "Yes, Human Resources, please."

Liza walked over to him, curious, but he held up a finger for her to wait. He was immediately passed to a different extension.

A pleasant voice on the line picked up and asked him about the nature of his call.

"Yes, hi, I'm calling for a reference check. On Eliza Dunning."

Greg smiled as the woman instantly recognized the name. They must have been acquaintances because as big as McKay and Fitz was he doubted the HR people would know everyone personally. The woman gave a glowing reference that Greg ultimately had to cut short.

"Can you tell me why she left, then?"

He listened to the answer then thanked the woman as he ended the call, before she could ask any questions.

"Well?"

"According to the HR person you were a wonderful employee. I think she knew you personally because she said you were sweet and thoughtful beyond being good at your job."

"That was nice."

"She said many people were sad to see you go, but you cited family obligations as your reason for leaving."

"Family obligations," Liza repeated. "I considered Hector my family. Not my boyfriend, my family."

"It makes sense. While he didn't raise you directly, he was there for you throughout your life."

She nibbled on her lip. "The fact that I left my job to join The Grande, makes me think he had a reason for asking me to come. Something that would have compelled me to work with him, despite not wanting to work for him in the past."

Greg nodded, seeing the puzzle she was putting together start to take shape. "What if…"

"What if he knew…"

The two of them looked at each other and Greg could tell they were having the same thought.

Liza's eyes lit up. "Hector must have had a suspicion something was happening with the books. He asked me to come help him find out what. It's the only reason I would have left a job I felt I needed to maintain my independence."

"It took time, but you dug into the accounts and found out what was happening."

"Jeanine said I scheduled an appointment for Sunday morning, but instead I went there the night before. What if I thought he was in danger?"

"Makes sense. Once the person realized Hector knew who was cheating him, he or she suddenly had a lot to lose."

"Did they have to kill him? Couldn't whoever did it just have left?"

Greg shook his head. "Whoever was stealing from Hector on that kind of level—I have to believe it was a kill or be killed kind of a situation. I'm sorry if it upsets you, but that was his reputation."

"Freddy said that Hector was trying to run a clean business," Liza said. "He wouldn't have wanted blood on his hands."

Greg instantly flashed back to the two men who had given him his last profound beating before he decided he was done with gambling. "In the gambling world there are different levels of clean. Hector was a man who understood the life. Whether he wanted to separate himself from that or not, I can't say. But if he let someone else cheat him, and go without punishment, it would have impacted his reputation. That's not something you mess with in AC."

Dark clouds started to move in, and there was a rumble of thunder, seconds before fat rain drops descended on them.

Liza squealed as they made their way out of the cage. By the time they had returned the bats and the helmets, they were running from a full-out rainstorm. When they reached the car, they were drenched and winded but laughing. Because, for whatever reason, getting caught in a thunderstorm brought its own fun. Like suddenly you were pitted against nature in a game, trying to outrun her. What wasn't funny was the tension that roared to life when Greg looked at his passenger. Liza's white sleeveless top clung to her skin and it took everything Greg had not to look at her nipples, which were hard and straining the fabric.

"Wow. That felt great."

Greg kept his eyes firmly on the windshield. "What part?"

"Running, laughing. Even swinging a bat. All of it. Thank you, Greg."

He didn't say anything. Yes, that had been his purpose. To make her feel better, to lift her spirits and maybe give her a break that would help her heal. He was thrilled he'd succeeded.

"I'd better take you home."

"Yes."

Except he didn't put the key in the ignition. Instead he looked over at her again as she was pulling the wet ropes of hair off her shoulders. He remembered how stunning he'd found her the first time he saw her. Even when she was covered in blood.

Now with the sadness that constantly surrounded her lifted, he could see she was beyond stunning. Beyond the beauty of any woman he'd ever imagined.

She said she had a feeling that men went out of their way to protect her. He didn't doubt it. A girl lost in the world, her parents taken from her by violence, growing up to be sweet of heart and more beautiful than anything around her. Of course men wanted to hold on to her. Of course they wanted to shelter her from all harm.

She chafed against it every time. They hadn't believed her when she was a teenager and said she hadn't tried to kill herself. But she let herself be sent to that hospital, let herself be treated for a depression she didn't have.

Why didn't she fight? Why didn't she shout and scream like she did with him.

I don't give a shit about who thinks what.

Greg couldn't help but wonder if that anger, that inner rage, hadn't been building in her for a long time. Long before she witnessed her last hope at family shot down in a dark alley behind a casino.

"What?"

Greg shook his head. "Nothing. I'm sorry."

He drove her home, not taking any peeks at her see-through shirt. When he reached her place, he checked every room and the basement and didn't leave until he was absolutely satisfied no one was in the house. He stood outside and waited while she activated the alarm, and he was happy to see a police patrol car drive by as he made his way back to his car.

She was as safe as she could be. And he wasn't a hero, so he should get in his car and drive away.

Instead he drove around the block, pulled up beside the patrol car to let him know who he was and what his intentions were. Then circled back to her place to park on the other side of the street.

He wasn't a hero. She wasn't a damsel in distress. He knew that, but he wasn't leaving. Because suddenly it clicked. Deep down in his gut where he couldn't pretend to himself any longer. He believed her. One hundred percent without question, he believed Liza Dunning watched for the second time in her life, as a member of her family was shot to death in cold blood. So close that the blood from his wounds fell on her hair and her clothes.

That person came back to this house. That person had a gun. That person wanted her dead.

No, Greg wasn't a hero. But he sure as hell wasn't going to let anything happen to her.

He settled into the seat of the car, wishing he had a change of dry clothes, and watched her house.

CHUCK CHECKED HIS PHONE after his text alarm sounded. Instantly, he lifted his hands off his ergonomic keyboard as if the person texting him could actually see what he was doing on his computer. Which was basically cyberstalking a lawyer he really needed to spend less time thinking about.

Snorting at his own guilt, he read the message.

Won't be home. Staying to watch over Liza. Don't be a dick about it.

Chuck considered any number of responses. His first thought was to ask if Greg was worried Liza would eat a poison apple and wanted to be there to wake her from her sleep with a kiss.

Prince Charming had nothing on Greg Chalmers. Which was probably why Greg wrote that last sentence. He didn't want to hear it. Not tonight.

It wasn't as if Chuck wasn't on the fence about the

whole situation, anyway. The dude they met with today should have confirmed it. Liza was banging Hector. Nobody else wanted to kill Hector. What had Ortiz called it…a personal matter?

But that theory didn't really jibe with the whole embezzlement scheme.

Not to mention that Freddy seemed a little too slick. Chuck had been hanging around Greg too long, not to detect some obvious tells.

The man had been nervous. Nervous, but trying to hide it. Chuck had felt the faint vibration in the floor as if someone in the room was bouncing their leg on the ball of their foot. The only legs in the room that had been hidden were Ortiz's.

That was what he planned to tell Greg as soon as he got home, although it didn't look as if that was going to be anytime soon. If some guy really had tried to take Liza out, then Chuck had to agree it was probably a good idea that someone stayed with her.

The mess they had gotten into by taking a call from a Brigantine Sherriff a couple of days ago.

Greg was locked in, and he imagined Elaine was now, too. They hadn't spoken since she'd told him about the amazing sex she'd had last Tuesday. They spent the whole drive home from AC in silence, staring at Liza's car in front of them.

But back to Liza. The people she worked with at the casino liked her. Greg liked her.

Chuck didn't not like her—he was just trying to

use his head instead of his dick, which was apparently where Greg was taking this. That was a flat-out bad idea and Chuck would bet that both Greg and Liza knew it. That didn't always mean you could stop it.

Hell, Greg was a goner from the moment she'd put tinfoil over his dinner to keep it warm while he'd been on the phone that first night. A soft heart, she was. Chuck always figured Greg would fall for someone with a soft heart.

You couldn't stop who you were attracted to. Chuck knew that all too well. Because if he had any control over this shit with Elaine, he certainly would have used it by now. How many girls was it going to take? Three more, four more, before he stopped thinking about her? Stopped wanting her?

Stopped stalking her.

On the internet, only. Did that even count?

Chuck looked at the screen open in front of him. Elaine's bank account transactions for last Tuesday. She'd swiped her card at a Chinese restaurant and she'd made an online movie purchase. Sure, that could have been a date. Guy comes by, they share takeout food and a movie and some sex. Then there was a transaction a little after midnight to some exercise equipment website. One of those gimmicky companies that advertise on late-night cable TV. Based on the amount deducted from Elaine's account, he concluded she had bought the complete

DVD set of workout routines that would turn her from Flab to Fab in two weeks.

Yeah, no woman had Chinese food and great sex, and then ordered workout DVDs.

So what did that get him? Chuck wondered as he logged out of her account. Which had been ridiculously easy to access. He needed to find a way to get her to come up with a more complicated password. Without telling her he knew hers.

She had lied to him, definitely. She hadn't been out with anyone. She hadn't had sex with anyone. But she wanted him to think that she had. To make him jealous. Which she had done. Jealous enough to invade her privacy.

Man, he was toast. If only he could stop thinking about her. Which he'd basically proved, for the past few months, he wasn't capable of doing.

Maybe there was another option. Maybe instead of trying to stop thinking about her, or being mean to her, or stalking her, or getting jealous over any guy she talked to, it was time to be honest with her. He'd considered it before and rejected it because he hadn't wanted to hear yet another rejection from her lips. The more time they had spent together, though, the more it was becoming obvious things weren't settled between them.

She was trying to make him jealous. He was falling for it. They were both snapping at each other and hurting each other, and it was as though neither one of them wanted to stop.

Because stopping would mean not seeing each other at all.

Chuck took a big breath. "I liked you, Elaine," he said to an empty loft. "I really, really liked you and I was pretty much crushed when you rejected me. Why did you do that? Why did you do that when I thought you felt the same way about me?"

Sadly, the empty loft had no answers. Which meant if he was going to get them, he was going to have to man up and ask her the same question.

CHAPTER THIRTEEN

LIZA LOOKED OUT THE window and saw his car across the street. Did she really expect anything less from a hero? She'd changed out of her wet clothes and dried her hair. She could only imagine how uncomfortable he was, sitting in his wet shorts and shirt.

Then she imagined him out of his wet clothes and that image convinced her she should leave him outside. Not inside, with her, for the whole night. That was where the real danger lay.

Except he wasn't interested in her like that. When she'd kissed him, he pushed her away.

Then why could you practically feel the heat coming off his body when you were in the car together?

It was a thought she hadn't wanted to pursue. She was aware he had deliberately not looked at her, as though it took all his physical strength not to. The effort was fairly telling. Even if he was attracted to her, it was evident he didn't want to act on it.

Which was exactly the right approach to take given the situation they were in. They couldn't have a relationship. How could she give herself to another person when she didn't even know who she was?

Liza considered the idea of having sex for sex's sake, but that didn't feel right to her, either. She was certain in her pre-memory-loss life she wasn't someone who had treated sex casually. So she couldn't have sex with him, and she couldn't have a relationship with him. But there was probably no harm in allowing him to come inside, dry his clothes and sleep in the guest bedroom, if that's what he felt he needed to do for his own peace of mind.

Liza disabled her alarm, unlocked the door and trotted down the walkway toward his car. His scowl seemed to grow as she approached, and he rolled down his window.

"This is not about me being a hero. This is just a precaution."

She couldn't help but smile. She would like to think that if she had ever looked for a relationship before that she had tried to find someone like Greg. Greg, who was so strong but who also had his weaknesses, so a person didn't feel inferior when they were with him.

"Come inside. You can get dry and sleep in the guest room."

He'd opened the door before she even finished her sentence.

"I'll cook us dinner," she said over her shoulder.

"Why am I getting so lucky?"

"You're not getting lucky!" Liza blurted the

words, before she understood he wasn't making a suggestion.

"Liza."

She didn't want to turn around. She didn't want him to see how mortified she was. He was the one who'd turned her away. He was the one who demonstrated so much control in the car when her shirt was wet, see-through and plastered to her. Yes, it had seemed as if he was deliberately not looking, but damn, he hadn't even looked once!

Pivoting on the ball of her foot, she tried to remember she was a grown-up and not a shy young girl with her first crush.

Billy Davis. Billy Davis was your first crush, your first kiss. Your first everything. But then Nonna died.

Liza closed her eyes as the memory came back.

"Hey, you okay?"

Liza nodded. She could feel Greg's hand on her shoulder and it was as if he was infusing her with all the caring he claimed he didn't have, but that she could feel.

"Another memory. It was nice."

"What was it?"

"My first kiss." Liza smiled. "Every girl should remember her first kiss."

Greg frowned. "Really? I would think every girl would want to forget it because most guys that age don't know what the hell they're doing."

"Yeah, well Billy Davis must have had some prior experience because I thought it was nice."

Greg frowned and Liza wasn't sure what that meant. She only knew she had effectively distracted him from whatever he'd been about to say to her before.

"Come on, you want to get dry and I need to start dinner. I'm thinking a simple baked ziti."

"Homemade baked ziti? I think I might cry."

"Wait until you taste it. I'll make sure I bring the tissues."

Liza walked ahead of him, thinking that she'd dodged the bullet. She was happy with the thought that not only had she had another memory, but she was also certain she could make a kick-ass baked ziti. She knew because she remembered now who'd taught her to cook. Nonna. Her grandmother taught her and she was an excellent cook.

"You're pretty, so it's not as important. But me, I had the big nose. I had to cook to make the man want me, yes?"

Liza hugged yet another memory—something from her grandmother—to her chest. Even with all the craziness of the past few days, Liza knew without a doubt she'd been loved.

Regardless of who Hector was and what her relationship with him was, she knew she considered him family. She hadn't been alone in the world.

Only now he was dead. Was that why Greg was

so appealing to her? Was she latching on to him to replace the last man who cared for her? She looked at him over her shoulder and then shook her head.

No, he was just really cute. She could own that. She didn't have to look at herself through the same lens everyone else did and determine she was weak and clingy. That when one man left her life, she searched for the next man to take over.

Those were things she knew she fought against.

She could be simply a woman who found a man attractive. It didn't make her weak. It made her, well, a woman.

Holding her head up, she led him inside. He was familiar with her guest room and she found extra towels for him and set them in the main bathroom. She also found an old flannel robe for him. It would be a little short but would allow her to take his clothes and throw them in the dryer.

Figuring he had everything he needed, she didn't linger. Though maybe there was a slight possibility that she watched through a sliver in the door when he took his wet T-shirt off, but that was more an accident of timing than anything else.

He did have a really nice back.

In the kitchen, she let herself loose. Her pantry and freezer were stocked with the ingredients she needed as if she made these sorts of dishes on a routine basis.

She knew her ziti wasn't exactly like her grandmother would make. Nonna would have made everything from scratch, including the pasta and the mozzarella. But after browning the meat and cooking the pasta, then putting it all together in a massive dish with sauce she must have made in large batches and kept frozen, she was certain it would turn out fine.

She was putting it in the oven when Greg walked into the kitchen. When she turned to face him, her heart skipped a beat. The robe was tightly cinched against his long, lean body and his hair curled more around his face now that it was wet.

His bare, hair-covered shins and long, bony feet seemed incredibly naked to her.

"Here."

In a flash decision, she decided to take whatever he was offering. Then she saw the pile of material in his hands. It was his shorts, shirt and a pair of boxer briefs.

Suddenly desperate to get out of his space, she reached for the clothes and skipped down to the basement to throw them in the dryer. She added a softener sheet—because who didn't like soft underwear—and then wondered how long she could hide in the basement before he got suspicious.

"This is ridiculous," she muttered.

She'd been sopping wet in a see-through shirt and he'd been able to resist her. She could get over some naked feet. If for no other reason than her pride.

Climbing up the stairs, she reached for a casualness she didn't exactly feel.

"Dinner will be ready in about an hour if you want to go watch TV or something."

"Liza."

He was sitting at her kitchen table, but the tone of his voice was similar to when he'd said her name earlier in the car. Her distraction, it seemed, was only temporary.

Maybe she should tell him the memory she'd had about her Nonna.

Or maybe she should go on the offensive.

"Look, Greg, if this is about the comment I made earlier about you getting lucky, forget about it."

"It's not about your comment, it's about the fact that you blushed several different shades of red after you made it. You know we... You know we can't."

Can't. Shouldn't. Won't. She hated all those words when it came to him. "Yes. You made it really clear when you practically fell to the floor getting away from me last night."

"You surprised me," he said.

"We both agreed it was probably from the shock of what happened."

"And we both know we were lying."

"You keep doing that," she accused him. "I'm fighting this really hard because, yes, I get that the timing sucks. I also know that you're acting like something happening between us is the last thing you want. Only you keep saying these things like—"

"I'm fighting it, too," he said grimly. "I am. I guess I feel like it's only fair to be honest. I mean, it's not just you, okay? It's both of us."

She shouldn't be excited by his admission. She couldn't be. It would only make things worse. But it made her feel slightly less desperate.

They were attracted to each other. It happened. Not the craziest thing in the world, for two attractive people of the same age to have chemistry between them. It wasn't one sided.

"Thank you for that."

He snorted. "Yeah, you're welcome. But I don't know how it helps anything."

"It makes me feel normal. Not needy, not desperate, not alone. You're a nice guy."

Greg winced. "You didn't just use the *nice* word."

Liza smiled. "I think I like nice guys. Also, you're hot. So you're nice and you're hot and you're a really good kisser."

"Better than Billy Davis?"

She smiled again. "Yes. Is that why you frowned when I told you about that memory? Were you worried that you didn't hold up to my first kiss?"

He shook his head. "No, I was disappointed that I was no longer the memory of your first one."

Her smile faltered. "See, you did it again. Saying stuff like that is going to make the fight even harder."

"Trust me when I tell you, it's already hard enough."

Liza bit down on her lower lip and tried not to be aroused by the thought of what Greg looked like hard.

"But we can do this," he insisted. "We can keep our heads. All we have to do is focus on the situation and acknowledge that complicating it won't help matters."

Liza nodded. "I already figured that out. I decided that I'm not the type to have casual sex. At least my instincts are to reject that as a possibility. The idea of a relationship while I'm still like this is crazy."

"Crazier than having amnesia?"

Her lips curled. "Exactly that crazy. But Greg… If things were different. If we had just met…"

"Yeah. If we had just met. If I had seen you walking into a coffee shop in Philly, I might I have followed you inside. Seen what you ordered and if it was normal, not like one of those two pump, extra hot, no foam, three shot deals, I would have flirted with you. Or tried to."

She ducked her head. "I'm not sure that would have worked. I think—I have the feeling anyway—that I'm shy. I might have made it too hard for you."

He stepped closer and she could smell a hint of the soap he'd used in the shower. Her soap. "I would have tried harder, then."

"Men scare me."

He blinked. "Is that a feeling or a memory?"

Her heart was suddenly pounding and Greg stepped forward to put his hands on her shoulders and rub her arms. She wasn't sure, but she knew it was the truth. She wasn't easy around them. "Memory, I think."

"And me? Are you afraid of me?"

"No. You make me nervous in a different way."

He smiled. "That's actually really sweet."

Liza wrinkled her nose. "I think sweet is almost as bad as nice."

"Sorry, I guess I like sweet girls."

For a moment they stood like that. With his long hands covering her shoulders and his body so close to hers all she had to do was reach out...

Buzz.

The sound of the dryer going off downstairs broke whatever spell they were both falling under, Liza backed away, her arms crossed over her middle.

"Sorry," she mumbled as she headed back down the basement steps to clothes that probably weren't dry yet. At least it would give her time to think about exactly how she felt. Because while she was nervous and shaken and rattled, she was also wildly turned on.

Men did scare her. She could feel that, not as a particular memory but as a pattern throughout her life.

Greg Chalmers, however, wasn't one of those men. That was even scarier.

HE SHOULD HAVE been asleep. Dead sound asleep. He'd eaten his weight in the most fabulous baked ziti he'd ever had. Instead of putting him in a carbohydrate-induced coma, it had only added to the allure of Liza.

Not that he cared whether a woman could cook or not; that was beside the point. It was watching her take such pleasure in the little things. The way she sprinkled the parmesan cheese on top of his plate so that it perfectly coated the dish. The way she used a towel to clean around the edges of the dish, removing the slightest imperfections.

The way she watched him eat.

She was confident in knowing he would enjoy his food and that look of despair she wore so frequently, as if she were completely lost in an unknown world, was gone for now. This was the woman she'd been before she lost her memory. She'd revealed a new facet of herself to him.

Which was a problem. Because every time she did that, every time she showed him another side of who she was, he fell a little bit harder. Greg wanted to hold on to the cynic he'd been when he first met her. But he could feel that cynicism dripping away with every moment they spent together.

His gut said she was innocent; his dick said she was smoking; his brain said she was out of bounds, but his heart?

Shit, he didn't want to think about his heart.

Hadn't thought about it in years, since his fiancée told him she could no longer put up with his bullshit, which he absolutely didn't blame her for.

He remembered some late night when Chuck had come home after one of his conquests, when they had shared a beer and Greg had told him how smart he was to stick to one-night stands. One-night stands were easy; relationships were hard. Then he'd told him about Irene and how she had dumped him, and Chuck had said how lucky Greg was to escape. Because a woman who couldn't be there for you in the dark times, wasn't the kind of woman you wanted in your life.

Because in life there were always dark times.

Greg thought of Irene and who she had been. Independent, smart, a corporate professional who always had her shit together. Greg used to think he mellowed her, relaxed her, and it was why she loved him.

He couldn't remember now why he loved her. Admired her, sure. Who wouldn't want a woman who was smart and beautiful? Who showed no flaws, ever. He'd never thought of her as intimidating. Greg was too successful in his own right. But after he lost Tommy and started to spiral out of control, he remembered thinking she was unforgiving.

Unforgiving of the idea that a kid might be so depressed he would take his life. Unforgiving of someone who would question his entire professional judgment over one mistake. Unforgiving of someone who couldn't dig himself out of the quagmire he'd gotten himself into. On purpose.

Greg tried to imagine Liza in that role. A fiancée or girlfriend of someone who was in trouble. She wouldn't be unforgiving. She couldn't be, because she knew too well what it was to hurt.

No, Liza would show sympathy and offer comfort. Would she be strong enough to try to pull him back on his feet? Sympathy was fine for a time, but when someone was digging a hole they needed a partner to reach down and haul them out of it.

He was trying to be that hand for Liza now. Offering the steady assurance of someone who could lead her out of this trouble. If their situations were ever reversed, would she be capable of doing the same for him?

He didn't know, but he suspected she would be. Maybe that was why, despite what his dick wanted, what his whole body wanted, he knew sleeping with her could be a trap. Liza might offer to put his head in her lap and stroke his hair and tell him everything was going to be all right.

That would be a nice place. Too nice of a place. A place like that and Greg feared he would linger there. Wallow in his pool of comfort and sympathy. It might make him weak.

Weaker, he corrected, with a silent inner curse. Even today, she'd wanted to congratulate him on overcoming his addiction. As if he'd done some impressive thing. As if he hadn't put himself in that situation to begin with. He hadn't been able to go with her to AC. Didn't she see that? He let her talk to people who were close to Hector without him being there to assess whether they were telling the truth or not.

No, she shouldn't be proud of him. She should be disgusted with him.

He'd let her go to AC. Yes, he'd sent Chuck and Elaine with her, but it wasn't the same thing. He'd let her go, even though he couldn't follow and that didn't make him any kind of hero for overcoming his addiction. It made him a slave to it, still.

Being with Liza, living in her world where she comforted him and cooked for him and gave herself to him…he wasn't worthy of it. That was the damn truth.

A noise down the hall caught his attention. He checked the clock on the bedside table and red numbers told him it was a little after four in the morning. A whole night spent obsessing over something he wanted, but wouldn't let himself have.

The short cry was cut off and Greg was instantly on his feet. He left the bedroom, practically sprinting down the hallway to the master bedroom. The house alarm was still engaged and certainly hadn't given any warning of an intruder.

When he opened the door, Liza was sitting up, breathing heavily, her eyes wide open.

"Liza, what is it?"

She blinked a few times as if not understanding who he was or why he was there, then she scrambled out of bed and flew into his arms. He only wore the boxer briefs she'd dried for him. She was in a sleeveless nightgown that showed off her creamy shoulders in the waning rays of moonlight.

He'd spent the past five hours doing everything he could not to think about this. Not to want this. To question all the reasons wanting it wasn't smart or noble or even within his right to want.

She was in his arms and her face was pressed against his shoulder, and he could feel her soft hair cascading over his arm as he wrapped it around her back, hopefully making her feel safe.

What a hell of a waste of time.

"Greg," she finally murmured. "I thought it was a dream, but I don't think it was. I think it was a memory."

"Tell me." Reluctantly, he pulled back from her body, already missing the contact of her pressed against him.

Her head snapped up. "You were right. He lied."

"Right about what?" he prompted. "Who lied?"

"Dr. Verdi. He wasn't only my doctor, Greg, he knew me. He was at the hospital with Hector. When they thought I attempted suicide. He knew Hector.

My God, how could he think…I wasn't just a patient there." She gasped as it fully came back to her. The complete memory of what happened to her at that time.

"Tell me!"

"He was Hector's cousin. He was there at my Nonna's funeral. *He* was the one who gave me the antidepressants after Nonna died. *He* was the one who said I tried to kill myself. Hector believed him and they both decided that I should go with him to that facility."

Greg's jaw tightened. He could remember the surprise on Verdi's face when Liza had walked into his office. What had he said?

I can't believe it. You came.

Of course it would have been hard to believe she'd return, if he knew how much she hated the place. Then there was the agitation when he talked about the difference of opinion he and Hector had over her care. Not the difference of opinion between a guardian and a doctor. They had been two cousins fighting for what they thought was best for Liza. Apparently, Verdi thought antidepressants were necessary.

Mostly, Greg remembered the doctor's urgency in wanting her to stay once he understood that Liza had no memory of the events surrounding Hector's death. How he actually believed she would want to stay in that hospital.

"I was scared of him," Liza said. "When I was

there…I was scared of him. That's why I kept those pills in my medicine cabinet. They weren't there for me to take, they were there for me to remember what can happen when someone else is in control of my life."

Men scare me.

Greg heard her words clearly in his head. It sounded as if Dr. Verdi might have been the first to frighten her.

He thought about tucking her back into bed with some reassurances that they would figure it out later after she had slept, but he knew neither one of them were going back to bed.

"Okay, listen. You go make some coffee. I'm going to call Mark."

Liza looked over at the clock next to her bed. "It's not even four-thirty in the morning," Liza told him.

Greg thought about all the times Mark had asked him to play poker when he knew Greg's situation. An early morning wakeup call was nothing more than a little payback.

"He'll live."

"But what is he going to do?"

"He's going to find out everything there is to know about Dr. Verdi. With some information we are going to make him a little less scary."

CHAPTER FOURTEEN

ELAINE HEARD THE KNOCK on her office door and looked up, surprised her assistant was in so early. It wasn't even eight and Elaine had already been working for the past two hours. She hadn't been able to sleep and work seemed like the best possible distraction.

Her law office consisted only of a shingle outside a room in which there was a desk for Beth and, behind a partition, an office for herself. She rented the space in a house that had been converted to offices, with four other private-practice lawyers.

Essentially her office had once been the parlor and dining room of a turn-of-the-century home. The converted house had a kitchen they all shared, a leaky roof they all complained about and, in the summer, air conditioning that could be spotty at best.

But Elaine had always thought the place had an old-fashioned charm. It was tucked away in a nice little upper-class neighborhood in South Jersey, where people could afford lawyers for things. Coincidentally, the same town where Liza lived, although she never recalled seeing Liza before. Then again, when she was there, she rarely left her office.

She cringed upon seeing Chuck's head pop around the door.

"What are you doing here?"

"Nice. You this friendly to all your clients?" he asked as he stepped inside the office.

"You're not a client. You're not even a friend, I don't think. It's eight in the morning and I'm working."

"You do that a lot? Work this early?"

Elaine could think of no reason for him to be here. Their last exchange had been embarrassing for everyone. After they had followed Liza home, they hadn't spoken one word to each other until he'd dropped her off at her condo and she'd muttered a goodbye as she bolted out of the car. She was finally coming around to the idea that whatever they'd once had as friends was well and truly over. Whatever they might have had if she hadn't been an idiot was over, too.

But here he was, sitting in her guest chair, slouched down a little as if he had no intention of going anywhere. She supposed he would eventually tell her why he'd come.

"I work when I can't sleep," she conceded to fill the silence.

"Why can't you sleep?"

Elaine looked at him, completely flummoxed. As if she was going to confess to him that he was the reason she wasn't sleeping. The worst part was she had a feeling he knew it, too. That he bothered her enough to affect her sleep. That he knew he'd managed to get under her skin and it pleased him.

"What do you want, Chuck?"

"Greg called early this morning. Too freaking early. They're going back to the hospital to talk to the good doctor again. Seems Princess Memory has coughed up a few new ones. Or old ones, depending on how you look at it."

"You still don't trust her?"

Chuck shrugged. "I don't know. But I know Greg is into her, and I either have to support that or start thinking about replacing him as a roommate. Because I have this crazy feeling if it came down to her or me he would choose her."

"That's ridiculous. They've only known each other for what, not even a week? That's nothing. Besides, Greg needs you. You're his rock."

"You think?"

"Don't you?"

"I think he did for a while. Now he's starting to realize how much better he is. The fact that he's reverted to his hero self says more than anything about where he is in his head. I always wished he trusted himself more."

"You've been a really good friend."

"Yeah, and we'll still be friends but it's not the same as having a woman in your life. A partner."

Elaine cautiously leaned back in her desk chair.

That sounded ridiculously mature from someone who the other day had explained the half-his-age-plus-seven rule.

"You think that's what Greg wants? With Liza?"

"I don't know," he said noncommittally. "Isn't that what everyone wants?"

Elaine could definitely say she had no idea where Chuck was going with this conversation. Part of her wanted to cut him off and tell him she had to get back to work. The other part couldn't help but go along for the ride.

The "mature Chuck, who talks about relationships" ride.

"I don't know. For some people it's important. A relationship, I mean. For others…" Elaine couldn't help but let the implication hang out there.

Chuck smirked. "You mean me?"

"It's not like you've made a secret of it. You ask out every woman you meet. That's not looking for a relationship. That's looking for…" Elaine didn't want to say it. She didn't want to put the specter of sex in the room. This was the most they had talked, actually talked, in months without fighting.

"What about you?"

"What about me?" she asked incredulously, as if he could dare compare him to her. Hell, Elaine was the one who couldn't even remember when she had her last date.

"Mr. Tuesday Night?" he said, reminding her of

her pathetic lie. "Mr. Amazing Sex. What's he? Is that a relationship or a sex kind of a thing?"

Elaine opened her mouth and closed it. Hell, she wasn't a very good liar under the best of circumstances.

"I don't want to talk about him." Lame. Completely lame.

"I know you didn't go out with anyone last Tuesday."

Her eyes narrowed. She knew what this man could do with a computer. God, had there been some kind of video surveillance of her that night getting home late from work, alone as usual, that he'd tapped into? If so, she was fairly certain she was going to kill him.

"Look, I spend too much time around Greg not to be able to tell when someone is lying. I guess I came here to ask why you did it."

Elaine laughed. "Seriously? You were making fun of the fact that I couldn't remember when I last had a date. Now you're shocked I would lie about something like that to save a little face?"

"I wasn't making fun of you," he said. "I was...I was just happy."

Elaine reached for a pencil on her desk, fighting the urge to break it in half and throw both pieces in his face. "Of course. I say no to a date with you, so you deem it fitting punishment that no one else

should ever ask me out. Is that it? You've got your revenge, Chuck. Congratulations. Why don't you go."

"No," he said sharply. "It's not like that. It's not
like I don't want you to date. I mean…yeah, I guess
I don't want you to date anyone. Not for revenge,
though, but because I don't like the thought of it."

Elaine was trying to follow his line of thinking.
As a lawyer she knew that asking the right question at the right time could mean the difference between learning the truth or letting the witness off
the hook.

"Why? Why don't you want me to date anyone
else?"

"Because I don't."

"Not a sufficient answer. Try again."

Chuck frowned. "I'm not on the stand, sweetie
pie. Take it easy."

"You call me 'sweetie pie' one more time and I
will shove this pencil up an orifice of your body and
I think you know the one I'm talking about."

He crossed his arms defensively over his chest.
"It's a cute nickname."

"It's not!" she said too loudly. Feeling herself getting worked up but not really certain what emotion
he was tugging on. "It's what you call every girl you
meet, everyone you flirt with. Honey, sweetie, cutie,
baby. I hate it."

"Fine."

"Fine!"

Only he wasn't standing with indignation, leaving her office and slamming her door on the way out. Instead, he was still slouched in his chair, looking at her as if he was debating whether to say something.

"I was glad you hadn't gone out with anyone because...I like you, *E-laine*. That's why I asked you out. I thought you liked me, too."

"I did!" Holy crap. She did. She hadn't known it, but she did and wow did it feel really good to finally say it. "I mean, I didn't know I did. I didn't think...I thought we were just friends. But now..."

"Then why did you say what you did?" he railed. "You didn't say 'no, thanks,' you said—"

"I know what I said!" Ugh. That one mistake. Opening her mouth before she thought, something she never did at any other time in her life except when she was with him. With him the words came out like a burp. Unplanned, uncontrollable. As if he had power over her speech.

Taking a breath, Elaine considered what she wanted to say, but then told him the truth anyway.

"I didn't mean it the way it came out. You took me off guard and I wasn't thinking about you in that way. I thought you were kidding. If you weren't, well then you always ask people out. The truth was it pissed me off that you would treat me like every other girl out there when I thought I mattered to you."

"I wasn't kidding. I was nervous," he grumbled.

"I know that now," she said sulkily. "If you were kidding you wouldn't have been so mean to me afterward."

"I wasn't mean, I was pissed."

"Well, you came off as mean."

"Sorry."

She felt the threat of tears and nodded.

"I've been out with a lot of girls since then."

Great. This was exactly what she wanted to hear. How he was over her by now, how he had met other women he liked better. How she had blown her only chance because he was never going to forgive what she said.

"I'm not going to lie. I had sex with some of them, too. Not all of them…but some."

The pencil she had threatened to stuff up his ass now felt better suited for her eyeballs. Because stabbing herself in the eyeball was preferable to listening to him talk about this anymore.

"Great. Good for you. Could you please go now? I actually do have a lot to do. Liza's case isn't the only thing I'm working on."

Chuck sighed, but he did stand. "I didn't tell you that to piss you off. Or brag or anything. I wanted to be honest because—"

"Awesome," she said, cutting him off. "You've summarized the situation really well for a non-lawyer. I haven't dated anyone. You've had lots of sex. This was fun. We should do this again, maybe in a hundred years or so. Bye now."

Chuck turned away as if to leave, but when he got to the door he stopped. "I don't know why we can't talk anymore. We used to be really good at it but now we can't do it at all without hurting each other."

She wasn't going to be sad. She wasn't. "Well then, I guess it probably wasn't meant to be. Even if I had said yes. We would have gone out, but it wouldn't have worked. Let's forget it ever happened, okay? Then maybe we'll be able to stand being in the same room for more than ten seconds at a time."

He nodded. "Yeah. Ironic, huh? You got a case where all she wants to do is remember and all we want to do is forget."

Elaine tried to laugh but it sounded more like a half gurgle, half cough. "Sure. Ironic."

The door closed quietly behind him and she thought the real irony was that even after everything he told her, she still wanted him to come back.

"Eliza! You've come back. Thank goodness. I've been trying to track you down ever since you left but it's been impossible for me to find someone who could give me your home address and you're not listed anywhere on the internet."

Thank goodness for small favors, she thought.

They had shown up at the facility midmorning, after dropping off Greg's rental car and stopping in at the county police station, so Liza could give her official statement about the shooting incident at her home.

She hated even thinking about it because it reminded her how close those bullets had come. Not to hitting her, but Greg. For being her hero, he might have cost him everything.

Because she didn't want to go there, she told the police what happened with as much detail as she could remember. It seemed they had already been in contact with the Atlantic City P.D. and looked as skeptical as Chuck did when she explained her current medical condition.

The only good thing to come of their trip was that Greg got his car back. She'd followed him to the body shop where he'd dropped it off to get the windshield replaced and together they left for the hospital.

While en route, Mark returned Greg's early-morning call, prefacing his information with a warning that someday he would return the favor for waking him and his wife. Liza saw the flash of a smile on Greg's face and wondered if he realized that, despite the way he referred to Mark and his wife as colleagues, it was apparent to her they were more like friends.

Then Greg put his phone on speaker, and Mark proceeded to tell them everything they needed to know about Dr. Anthony Verdi. The more Mark spoke, the more so much of it seemed familiar to Liza.

Anthony Verdi was the child of Angelo Verdi and Mary D'Amato. Hector's aunt. Apparently, the two families had never been close as Anthony's father hadn't been convinced that the D'Amato family had completely removed themselves from the mafia, but Hector had helped pay medical school costs for his doctor cousin.

When they pulled up to the hospital gate, Greg asked Liza if she was ready to do this. This time with at least some memories of the place.

She realized she was ready. Something told her this confrontation had been brewing inside her for some time. They were shown to Dr. Verdi's office again. This time she was partially aware of who he was and what he'd done to her. Greg shut the doctor's office door firmly behind them and Liza could see he pressed a button to lock it, as well. There would be no chance of interruptions.

"Dr. Verdi, we're here for a few more answers," Liza began.

"Yes, of course."

"Let's start with why you lied to me during our last visit. You weren't just my doctor. You were also my godfather's cousin." Liza wouldn't use the word family. In connection to him, it felt wrong.

The doctor's expression was grave, as though he'd just been told about the death of a family member.

"Who told you that? Was it Ortiz? What's he been saying about me?"

That name coming from him shook her. It was like the last time she was at the hospital, when he said he'd tried calling the casino after he'd heard about Hector's death. This man, who should have been firmly in her past, she was now understanding was also part of her present. Yes, knowing that he and Hector were cousins made it more understandable that they were connected. But she couldn't imagine, knowing what she did about him, how she felt about him, that he would want her anywhere near him.

He knew she worked at the casino. He knew Freddy Ortiz. What did that mean?

"No, he never mentioned you."

"Then, your memory has come back?"

"I ask the questions. Why didn't you mention this very pertinent fact?"

Liza let her anger defuse any fear she might have felt. This time when she'd passed through those gates, she hadn't felt agitated or nervous. She wasn't a seventeen-year-old girl who didn't know what the hell was happening to her. She was one very pissed-off grown woman and she had a good friend at her back.

The dream last night hadn't been as clear as a memory. More like disparate scenes that played through her mind in a fast-moving kaleidoscope. She remembered Verdi at the funeral, at the hospital and waiting for her at the end of the driveway when Hector drove her through the facility's gates.

There was another memory, too. Far at the edges of her mind. It was as if her brain knew it was upsetting and was deliberately trying to prevent her from accessing it. But Liza knew she had to get there. "Doctor?"

"I...was concerned of course. I knew you had lost Hector. I was uncertain how you would react. When you told me about your memory I didn't want to startle you."

"Lie," Greg reported.

"Try again," Liza said.

"That's the truth!"

"Greg says it isn't. Let me be clear, I trust him more than I trust you."

The man blustered, but walked around his desk as if uncertain where to turn.

"Eliza, I've only ever wanted to help you."

Liza looked to Greg. He shook his head.

"That *is* the truth."

"Really," Liza pushed, focusing on his face and struggling to make a clear story out of what were only images. "Were you helping me when you gave me the drugs?"

"You were distraught," he rasped. "Hector didn't know how to console you. He called me and I prescribed a mild sedative. Then you stayed so sad for days on end. We didn't know what to do, so I thought something stronger might help."

"I was grieving the woman who raised me! She was my mother and my father, my Nonna. I wasn't allowed to be sad?"

"No, no, of course you were. I only wanted to help. Hector was counting on me. The antidepressants did seem to help but then you ran off with that boy."

Billy. He came by to take her out for a drive. He wanted to give her a break from her family. He brought a six pack of beer. A drive, a couple of beers, a few kisses. He made her feel normal. It was what she had wanted so badly.

"You were told the medicine couldn't be taken with alcohol but you did it, anyway. What were we supposed to think?"

"That I was seventeen!" Liza roared, slamming her hands on the desk. "I told you that I didn't mean to kill myself. I screamed it at you and you looked at me with this pathetic expression and told me you knew what was best."

The older man, who suddenly looked even older, held out his hands. "I wanted to help you."

"Lie," Greg announced. Liza looked behind her, almost startled to see he was still there. She looked at him and he turned his head to her, away from Verdi. He was wordlessly telling her that he wouldn't interfere beyond letting her know when the man was lying. This was her business. Her history that she had apparently never dealt with.

She tried to think about why Anthony had done it. Why he'd forced her to come to this hospital when she'd told him it had been an accident. She hadn't wanted the damn pills in the first place. What possible motive did a man have to pronounce a girl sick when she wasn't? Liza thought about the other piece of information Mark had relayed to them on the car ride over. About the financial situation of the hospital. On the surface, it appeared to be prospering but that prosperity was only surface deep.

No, a doctor didn't want to keep a healthy person locked up unless he wanted to be paid for making her better.

The Verdis, puh, they are so proud of their beloved boy, but who put him through medical school? Who funds that fancy hospital? They don't want to touch my dirty casino money until they need to touch my dirty casino money.

Liza could remember Hector talking about his estranged family. He'd had nothing to do with them other than to answer their requests for money. He gave them money because at the end of the day he would say family was family and he had more than enough to spare.

She'd been sad. Nonna was gone and she had been so sad. Hector never could stand to see her cry. Any hurt she had, he wanted to take away. Any problem she faced, he wanted to solve. He'd always wanted to keep her in bubble wrap, and she had always wanted to be free.

"How much money did he pay you to *cure* me?"

"Eliza, it wasn't about the money…"

"Lie." Greg took a seat then, as if to settle in for a long exchange. "You do understand this is what I do, right? You can't get away with this bullshit. You're not even particularly good at it."

"Fine. I was paid. This is a business. It has to run. Hector was always very generous. I am telling the truth when I say my first concern was you."

"There you go," Greg announced. "That was honest."

Liza considered what that meant. He'd lied about wanting to help her, but he'd told the truth about her being his first concern. Of course it could still be about the money. As long as it was coming in from Hector, he had every reason to keep her there.

Until the day she decided she'd had enough.

The memory was almost like a stabbing sensation in her head. "You had interns strap me down…"

It was *the* memory. The one that had lingered on the edges of her conscious. The one her brain wanted to shield her from, but couldn't any longer. "I was done with treatment. I wanted to leave. I knew there was no reason to keep me here because I knew I wasn't sick. You had them hold me down, you had them use restraints on my wrists and ankles."

Liza backed away from him. A few steps until she could feel Greg's hand reach up to hold hers. She squeezed it and let it go. She didn't need him, but he took away the fear. And she needed that. She needed to no longer be afraid of this man.

Men scare me.

No, she thought. This man scared her. This was the first man who scared her and made her wary of all men since.

"You liked that, didn't you? You liked seeing me tied to the bed."

The man's eyes fluttered. "No. Of course not."

"Lie," Greg said softly.

"I could see it. The way you were looking at me. I knew. You would have touched me, you would have…but you were too afraid of Hector. Of what he would do to you. I could see that, too. You left me there for hours and when I calmed down you let me go. Then you prescribed those other pills. The ones I would never take. The ones that would have made me not myself. I called Hector and told him he needed to take me away from this place. That if he didn't come I would run away and he would never see me again."

"Hector, he always gave you what you wanted."

Yes. He did. Liza could see that in so many ways he'd contributed to her feelings of weakness, by never letting her be strong for herself. But she was strong that day. She was determined to get away and she did.

"If I had told him, if I had even insinuated that you had looked at me funny, he would have killed you."

The man sneered. "Yes. The sanctimonious, noble Hector D'Amato. Only you don't know how much blood was already on his hands. From the days before he became the man who cleaned up The Grande. From the days when your father used it as his own personal palace of sin. Do you know what you come from? Hector, he shielded you and I could see why. It was as if the devil had given birth to an angel."

"And we're done," Greg said. "You're not going to listen to this."

"See, Eliza. There will always be a hero for a woman who is an angel."

Liza walked around the desk and stood in front of the doctor.

"You're a sick man," she said, stabbing a finger into his chest, and whether it was the specter of Hector or the fear of Greg leaping across the desk, the doctor stayed rooted to the floor. "I'm going to see to it not only that this *facility* is shut down but that you lose your license. That's going to be me, not anyone else. I'm going to make that happen."

His fearful gasp made him sound like a child instead of a man. "Eliza, you can't."

"It's Liza, you pig." Then with every ounce of anger she felt from her days spent in the hospital, she raised her knee through the skirt of the dress she was wearing and slammed it into his crotch. The doctor doubled over and the profound sense of power she felt was like nothing she'd ever experienced before.

"Ouch," Greg said from where he stood. "I bet that hurt."

"You can't take away this hospital," the doctor groaned as he fell to the floor. "Hector promised me. We're family."

"You're not my family," Liza said. "I don't care what Hector promised you."

Liza circled back around the desk. Greg smiled at her and took her hand. She could feel his pride and it made her glow from the inside out.

"Ready to leave?"

"Never more ready in my life."

As she reached the door, something else came back to her and she stopped short. Another memory, this one much more current. "What Hector promised you..." she repeated. "You were there. In my office at The Grande. You needed more money but Hector turned you down. You found out I was working there and you came to see me... Oh gosh, Greg."

"Take a deep breath," he said calmly in her ear. "Let it come back."

The doctor nodded as he pulled himself into his chair. He obviously didn't see the point of lying anymore.

"Hector and his money. I hated him for it. All

anyone thinks they need anymore is drugs. No one needs therapy, or a place to stay and recover. Just the drugs. This place, it was dying and Hector knew it. He told me giving me any more money would be bad business. This isn't a business! Hector had always given you anything you wanted. I only needed to convince you to talk to Hector about the money."

Liza tried to recall the answer she had given him. Tried to remember how she would have felt seeing him for the first time in ten years. Scared, angry, disgusted.

Weak?

"Tell me," she said. "Tell me what I said when you asked me to talk to Hector about the money."

His head looked like a heavy weight on his shoulders. "You said no."

Liza smiled. "I said no."

That would have taken some strength, to stand up to the man who made her afraid of other men.

Knowing what she'd done felt almost as good as watching him double over in pain.

"When did this happen? When did we have that meeting?" Liza asked the question, but as soon as she did, she already knew the answer. "It was that Saturday. In the morning. Then later that night, Hector was shot."

"Did you do it?" Greg asked, getting as close to Verdi as his desk would allow. "Did you kill him?"

Verdi shook his head and smirked. "I wanted to. How about that for an honest answer."

Liza didn't need Greg to confirm that he was telling the truth.

CHAPTER FIFTEEN

GREG LOOKED OVER AT LIZA as he drove them back to her place. She was breathing heavily and had a hand over her chest. He might have been worried about her if it wasn't for the expression of joy on her face.

"Are you okay?"

She looked at him and he could see for himself that she was.

"I'm euphoric. Did you see that? Did you see what I did? I've never been a violent person before. I don't think violence is right in any situation, but I did it. I hurt him like he hurt me. He cost me six months of my life, my senior year in high school—"

"Your boyfriend. Don't forget Billy Davis."

Liza laughed. Laughed and shook. "Yes, well that wasn't such a loss. He broke up with me in my get-well card. Seriously, it said 'hope you are doing better, but I think we should break up.'"

Greg didn't want to comment on how much of her memory was returning. Something told him the less she focused on what she did and didn't remember, the quicker it would return.

Her brain had received a traumatic blow. Not a

physical one, but an emotional one. All it needed was time to heal.

"I feel like…"

"What?"

"I don't know," she said, shaking her head. "Like I'm free for the first time in a really long time. I mean, I let that whole thing weigh on me for so long. Why did I do that? Why didn't I tell Hector or confront Verdi years ago?"

She was reaching again. Trying to make the pieces fit. "Stop. You beat yourself up because you think you're weak, now you've stood up for yourself. Don't diminish what you did because you didn't do it sooner. You were awesome in there."

"I felt awesome. I felt powerful."

"We should tell the detective," Greg said. "Let him know that Verdi was at the casino, and that he had motive."

"Yes. I mean, my amnesia makes even more sense now. With my history with Verdi, if I had seen him kill Hector, I might have lost my grasp on everything."

"With good reason," he pointed out.

"I don't want to think about that. I don't want to think about losing myself when, right now, I feel like…like I could…do anything I wanted."

"Okay," Greg said, happy to oblige. "We've got the rest of the day. What do you want to do?"

Liza reached out and touched his thigh. Greg

wasn't certain if her intent was sexual, but her simple touch made him hard.

"Liza," he growled, ready to reach down and move her hand. She wouldn't have any idea what her touch did to him. Hell, he didn't even understand it. He was like a seventeen-year-old kid around her and it messed with his head.

Before he could move her hand, she was moving it again. Higher, until it fell between his legs and he groaned in response. He closed his eyes for a second before he remembered he was the one driving. Along a fairly busy road, although it wasn't so busy in the middle of the afternoon.

"Liza…"

"Don't stop me. Don't stop us. I'm not weak. I'm not vulnerable. I want you and you want me. What's so wrong about that?"

She pressed her hand more firmly against his now fully formed hard-on and any argument he had formed about why this was a bad idea vanished. She was right. He wanted her from the start and it didn't matter that she was involved in this situation. Like he said, if he'd seen her on the street, walking into a coffee shop, he would have followed her. He would have asked for her number. He would have wanted to know who she was because something about the way she looked at him made him feel clean and good. Like there was decency in the world.

He wasn't taking advantage of her or her situation. Hell, if anyone was taking advantage of anything...

Greg looked at the road in front of him, calculated how far they were from her house and more specifically her bed, and made an instant assessment: it was too far. When she undid her seat belt and leaned over to start messing with the buttons of his jeans, he decided that to continue driving at that point was unsafe.

An abandoned furniture store was perfect. He pulled into the lot and circled around the back to where he knew there would be enough room for a truck to pick up and drop off furniture. He pulled up to the store and thought about what they were doing.

"Liza, we could wait until we're back at your place."

"I don't want to wait."

And she didn't. She'd succeeded in getting his jeans' button undone and was slowly lowering the zipper. Finding out how far she wanted to take her power trip was probably going to be the most fun Greg had ever had with a woman. He undid his seat belt, moved the seat as far back as he could and lifted his hips to let her slide the jeans far enough down so that she could reach into his boxer briefs and... Oh, yeah...

Her hand was long and slim and he could tell she didn't really know what she wanted to do with his erection, but her small tight strokes blew his mind.

The way he was feeling now made him think that having her, coming inside her, might actually kill him.

He would have thought he'd had all he could stand but then she was leaning over him and he watched her head sink lower and lower into his lap until her mouth was taking in the head of his cock.

He rocked his hips and she pulled back, but then she took him in her mouth again with a soft moan. Her lips and tongue sweeping over his head was the most delicious kind of torture he could imagine. She didn't move down on him, she didn't suck him deeper like his body craved. He almost howled at her to do something, but instinctively he knew that this was her first time doing something like this and he didn't want to give her any reason to never do it again. So he sucked in his breath through his nose and let her lick him and hold him there, just inside her hot wet mouth. When she lifted her head, her smile was so smug he wanted to laugh and cry at the same time.

"My turn." He moved quickly before she could torture him any further. "Backseat. Flat on your back with your knees up."

He started pushing her through the opening between the front seats. She quickly got the idea and positioned herself so she was lying as directed on the backseat, her knees forced up to allow her to fit. Satisfied he had her where he wanted her, he opened the car door, got out and then opened the back door as if he was opening the door to a magical palace.

Kneeling on the hard edge of the door ledge, he swept his hands up the skirt of her dress and pulled away her panties in one sharp tug. He wanted the dress off completely, but he knew it zippered up the back and suddenly that seemed like too much work. Instead, he flipped the wide skirt up and was rewarded with the most beautiful nest of blond curls he'd ever seen.

"Ever done this?" he asked, running his hands up her thighs to let her body know where he was going.

"Umm, what in particular?"

Her voice cracked and he smiled devilishly. "This."

His tongue went right to her center. It was like plunging into a dish of honey, so slick and luscious. She was wet for him and all she'd done was touch him and lick him a little. With his tongue still teasing her, he reached his hand up to cup her breast, frustrated with the snug cotton dress that stood between him and her naked flesh.

"Greg, oh no, I don't know… Oh my God!"

He played with her, teased her, used his tongue to torment her until he could hear how close she was to coming. It wasn't enough. Not enough to plunge into her and with a few thrusts—because he really didn't see himself lasting more beyond that—have it be over. Not this time.

Their first time.

Leaning back, he studied his subject. She was pink and flushed and her eyes were so wide open, he knew what the answer to his question was. While she watched him, he licked his lips and thought about how shocked she was going to be when the next place he put his tongue was in her mouth. Because that's what he wanted to do. When she smiled at him, when she laughed, he thought she was everything that was good in the world. So when it came to the sex between them, of course he wanted to be everything that was dirty and sinful and would give her more pleasure than she could ever imagine.

As he palmed her breasts, he could feel her taut nipples beneath her dress. The frustration of not being able to touch her skin, of not knowing what her bare nipples felt like under his fingers was another kind of torture.

He wanted to give her some of that delicious torture back. With his other hand, he slid his finger inside her sheath. Just the tip at first, then he added a second finger, again just the tip, just enough to open her. Enough to let her crave more. He waited and watched as she started to squirm.

"Greg," she sighed. "Please."

"Oh, you need a little more, do you? A little deeper? Sorry, this is payback. When you had your mouth on me, the head of my cock in your lips, it felt like this…so good, but so maddening. Now it's your turn to feel this. To want."

Apparently, she wasn't very good at taking his sexual commands because the way she moved her hips, thrusting into him brought his fingers deeper into her by default. It was the sexiest little move he had ever seen in his life. Like she was working for her pleasure.

Not able to wait, he stood and placed his knees on the backseat. He pulled her hips up and over his thighs, positioning his erection right where he knew it would slide deep. It was then, as he was about to plunge into her, that he remembered he didn't have a condom.

"Baby, please tell me you at least remember if you are on birth control."

"Greg, please…I need you. Please!"

"I don't have a condom."

"I don't care. God, Greg. Now!"

Screw it. He plunged into her and groaned at how tight she was, almost resistant, but then she was there with him, surrounding him, taking all of him inside her, deep to his balls. He would pull out when he came. That was what his lust-addled brain told him. He would pull out and the chances of her getting pregnant would be slim. For now they both needed this connection too badly.

She was writhing on her back and the squeeze of her muscles all around him told him she'd gotten there. He wanted to take her there again. He could hold out, he could let her come down and then build her back up again. He would give her everything, because what he was starting to realize was that she was giving him everything back. His life. His belief in people, in love, all of it.

Yes, he could do this forever, give her more pleasure, but then she was twisting her hips up against him and the keening noise she was making made his control slip. He needed to pull out, to finish out of the car and onto the pavement, to give her at least that.

No, it's okay. She's yours.

It wasn't the devil on his shoulder. It wasn't his macho inner voice that only cared about getting to the end, to the pleasure of coming. It was true and it was real and when she tightened around him again, her legs circling his hips to bring him closer, he let himself go.

"Oh, Greg! Yes!"

Yes! For the first time he knew what it felt like to come inside a woman with no barrier between them.

His inner caveman, the one she brought out of him more than any woman had done before, reveled in the feeling. He was marking her, he was feeling all this pleasure, all this wonderful, gooey, blood-thrilling pleasure, but he was doing something else too. He was connecting her to him in a fundamental way.

"Mine," he growled like any good caveman would.

He leaned over and kissed her. Pushing his tongue inside her, letting her taste herself, letting her taste them together. This moment, he thought crazily, would be their real marriage ceremony. It felt different than any other sex he'd had in his life and he supposed that was how a man knew, really knew when she was the *one*.

He crushed her into the backseat and reveled in the feel of her beneath him. This time when she squirmed he knew it was because he was too heavy. Gently, he pulled out of her, feeling the incredible slick slide-out as he never had before. He stepped outside of the car, bracing his arms on the roof while she sat up. Her face was beet red, her hair a mess around her shoulders. He wanted to get back in there and do it all over again. Instead, he sat next to her and closed the door behind him, sealing them together inside. The smell of sex was a powerful aphrodisiac.

She ducked her head next to him, trying to straighten her hair, her dress. Not wanting even that much separation from her, he pulled her into his lap. She tensed at first, but ultimately relaxed against him like a wet noodle.

A well-loved wet noodle.

"I didn't use a condom." He needed to tell her again, now that they were both clear headed.

"I know," she said softly.

"Yeah, but I didn't…do anything to try and… Oh hell, Liza, I came really hard and really deep inside of you."

She giggled against his chest. Giggled. Then she kissed his neck. "I had birth control pills in my purse. I might have missed a few days, but I've been taking them since. We should be okay."

Why that made him sad, he wasn't sure.

"You sure you're all right?"

She nodded against his chest. "I wasn't a virgin or anything, if that's what you're worried about. I'm afraid to say Billy took care of that deed, as well."

"I am really starting to hate Billy Davis."

She giggled again. "I guess you could tell by my technique that I haven't exactly been very experienced."

"Honey, if that's you not experienced then we need to keep you this way, because if you get any more experienced you're probably going to kill me."

More laughing, more snuggling. He felt awesome.

Closing his eyes, he rested his head against the seat and reveled in the aftermath of sex. That blissful, boneless feeling. They had nowhere they had to go, no plans for the hours before them other than touching base with the police. He figured they could nap, drive home, eat, make love again, and he would count it as the best day of his life.

Which was why the tap on the window completely startled him.

"Sir, could you roll down the window?"

Greg blinked a few times at the police officer standing next to the car and considered how soundly the two of them must have been dozing to miss the sound of the police car pulling up next to them.

Liza squealed and immediately pushed herself off his lap to sit on the other side of the car, leaving Greg to deal with the situation. He searched for the window button not knowing where it was in her car. Finding it on the arm rest, he pressed it once and the window slid all the way down.

"Can I ask what you're doing back here?"

"Uh…we needed to…rest."

The officer nodded. "I often find kids back here doing things like…resting. Seems like you might be a little old for that."

"Never too old to need a little…rest."

The officer scowled. "Right. But this is private property. You need to leave."

"Yes, sir. Thank you, sir."

Greg got out of the car as the officer was walking back to the patrol car.

"Oh," the man said over his shoulder. "You might want to pick up your lady's panties. They must have fallen off while you were…resting."

Greg looked down at the panties. They were pink and he hadn't appreciated how cute she'd looked in them before he'd pulled them off her. "Thanks again, Officer."

While Liza scrambled into the front seat, Greg got behind the wheel.

"Resting?" she asked. "That was the best you could do?"

He started the car and steered them back onto the road. "Oh, don't blame me for this. This was all your idea. Now, no illegal touching while I'm driving. At least not until we're pulling up into your driveway."

"Can we hold hands?"

He looked at her then, this beautiful woman. A knot in his throat made it hard to swallow. Then he reached over, took her hand in his and squeezed it. Yeah, he thought, holding hands was nice.

GREG SAW THE police car in Liza's driveway and winced. Wow. Were they seriously going to take a little car sex this far and issue a violation? The thought evaporated when he considered that he hadn't given his name and license information to the officer who had caught them in the parking lot.

Then his gut tightened as if someone had thrust a hand inside his body and squeezed his stomach when he saw Elaine talking to the officer. They must have called her.

"Greg…"

"It's going to be okay." Although he had no idea if that was true or not.

The two of them got out of the car and slowly approached the officers who were walking toward them.

"Eliza Dunning?"

"Yes."

"You're under arrest for the murder of Hector D'Amato."

Greg heard the words, but they didn't register. This wasn't happening. This was Liza and she was innocent. They should be looking at Verdi!

Damn it, they had been having sex when he should have been calling the police, letting them know Verdi was at The Grande the day of the murder, that he wanted Hector dead. That there was another suspect.

Instead he'd had sex with her. Unprotected sex because he knew it was going to be okay, because the idea of having a baby with her felt right and good in the moment. Like they could be a family. His future wife was not a murderer. He knew it. Only they were putting handcuffs on her and reading her Miranda rights while she silently sobbed his name as they placed her in the back of the car.

"Elaine! What the hell is happening?"

Elaine jogged over to him, stumbling a bit in her clunky clogs. He felt like taking those quirky shoes off her feet and hurling them as far as he could because they were preventing her from getting to him faster.

"Sorry, I tried calling you but you weren't answering your phone."

No, because he'd been having the most incredible sex of his life in the backseat of Liza's car.

"What happened?"

She winced, which told him his tone and facial expression were relaying his fury at what he knew was an injustice.

"They found the gun. Alongside the highway where she was picked up. Her prints are on it."

Greg didn't answer, walking over to the cop car and opening the door, instead. The police officer was about to object, but Greg held up a finger as if to suggest he needed a minute.

A minute. Or maybe a lifetime. That's all he wanted with her.

She was sniffling, trying to hold her shit together. "Why?"

Greg crouched down so she could see him. "They found the gun and your prints were on it. Can you think about why that might be?"

She shook her head. "I'm remembering so much, but that day, it's like it still didn't even happen."

"Okay, we're going to get you out of this. Listen to me. They are going to take you back to Atlantic City and charge you. I'm going to get Mark to pull some strings for us and we'll get you a bail hearing today."

Elaine who had come over to stand behind Greg said, "It's murder, Greg. Bail won't be set for anything less than a million."

"Fine. That's a hundred thousand I'll need to put up. Find a bondsman you trust, and I'll make it happen."

"No," Liza said. "I can't ask you to do that. It's too much."

"Honey, you didn't think I was playing only for poker chips when I was gambling, did you? I'll put the money up and we'll get you out of there and then we'll figure out what happened. I promise."

"I doubt she'll need to rely on you for the money."

Greg stood up. It was the detective from AC, the one who had originally questioned her. Greg could see his car in front of the patrol car. He must have wanted to be onsite for the arrest. That was who Elaine had been talking to.

"What's that supposed to mean?"

"Turns out Ms. Dunning is D'Amato's sole heir. Being able to get your hands on a couple hundred million dollars, I would say that's a pretty good motive for murder."

CHAPTER SIXTEEN

"WILL YOU RELAX? She's on her way home."

Greg looked over at Mark. He didn't know how he was ever going to repay him, given everything that the guy had done for him. Since the day he'd lost Tommy, Greg had deliberately held people at bay. He didn't want ties to anyone. Chuck was the only friend he allowed himself to have because he needed the support. Also, Chuck had been like a pit bull when they met and Greg hadn't been able to shake him off.

Now he was here, having to rely on Mark, and being indebted to him felt strange.

They were in Liza's house, the police having already conducted their search for evidence. Of course they found nothing, because there was nothing to be found. Mark had been Greg's first call after the police car drove off with what felt like his future inside of their car. Elaine was heading down to AC with a promise to Greg that Liza would be out on bail tonight.

Then Mark had called in a few favors with the police to make sure the arraignment was done im-

mediately after they processed her. After that, he'd
come to stay with Greg to offer his support and company. Which mostly consisted of watching Greg pace
back and forth.

Mark hadn't been able to tempt Greg with beer,
food or a baseball game. So Mark being Mark had
suggested a game of cards.

The prick.

"You don't get it. I can't relax," Greg said.

It was pitch-black outside now. Eight hours since
Liza's arrest. Eight hours since he'd watched her
leave and hadn't followed her. Instead, he'd asked
Chuck to come over and go with Elaine. To be there
as his freaking proxy. He'd instructed Chuck to call
him hourly to let him know if anything changed.
The last call had come twenty minutes ago. They
were done with what they needed to do and Chuck
was driving Liza home.

"Oh, I get it. You forget what I was like when I
met JoJo."

Greg did remember. Mark had been a little crazy.
Trying to help her deal with her family issues by
springing Greg on her at a restaurant. As if surprise therapy was something every girl wanted to be
wooed with. Greg remembered thinking how obvious it was that Mark had feelings for his then employee. He was different around her, hypersensitive
about everything when it came to her.

What he'd done to JoJo had been stupid, but it had

been done out of love. Mark hadn't known it at the time. For that matter, neither had JoJo.

Is that what this is? The real deal?

Greg couldn't wrap his brain around that concept. Yes, when he'd made love to Liza he'd thought in terms of *the one.* But he was a man who had already proposed to a woman in his life before. Which meant, at one point, he must have thought that was love, too.

This didn't feel like Irene. Losing Liza…no, he wouldn't go there. It was too much, too scary. None of his thoughts about relationships and women had ever touched this crazy part of him, deep inside, that he realized he'd kept hidden from the world for a very long time.

His last barrier of protection from the lies, big and small that people told. Lies like *I love you* when you didn't even really know what those words meant. Liza hadn't just gotten beyond that wall. She was inside of him. Deep inside of him. It was how he knew that if he lost her, he might physically feel the wound of her separation.

"This is…this is too much."

Mark nodded solemnly. "I know, man."

Greg sat heavily on the couch next to him and dropped his face into his hands. "I hate being here. Not with her. Where I should be."

"You wouldn't have been with her. You would have been cooling your heels in the police station lobby like Chuck did all day. It's done now. She's been processed, she's made her plea and Chuck is bringing her home."

Nodding, he tried to imagine what she'd gone through. The fingerprinting, the mug shot. The humiliation of people treating her like a criminal. Now, instead of being in a car with him and feeling safe, she was with Chuck who had never really believed her story. Greg had warned him not to say anything, but what if Chuck couldn't help it? After all he had more reason now than ever to believe he was right. The police were on Chuck's side.

Except Greg knew Chuck and the police were wrong. They needed to look at Verdi.

"Was that information I gave you helpful?"

Greg had to focus on what Mark was asking. "Yes. She remembered everything about her stay there. About what Verdi had done to her so D'Amato would keep financing his hospital. Now that D'Amato's dead, I don't see him staying in business much longer. One more reason why Verdi might have killed him."

"You think there's an angle there?"

Greg clenched his fists. "I know there is. He was at the casino that day to see Liza, to get her to convince D'Amato to keep paying him but she kicked him out of her office. I asked him if he did it, if he killed Hector, but all he would say was that he wanted D'Amato dead. I can tell you he was telling the truth about that."

"You tell the cops?"

"Yes, but I could see they weren't taking me very seriously given that I was shouting at them to look into Verdi while they were taking Liza away. I'll call them tomorrow and tell them everything once she's back here. With me. Until then I can't think."

"It's a stretch," Mark said, apparently mulling over the idea. "What does he gain? Did he think he might be in the will? Did he think Liza would be more receptive to giving him money once Hector was dead?"

"He hated him." Greg could see it in his eyes when he said he wanted him dead. "Isn't that motive enough?"

"It depends. On how powerful the hate is. If you go to the cops with this you're going to need more than that."

Greg nodded. Until Liza could remember what happened, until she could clearly recall the events of that day, the only way out seemed to be finding the person responsible. "How do I get it?"

"You're certain she didn't do it?"

"Yes." It wasn't even a question. Hadn't been a question, really, since shortly after meeting her. The most violent thing Liza Dunning had ever done in her life was shove her knee into the crotch of the man who had made her feel mentally unstable and sexually threatened.

"She was there, she had motive and there is a gun with her prints on it."

Greg dismissed the obvious. Of course she was there. Yes, she saw what happened. Maybe she picked up a fallen gun, but that was the extent of it. "Motive? What motive?"

"She stands to inherit a fortune."

"Mark, look at this house."

Mark looked around as if he was seeing the house for the first time. "It's not the Taj Mahal."

"That's my point. She had a good job with a large accounting firm. What did she do with her money? Bought a small, manageable house. A conservative car. Nice clothes, but not ridiculously expensive. The way people talk about her and Hector, he would have given her anything she wanted. She chose to live this way. There was no reason to kill him for the money."

"Okay. But you also told me she had accounts on her computer that indicated someone was stealing money from The Grande. How does that tie in with Verdi?"

Greg pressed his fists against his eyes. He didn't know. For hours he'd been running different ideas through his mind. Different scenarios that the police would find plausible. He even considered if Verdi could be working with someone on the inside. If those checks made to that fraudulent vendor had somehow made it to Verdi instead.

"I don't know. Maybe they weren't connected. I only know that she was brought there by D'Amato to find out what was happening. He needed someone he could trust. The only person he could trust."

"Okay. D'Amato brings Liza in to audit the books. She finds proof of the embezzlement. Someone kills Hector then takes a shot at Liza. Does that rule out the doctor?"

Greg cursed under his breath. He hated Mark's sound reasoning skills in that moment, because he couldn't find a convenient way to connect the dots. Everything was hypothetical. A theory, not hard fact.

"I don't know."

"Sounds like you need a private investigator," Mark said. "Good thing you happen to know one."

Greg smirked. "Yeah, I'll call JoJo first thing tomorrow and get her on the case."

Mark laughed. "You know that would be funny, except, I have to admit, there are times when my wife is better at tracking information than I am. We'll work on it together. We'll find out what happened."

"With proof. I need proof if I'm going to clear her name."

Mark hesitated. "Is this about clearing her name or is this about finding out the truth?"

Greg suddenly wanted to hit the man very hard.

He'd fallen for a woman; he hadn't become an idiot overnight because of it. He wasn't some damn version of Sampson who had his hair cut off by Delilah and couldn't distinguish any longer when someone was telling the truth or lying. He struggled to rein in his temper.

"You've done all this for me. It sort of puts me in your debt…"

"Or it just means I'm a friend."

He was right. They probably had become friends without Greg realizing it. Swell. He was friends with a prick. A prick who had skills that could help him.

"Okay then, as my friend, you need to trust me. I'm trusting you with her life. You need to trust me that I'm right."

Mark stood and walked over to where Greg had stopped pacing.

"Okay. Good enough. JoJo and I will head to the casino first thing tomorrow and start asking questions."

Greg frowned. "Quietly. You start asking questions, you might make yourself a target."

Mark shrugged as if to indicate he wasn't overly concerned. "Seems strange. Someone comes after Liza. He breaks in here, either looking for something or waiting for her. Ostensibly to kill her because she was a witness."

"What's your point?"

"Why did he stop?" Mark asked. "If it was me and

I needed someone gone, I would tail them night and day until they were gone. This guy takes one chance and then nothing since."

Greg thought about it. "I took her back to the loft after it happened. He would have had no way to know who she was with and where I was keeping her. She's been back here since but I've always been with her. Hell, I took her to the batting cages, completely out in the open without any incident."

Mark's eyebrows shot up. "The batting cages? Oh hell, then it must be love."

"Did anyone ever tell you you're a prick?"

"Many people. I refuse to believe them."

"It's not love," Greg insisted. "It can't be love. Yet."

Lie. It's love and you know it.

"Why not?"

Because I'm not ready for this.

He rejected his inner voice. Yes, what he was feeling didn't match with what he was thinking. So he would disregard what he was feeling because in so many ways it was awful and uncomfortable and he would think only about what made sense.

He'd only known her for a handful of days. He only knew the half of her she remembered. Great sex didn't always mean everlasting love. Those were sound logical arguments against it being love.

Lies. All of them.

"You know when I knew it with JoJo?" Mark

asked, apparently not needing an answer to his question. "I remember she walked into my office with her attitude and this turtleneck she thought could hide the tattoos on her neck. When I think back on it, when I'm really honest with myself, I knew then. It was that quick."

That was ridiculous to Greg, who could explain the psychology behind the phenomena of instant love. Except, of course, he could see Mark believed every word of what he was saying.

"We were talking about trying to find a killer."

Which currently was a much easier topic for him to deal with than the fact that, despite every logical answer he'd listed, despite being engaged once already in his life, despite all the shit that was falling down around him and Liza, he knew without a doubt that this feeling was unlike anything he'd ever experienced in his life.

It scared the freaking crap out of him.

"Right," Mark said, allowing himself to be redirected. "Okay, so why did our guy...you're sure it was a man?"

"Positive. Big build, strong, fast. Either it was a man or a woman on a pretty big dose of 'roids."

"Could it have been the doctor?"

Greg considered that. "Right height, but if I'm being honest, he moved pretty fast for a man the doctor's age. Still if you're there to kill someone, the adrenaline has got to be pumping pretty hard."

"So why does he stop there?" Mark asked.

The answer came to Greg, and the two men's eyes met and he knew Mark had gotten there, too.

"He knows she doesn't remember. He thinks he's got time," Mark said for both of them.

"Or better, he thinks that without her memory she's sure to be charged with the crime. Rather than kill her, he lets her take the rap for the murder."

"Now that she's been charged, Elaine will have access to the evidence the police have on her. We'll start there and see who the witnesses are against her. If we can find someone who is making a strong case, we'll dig a little deeper into that person."

It was a start. Mark was right. With Elaine having access to everything the prosecution was going to have, they stood a much better chance of finding the truth. Greg had no doubt the ACPD were only looking for proof that Liza was guilty. A not-so-smoking gun basically took care of that for them. But he doubted they knew about the stolen money, especially when the arresting detective cited her motive as being her inheritance.

"We'll find him."

Greg nodded tightly. "I'm counting on it."

"Can I ask another question that's probably going to make you call me a prick again?"

Smiling, Greg sat. "Please. I would love the excuse."

"If you are committed to this, if you are committed to *her,* why didn't you go down to AC with her? Like I said before, there was nothing for you to do, but I'm still curious."

It felt like being kicked in the nuts. Because when a man is kicked there all his breath is immediately replaced with pain and he's vulnerable to everyone and everything. He thought of a thousand things he could say. The truth being the last on his list.

I'm a coward. I let a woman I made love to that same day go alone to a place I was too afraid to go. When she was scared and she needed me. A woman who I'm crazy about.

"Is it the gambling thing?"

"No," he said, realizing that much was the truth. He wasn't afraid of finding himself at a poker table. It wasn't fear of regression that kept him away.

It was just fear.

"Then what? We're friends now. We made it official. I'm here for you."

Greg looked at his…friend. Holy crap. Who would have ever thought they'd be friends? And he wondered what Mark would think of him if he knew the truth. Maybe it was time to find out. Maybe he needed to get the truth out of his system before the ugliness of it took over everything.

"Before I started working for Ben, when I was officially gambling full-time, I used to get kicked out of a lot of casinos. The last one, ironically, happened to be The Grande."

Mark's eyebrows raised a fraction. "When you say kicked out…"

"I mean *kicked*. My last exit cost me a broken nose, two cracked ribs and a bruise on my back I'm fairly certain still isn't gone."

"Oof. I guess that's a good reason to stay away from a place."

"It's not the fear of getting beaten up again," Greg said. That would have been almost easy to deal with. No, he didn't care about what might happened to him physically. It was all the stuff in his head—that was where all the bad stuff lived.

"When I was lying there on the cement, alone in the parking lot with blood and snot running out of my nose and mouth, my body screaming in pain, I thought…this is it. This is as low as a person can fall. I had to freaking crawl to my car. The humiliation, the shame of what I had done, what I had let myself become was all there. When I think about that place, that city, it all comes back. That's what I fear the most, that somehow I'll break down and mentally I'll be back there in that pit of disgust. So I can't go back. I let her go, knowing I wasn't following her, because of my own damn weakness. Hell, she would have every right to come back here, slap me in the face and tell me she never wanted to see me again."

"Well, I guess you're going to find out," Mark

said, his eyes drawn to the windows in the front of the house. "Looks like a car is pulling up."

Greg hurried outside in anticipation of seeing her. Would she be angry? Hell, would she knee him like she had Verdi? The only thing he could do was say he was sorry and he wanted to say it immediately.

Chuck pulled the car to a stop in the driveway and the passenger door flew open. The next thing he knew, Liza was running toward him and, without thinking, he opened his arms. She flew into his body and the impact of her pressing against him from head to toe was instant and almost orgasmic in its relief. Her sobs were loud in his ears and he lifted his head to glare at Chuck as if the man he sent in his stead as his trusted friend was suddenly his worst enemy.

Chuck raised his hands as if to suggest his innocence. "Don't look at me. She wouldn't say a word to me the whole ride home."

Right, because she didn't trust Chuck. Because she knew Chuck didn't trust her. Greg had done that to her, had forced her to make that hour-long drive back from Atlantic City without him because he was chickenshit. He hated himself in that moment, but at least she hadn't kneed him. He had to be grateful for small favors.

Instead, Liza simply buried her face against Greg's neck. So he did all he could, which was to hold her. And to apologize.

"I'm sorry. I'm so sorry."

"You couldn't have stopped it," she sniffled against his shirt.

"No, I'm sorry I wasn't there. With you. Sorry I wasn't there to bring you home."

She lifted her head and looked at him. "You can't go to Atlantic City. Because of the gambling. I understand."

No, she didn't. Now wasn't the time to explain it to her. It wasn't about him anymore, it was about her. From her morning spent confronting Verdi, to her arrest in the early afternoon and finally her arraignment, he had to imagine this might have been the longest day of her life.

That wasn't counting get nailed in the backseat of a car, either.

"I want to take a shower. I want to get clean."

The fact that his body responded to that, to the idea of her being naked and dripping with hot water, made him cringe.

Yeah, Greg thought, he was a real class act.

"Come on, let's get you inside."

Greg was expecting Mark to be inside, but as if the man sensed that what Liza needed most right now was quiet, he had let himself out the back door instead. Greg could hear the rumble of two cars outside and watched as both Mark and Chuck pulled out of the driveway.

Liza made her way down the hall while Greg

secured all the locks and set the alarm. Then he made his way to the kitchen and thought about what he might want to have after being arrested.

The answer was too easy. He found the bottle of bourbon she'd put away the other day. He poured a few fingers over some ice and, when he thought enough time had passed, he walked down the hall-way to her bedroom.

She was in her robe fresh from her shower, a towel wrapped around her head in a way that certain women could make look really sexy. Probably the same women who were, by definition, sexy.

Greg had spent so much energy refusing to see her for what she was that it almost made him gasp to think about how she had looked laid out on that backseat, her skirt around her waist, and the feel of her as he'd pushed his way inside her body. He wanted to tell her how amazing he thought she was.

Down, boy.

"Here," he said, handing her the glass. "I considered hot chocolate but thought you might need something stronger."

She nodded and took the glass from his hand. Her fingers shook and the ice rattled as she took a sip and sat on the end of the bed.

"You okay?"

She nodded.

He wanted to ask if he could stay with her tonight. The words came to his lips, but he stopped them.

He didn't want to give her the option. He wanted to hold her in his arms and whisper into her ear that everything was going to be okay until she fell asleep.

He recognized the selfishness of that desire. What she needed was what she wanted, not what he wanted.

"Okay, if you're good I'm going to sleep in the guest room…"

"No." She stopped him. The look on her face was enough to break his heart. She looked as lost as the day he'd shown up in the interview room of the Brigantine police station. "Please stay. I mean if you want. I don't want to… I mean, I'm not up for…"

Greg tossed off his T-shirt and unbuttoned his jeans, letting them slide down his legs. He was already barefoot when he padded over to the other side of the bed where she wasn't sitting. Still in his boxer briefs, he slid under the covers and into bed.

Liza swallowed the last few gulps of the brown liquid and coughed again like she had the first time. She pulled the towel off her head and laid it over the pillow. Greg watched as her hands went to the tie of the robe and he closed his eyes. He could summon the willpower to hold her all night. He didn't know if he could do that if he saw her completely naked first.

When he peeked—because he wouldn't be a man if he didn't peek—he saw that she had a nightgown on under the robe, sheer and sleeveless and as sexy and innocent as she was. She pulled the covers back on her side and got in next to him.

"I'm not exactly sure what—"

"Shh." Greg turned on his side. He pushed his arm under her and pulled her until her back was tucked up against his chest and her head rested against his shoulder. Her shoulders started to jerk and he knew she was crying again, but that was okay, too. As long as she knew he was there for her. As long as she knew he wasn't going to let her go.

"I've got you," he whispered into her ear as she continued to sob into the pillow. "I've got you."

He continued to say it until her shoulders stopped shaking, until her breathing evened, until she was asleep and the only person to hear him say it was himself.

"I've got you. I promise."

CHAPTER SEVENTEEN

LIZA OPENED HER EYES AND looked out her bedroom window and waited as she had every day since that awful day to see if she knew who she was. She had a tragic loss as a child, but then was raised by a wonderful, loving adopted grandmother who taught her how to make good Italian food. She was devastated when she lost her grandmother, but she wasn't so depressed that she needed medication, and in defiance of that prescription, she let her boyfriend feed her beer that reacted with the pills and put her in the hospital.

She gritted out a few difficult months at a mental-health facility, but then because of her own determination, she forced her guardian to see reason and let her go back to school. She went to college, got a degree and was happy, if maybe a little lonely.

She was in love with a wonderful but complicated man who believed her when it seemed like no one else would.

And she had been arrested for a murder she knew she hadn't committed but couldn't remember.

Liza groaned and turned onto her back. She wasn't

sure which was the worst part about her summation. That she was in love, maybe for the first time, with a man she was in no position to begin a relationship with…or that she'd been charged with her godfather's murder.

For a moment she let herself feel the impact of knowing Hector D'Amato was dead. She didn't think they had been close, but she did know she thought of him as family and now that family was gone. Sadness built in her chest and an overwhelming sense of grief bubbled up inside her until tears were leaking out of her eyes. Not wanting Greg to see her crying again, she was glad when she turned her head and saw the bed was empty.

Then she heard the shower running on the other side of the bathroom door.

Would he understand that she mourned her godfather, despite knowing that at least at some point in time he had been connected with her father who by all accounts was not a good man? Liza struggled for a clear picture of her parents, but the only one that remained was from the picture on her dresser. She didn't grieve for them because she didn't know them. She imagined she would need to add another photo to her shrine of family.

Freddy had said there were pictures of Hector and her in his penthouse suite. A vague memory of large rooms and even larger windows that looked out onto the ocean came into focus. Freddy had said that Liza

had eaten dinner with Hector once a week, sometimes in his penthouse. If she was working for him,
she imagined she would be updating him on her
progress at those dinners. Maybe already telling him
about what she'd found. Or would she have waited
until she knew who was responsible before telling
him anything?

Is that why he'd been killed? Had she identified
the person who was stealing from him and Hector
had confronted him? She closed her eyes and tried
to think, but the large windows were the only thing
she was certain about.

At least it was something. She did have a sense of
who she was now. She did know what kind of person she had been.

Otherwise how could she have fallen in love?

Another groan escaped her throat. How pathetic,
she thought, to actually fall in love with her rescuer.
It was bad enough that she could see Greg had a natural heroic instinct that drove him to rescue people
and help those in need. Maybe he forced himself to
stop trying after he lost his patient, but those basic
instincts hadn't gone away, they had only been buried for a time.

She wondered how many other women had fallen
for him when he helped them. She wondered about
the fiancée who wouldn't stand by him when his life
had gotten difficult. Had he rescued her first, only
to be dumped when he needed rescuing?

Liza knew she wouldn't have left. The thought of saving Greg actually appealed to Liza. Saving Greg, helping him through whatever was happening to him in his life. Believing in him, when he lost belief in himself for a time. She could close her eyes and still remember the soft words he spoke into her ear.

I've got you.

She wanted to tell him the same. She wanted to be free of this nightmare so that she could tell him that he needed to go back to helping people because it was what he was born to do. He needed to leave the pain of what he perceived as his failure and focus instead on the good he could do.

Greg Chalmers was a superhero. He'd just forgotten how to be one.

Liza smiled at the fantasy of being taken hard on the backseat of her Ford by a superhero. It had been quick and intense and conceivably very stupid if she found herself pregnant next month. But she wouldn't regret it. She wouldn't regret any of her time with Greg.

What happens next?

Liza shook her head. She couldn't go there. It was hard enough to stay in the moment when her most recent past was such an empty pit. Her first objective was to get her memory back, which would hopefully explain what happened to her on the day of Hector's death. Her second objective was to prove herself innocent.

Greg, and her relationship with him, shouldn't even crack the top ten on her to-do list. He was the only thing she could think about, though. The only thing she wanted.

Now.

Pulling back the covers, she swung her legs over the bed until she was standing on the carpet. Then, in a burst of bravery, she let the straps of her nightgown slide off her shoulders until the white cotton pooled at her feet. Quietly, she made her way to the bathroom door where she could hear the sound of water and…was that singing?

Greg was a Van Morrison fan it seemed. She opened the door and was enveloped by a cloud of steam. His singing instantly stopped and it disappointed her. He had a good voice and she had this lovely idea about him crooning to her in the shower.

"Liza, is everything okay?"

Beyond the bathroom she could hear a phone ringing. It could be Elaine, or maybe the police. Or Freddy, who'd heard about the arrest. None of that seemed to matter. She pushed aside the shower curtain and stepped inside, gasping as the hot water fell over her in streams.

Without a word she put her hands on his chest and let her fingers glide over his lean, strong muscles. He didn't move. He didn't even breathe when she ran her hand low over his belly until she found him hard and powerful in her hand.

Yep. A superhero.

"Liza," he groaned. "We can't do this again. I don't have a condom."

Last she heard, a person didn't need a condom for touching, which was all she planned on doing. Which was all he did when his hands found her breasts. Immediately He dipped his head and took an already hard nipple into his mouth.

"I wanted this so bad," he said before his lips closed over the hard nub and she felt the answering tug deep between her legs.

Her hand circled his heavy erection and she loved the movement of it as it glided through her hand. Loved watching him shift his legs a little wider to plant himself as he started thrusting in time with her strokes.

"Shit," he said as he backed off, reaching down to grab her hands, keeping them inches away from where she wanted them. He was gasping a little for breath and the image of his body so tall and lean and perfect as water dripped from him made her mouth water. She leaned into him and felt his hard-on push against her stomach until she was cradling it against her body.

She kissed his neck and decided Greg was delicious both at room temperature and slightly cooked.

"Liza, you can't know how hard this is."

"Wanna bet?" She giggled, actually laughed, and it felt so good. She knew what was waiting for her outside the bathroom door. Knew the horrible world she had left behind, but right now she was there with him and there was nothing else.

"Liza…"

She lifted her lips from his neck, and met his eyes. His dark, soulful eyes. "Greg, what would we do if you were just Greg and I was just Liza, and we met at the coffee shop and you asked me out?"

His lips twisted into a smile. "Did you say yes?"

"I did. Because I thought you were kind and I thought I could trust you. So I took a risk. If that was us now, what would you do?"

He wrapped his arm around her waist and lifted her with shocking ease as he pressed her back against the tile wall. Then he pushed his hips between her thighs until she was lifting them and circling her legs around his back.

His penis pushed against her folds, once, twice, until he was sliding inside. She still ached a little from yesterday, but the profound pleasure of having him inside her outweighed any minor pain. He didn't move his hips, but kept himself pressed against her high and tight. His breath was heavy and rasping.

"I would do this," he said against her neck. "I would tell you I had to have you and I couldn't resist. I would tell you this time I will pull out because you missed those few days on the pill, but I like not having anything between us. I like that I can…"

The words he whispered in her ear then made her clench her body around him.

"…Anytime, anyplace," he finished as he started to move inside her. The tug and push of his body against her hips while her upper body was still, forced her focus to center between her legs.

Her head dropped and she looked down to see them, to watch it happen, but his head was in the way. She ran her fingers into his wet hair and tugged. He lifted his head at her request. Then he saw what she was doing. Saw how shameless she was.

"You like to watch," he said. Not a question. A statement.

She liked to watch him, she thought. It was so elemental, so sexual to see his flesh disappear again and again into her while she could feel the impact of him filling her, connecting her to him.

As if to tease her, he slowed down his penetration, taking his time to withdraw before thrusting harder and deeper into her, pushing her bottom into the tile until she felt pinned there by his erection alone.

What if this was really them, what if they could just be a couple waking up on a morning together, enjoying sex and a hot shower together?

Her climax, when it came, surprised her. "Noo," she moaned, sad that the intense pleasure of making love was now over, replaced by the quick and euphoric feeling the end brought with it.

"Damn it," Greg growled as he pulled himself free

from her body, his hand reaching down between his legs as he stroked himself to his finish. She couldn't tell if it satisfied him or made him even more frustrated that he'd had to leave her. Then he was groaning against her neck, and she thought even when he wasn't inside her she was still connected to him in this moment.

Finally she let her legs drop until she was standing on her own power, but she didn't let go of him. She wrapped her arms around his waist and was content to simply breathe him in. He, too, seemed content to cup her bottom with his hand so that she was pressed against his still semi-hard penis while he brought his breathing under control.

"It's okay," she said as she ran her hand along his back. "I've got you, too."

Breakfast was awkward. Liza wasn't sure what the brooding expression Greg had worn since they finally finished actually washing up in the shower meant. She wondered if he was annoyed that she'd started something he hadn't wanted, but couldn't resist as soon as it began. But the way he had kissed her when she whispered his words back to him, so gently and reverently, made her think he couldn't be angry with her.

But they were already into cereal and toast and half a pot of coffee and he hadn't said anything more meaningful to her than "Can you pass me the milk?"

It would have been easy enough to distract him with a discussion of the case. Of what they were going to tell the police about Verdi. But Liza found herself reluctant to go there. She had wanted the morning off. She wanted to feel like she felt at the batting cages with him. Fun and light and not filled with the dread of what happened yesterday or what tomorrow might bring.

He clicked his knife against the butter dish and she watched as he destroyed the slice of toast rather than waiting for the butter to melt a bit before trying to spread it. Either he was impatient when it came to toast or he was definitely agitated.

She hated to do it, hated to end at least the pretend moment of peace. But she couldn't sit across from him anymore feeling so completely distant from him.

"Did I do something wrong?" Liza winced at her choice of words. She hated to sound so weak. As if it was obvious that any issue he was having, was a result of something she did wrong.

Sitting straighter in her kitchen chair, she shook her head. "No, never mind. I don't think I did anything wrong. Except give you good shower sex."

There. That felt good. That felt like someone who wasn't a doormat. Who wasn't afraid to stand up for herself in a relationship.

Whoa. Was this a relationship?

Now it was her time to brood. He was half smiling as he lifted his coffee cup to his lips. "You gave me excellent shower sex."

"Then why aren't you talking to me?"

He sighed and leaned back in his chair, his jean-covered thighs spreading out in front of him. "Because I don't know what to say. No, that's not true. I have lots of things I want to say, but I don't think I can. I'm not even sure I have the words."

"I don't know what that means."

"Liza, we can't keep doing this. It's wrong."

A sudden thud in her chest had her looking away from him. She didn't want him to see her disappointment. She definitely didn't want him to see her pain. It was too soon for there to be pain. After only what, a week? It was there nonetheless.

"Shit, I'm messing this up. I only meant to say we can't start something until we finish this. We both know that. It's why we both resisted whatever this thing between us is…"

"What is it?" Liza wanted to know. She wanted to know what it was from his perspective. They had talked about attraction, and there was obviously lust. Lust they hadn't been able to contain. Was that what he meant? "What is this *thing*? For you."

For a minute he said nothing, only watched her as he might study one of his patients. As if he was trying to discern information from her question.

Finally, he said slowly, "I don't know. I don't know how to describe it."

Liza got up from the table with her bowl and dumped the contents into the sink. "So let's change the subject. What happens next? I think I need to hire investigators. I don't know if Elaine does that, or I do. I also want to get a better handle on my financial situation. I'll need to pay Elaine and any investigators she hires…"

"Stop." Greg put his hands on either side of her, trapping her against the counter. His chin rested on her shoulder, and she wanted to tell him it was a little pointy, but she loved his somewhat pointy chin.

She loved him. And he didn't know.

"I'm not…I'm a mess, Liza. I'm so much of a mess I couldn't be there for you when you needed me and that scares me. It makes me question if I'm worthy of you, worthy of having anyone's faith or trust. You make me feel…like it's worth reaching for, but I don't know if I can. Forgetting all the shit you are in, forgetting all the reasons why adding our feelings will only complicate your situation, I have to be honest with you. I have to tell you that I don't know what this is. Or where this can go. Because of me. Not you. Me."

She turned in his embrace and could see the honesty in his expression. Which only made her sadder because he thought he didn't have enough to offer and she thought his greatest strength was everything he did have to give someone. She cupped his face and smiled gently. "Did you just give me the 'it's not you, it's me' line?"

He rested his forehead against hers and she breathed in the feel of him surrounding her. Took her own strength from him, like a thief.

"What happens when it's the truth?"

"Sorry, it still feels like a cop-out."

He backed away from her and she could see that she'd annoyed him and took a perverse thrill in that. That she had the power to make him angry.

That she had power at all.

"What do you want?" Greg fired at her. "Where do you see this going? You think we should try to build something? That we should think about moving in together and buy freaking towels and plates together? While you're fighting to prove your innocence? That's crazy."

Liza smiled. "No. My life. Right now. That's crazy. This *thing* between us has been the only normal thing in my life since a police officer found me on the highway."

"Liza…"

She held up her hand. "Now you stop. I'm not saying this to push you into anything. The truth is I'm not exactly sure what I want either. I only know this is special to me. You are special to me. Okay?"

He nodded.

"You have way more to give than you think, Greg Chalmers. If anything, I think you've given too much of yourself to the people in your life. It's why, when things don't happen like you expect them to, it hurts so much."

"That's not—"

"Yes, it is. You're not the only one who can see people. Understand them. I don't know if I have that skill with other people, but I certainly have it with you. You used to trust people, I know that because you're trusting me now. But you let pain separate you from that instinct and that's why you think you're a mess."

Greg sat down at the table and stared into his coffee cup.

"Maybe you should forget accounting and go back to school to become a psychologist."

"Maybe I will," she said flippantly. "You know, right after I prove I didn't kill anyone."

"Yeah. Right after that. Speaking of which, you don't have to hire an investigator. I already have Mark and JoJo looking into it. Anything they find, they'll let us and Elaine know."

Elaine. Liza looked at the phone hanging on the kitchen wall and remembered she had heard it ring before being distracted by Greg's body. If it was Elaine calling then she might have important news. She reminded herself that she needed to call the phone company to get her password reset, too...

"Four is always my lucky number. I was marked with it on my birthday. April 4, 1940."

It was as if her Nonna was in the kitchen with her, smiling at her as she said something Liza knew she had repeated often. The memory was that clear.

Four was her Nonna's lucky number. Liza picked up the phone and hit the voice-mail button. She waited for the voice to prompt her for her password and then keyed in 4440. Immediately, the voice told her she had four new messages. Hitting the number one, it started with what she imagined was the oldest.

"Liza, you need to call me. We need to talk. Now."

Liza recognized Freddy's voice. The machine rattled off the date and the time when he left the message and she realized it must have been the day of the murder.

"Next Message. Beep."

"Where the hell are you, Liza? You need to call me and tell me where you are."

"Next Message. Beep."

Liza waited for the next message, but there was only silence and then a click.

"Next Message. Beep."

"Liza, it's Freddy. I heard from the detective that you've been formally charged. You need to come back to The Grande so we can talk about this. Things are hectic here...I can't get away. Also I don't know if you want to start thinking about what you're going to do with Hector's things...maybe now isn't the time. Anyway, I want to help. Hector would have wanted me to help you. I know you said you had represen-

ation, but this is serious. You'll need a team of law-
yers experienced with murder cases. Call me."

Liza frowned as she hung up the phone.

"What? It can't possibly be more bad news."

"No, it was Freddy. He heard about the arrest and
wants to hire a team of lawyers. There were several
other messages where he seemed very upset, which
he must have left after learning of Hector's death."

"Are you considering taking his advice?"

"No, I'm happy with Elaine. He did mention that
at some point I'll need to go through Hector's things.
It made me think, maybe that would help. Maybe if
I'm back in his place, where he lived, where I spent
time with him, I might remember more."

"No."

Liza blinked. "No, what?"

"You're not going back there. It's too dangerous. Are you forgetting someone shot at you? I
don't know if it was Verdi or someone else but you
shouldn't be putting yourself out there."

Liza shook her head. "I can't sit around here,
tucked away in this house not doing anything to help
my case. Verdi mentioned Freddy's name. I should
ask him what he knows about him."

Greg shook his head. "I'm not letting you go down
there by yourself. Mark and JoJo are tied up with the
investigation, Elaine needs to focus on the case and
I can't ask Chuck to go with you again."

Liza took the chair next to him. "Listen, I'm not

trying to be brave or stupid, but don't you see? This feels like a race. I have to get my memory back to prove I didn't kill Hector. I have to get my memory back to hopefully learn who did. I can't sit here and let everyone else around me work to figure this out, when *I'm* the one who is at risk. This is my life, my future. If it were you, wouldn't you do anything you could to save it?"

He closed his eyes and nodded.

"I'll be safe."

"Yes," he sighed. "You will be safe. At least as safe as I can make you. Because I'm going with you."

"You don't have to do this, Greg."

He met her eyes and she could see the determination in them. "Yes, I do. If I'm going to be worthy of you, I have to do this. Please, let me do this."

"Okay," she said softly. "Then I guess we're going together."

CHAPTER EIGHTEEN

THE INVISIBLE VISE AROUND his chest wasn't making it easy to breathe, but he hadn't passed out yet.

Greg walked himself through the panic attack. Shortness of breath, light-headedness, cold sweat. It wasn't by coincidence that he asked Liza to drive. As they pulled into the multilevel parking garage, the scene of his demise, Greg felt his breath bottom out, so much so that he could see spots in front of his eyes. He focused on taking slow deep breaths and waited for his vision to clear.

He could feel the sweat under his arms seeping through his shirt and he thought he was going to have to take another shower when they got home.

That was it. He needed to think of the shower. The feel of her pressed against him naked, her amazing hands on him, stroking him. Her pretty, firm breasts, the tips of them in his mouth.

"I've got you, too."

No, that he didn't want to think about. Not those words she whispered in his ear that had ripped right through him.

She had him? Nobody had him. That's not the

way it worked. He took care of others, he helped others. Others didn't help him. At least that was how it used to be. Prior to failing Tommy, prior to failing himself.

He told her letting people help didn't make her weak. He figured he proved that by living with Chuck, who had kept him clean for a year. Now he knew he didn't really mean it. He felt fragile and he hated that about himself. Hated it with a passion.

Which was why he'd put his butt in a car headed for Atlantic City. Which was why he was close to hyperventilating in a parking garage.

He would beat this. He would. It was the least he could do for her.

"Are you okay?"

"Yes," he said tightly. "I'm fine."

"Greg, if this is too hard…"

"It's not. Trust me, I have no desire to play poker right now."

Only Mark knew the real anxiety that kept Greg far away from this place. He hadn't even told Chuck. It was all too humiliating. Too embarrassing. Too pathetic.

Damn. How many times had he scolded Liza for saying the same thing about herself? Look at how wrong she'd been, too. Every action she took was brave. She hadn't tried to kill herself, she'd stood up to the doctor. She'd stood up to him.

She was completely honest about her feelings, about what she wanted.

He wasn't. He wasn't sure what that said about him, but he was pretty sure he didn't like it.

The car was stopped and she was looking at him. "I think we should go back. It's not worth putting you through this in the hope that I'll get a few memories back."

She was biting her lip and he probably looked like a man who was about to have a mental collapse any second, but he was determined to see this through. If he could do this, if he could handle being in this place, then maybe he would feel strong enough... to what?

To feel this love. To own it.

Greg couldn't think about that now. One step at a time. The only thing he needed to accomplish right now was getting out of the car. Which he did before Liza could make good on her threat to drive them away.

She got out after him and followed him without a word. He didn't need directions to the entrance to the casino. He knew the path. When they made it through the garage and into the connecting hallway, he was filled with a pounding in his head.

Or maybe it was simply the sounds. The bings and bongs, the bells and whistles, the people cheering and groaning. The lights. The oxygen-rich air that kept people alert and awake even as the watered-down alcoholic beverages made them fuzzy and unclear in their thinking. The best way to part a fool from his money.

They had parked on the third level. The view from where he stood was of the gambling floor below, where a wide staircase waited for people to descend into the masses. Into a place where the spectrum of emotions ran the gamut from fear and despair to exhilaration and euphoria to the most powerful one of them all: hope.

Everyone who gambled hoped. At least in the beginning. Everyone except for him. He hadn't used gambling as a method of entertainment, or a way to make money. He'd wanted to prove to himself that he was infallible.

How ridiculous was that? All these years he'd punished himself for what he believed was his failing, but to do that meant he thought perfection was in his grasp. That never making a mistake was something attainable.

He'd been an idiot.

"Greg, say something."

He turned away from the scene and felt the band around his chest start to recede. He wasn't perfect and it was okay to admit that. It was okay, because no one was perfect.

"Let's go see if we can drum up some memories for you."

"Are you sure? You're really okay being here?"

He nodded. "I'm really okay." He took a deep breath and knew it was true. Then he smiled at her. "But if you see me heading for the poker room, tackle me."

She smiled. "Okay, let's go. Jeanine will have a spare key to Hector's suite."

"Hunch or memory?"

"Memory," Liza told him. "They are all memories now."

GREG STOOD BACK and let Liza slide the key card into the lock. The yellow police tape across the door had already fallen by the wayside, suggesting they weren't the first people to enter this room since the police had done their thing. Once inside, Liza deactivated the alarm system and then he followed her into the apartment. The place was as expected. Massive and luxurious. So over the top that it might be considered garish. It appeared that Hector was a student of the Donald Trump school of interior design.

The idea that Liza would have killed the man for this was almost silly. She was the opposite of garish. She made simple beautiful.

"It's pretty awful, isn't it?"

"Not if you like gold and mirrors," Greg said as he wandered around the space that was filled with expensive things. Furniture, glassware, paintings. "Does it bring back any memories?"

Liza walked over and pulled on a cord near the

edge of the window to expose the view. The Atlantic Ocean won hands down in terms of things Greg would rather be looking at. Except, of course, for Liza.

"I remember this."

"Of course you do. It was the only place you could have looked without hurting your eyes."

Liza glanced at him and then back out the window. "I felt sadness this morning. Grief for him. I don't think we were close, I don't think I let myself be close with him. But I know he tried to do right by me. He should be grieved for that, at least."

Greg wasn't so sure. "If he was doing right by you, he wouldn't have made you quit your job and involved you in an embezzlement scam. He had to know that would be putting you in danger."

"I'm sure he thought he could protect me. My vague memories of Hector are that he was a control freak. I mean, look at this place. He thought he was a king and this was his palace."

"Yeah, a palace someone else wanted."

"Oh my God, it just occurred to me I own this now. What the hell am I going to do with it?"

"Whatever you want, I suppose." Although the irony that he was now involved with a woman who owned a casino was not lost on him.

Liza wandered over to a table filled with pictures in the living room. He watched as she lifted each one, studying it, hoping no doubt that one of them would bring it all flooding back. He walked up behind her and looked at the picture in her hand. She was in a cap and gown. Hector's gleaming white teeth contrasted sharply with the dark hair, eyes and skin of his face. He was looking at her instead of the camera and there was a sense of satisfaction in his expression. As if he was applauding himself for what he'd done.

Liza simply looked young and happy.

"You are beautiful."

His words made her jump. "Stop."

"It's true. I look at you every day and I can see it, but I don't think about you in terms of your beauty. Looking at this picture, I'm reminded again. You're stunning."

"Yes, she is."

Greg and Liza swung their heads around to the door that was now open. Greg didn't recognize the man standing in front of two others behind him. He was guessing, based on the expensive suit that didn't seem to fit quite right and the Italian leather shoes, that he was Freddy Ortiz, the current acting CEO of The Grande.

He sure as hell knew the other two men. They had become intimately acquainted with his face a lifetime ago. Thick Neck number one and Thick Neck number two, if he recalled their names correctly.

That earlier feeling of disgust and shame overcame him again. They were here. With Freddy. Liza was going to know what he did, what he became.

She was going to learn how pathetic he'd been. Had allowed himself to be.

His stomach cramped.

Freddy stepped forward and the two men followed him. "Liza, what are you doing with this man? Is he threatening you?"

Liza choked on a half laugh. "No, of course not. Freddy, this is Greg—"

"I know Mr. Chalmers by reputation. Mr. Chalmers, your face was picked up by one of our surveillance cameras as you entered the facility, which alerted security to your presence. You can imagine my surprise that you would consider returning to a place where you know you are not wanted."

Don't say it. Don't say it out loud.

"Liza, do you know who this man is? He's a cheat who's been banned from every casino on the boardwalk, not to mention Vegas."

Greg winced. "Cheat isn't exactly fair. More like overly skilled."

He didn't carry the guilt of cheating. Only that he'd played. That he'd needed to play because he needed to win. That he couldn't stop. His addiction cost him his job, his friends and his fiancée, and left him bleeding on a cement floor. Now Liza was going to know how ugly it had been.

"Liza, what are you doing with him?" Freddy repeated.

Greg thought it was an excellent question. What was this remarkable woman doing with *him?*

"He's been helping me. With recovering my memory."

"Your memory is back?"

"No," she answered carefully. "Not all of it. But parts of it are starting to return."

Freddy nodded. "That's good. Excellent. I mean, if you're going to try and prove your innocence, you're going to need to know what happened that day."

"Freddy, do you know a Dr. Anthony Verdi?" Liza asked him.

Freddy made a sour face. "Yeah, I know him. He was Hector's cousin. Always hitting him up for money for his crazy hospital while at the same time looking at Hector like he was dirt underneath his feet. Hector finally cut him off."

"I know," Liza said. "He came to me that day, the same day Hector was killed, asking me for money."

"Seriously? Liza, if Hector knew that… If he knew Verdi had talked to you that wouldn't mean good things for the doctor. Wait a minute. You think he might have killed Hector?"

"I know he wanted Hector dead," Liza said.

"Maybe you can tell us what you remember about that day and night?" Greg interjected. "Were you here at the casino?"

Greg could feel the two thick necks eyeing him the way a hungry dog looks at a piece of raw meat. Ready to start pounding their fists into him at the first sign from Freddy.

"I was. I was working."

"Did you see Hector that night?"

Freddy opened his mouth to answer and then closed it, carefully folding his arms over his chest. "Last time I checked you weren't the police."

"No, not the police. Only curious how a casino filled with cameras so sophisticated they ID'd me in less than ten minutes, failed to capture the owner's violent death."

"That's what we're going to hope the police figure out, isn't it?"

"Obviously they're done figuring anything out because they've already charged Liza."

"Well, now it's my turn to help her," Freddy said pointing at his chest. He looked to Liza and nodded. "We're going to hire as many lawyers as it takes, Liza. I promise. If you think Verdi is involved, we will turn his life upside down."

LIZA STARED AT the man filling the room with his broad shoulders. Hector's number two, she thought. It made more sense to her now than when she was first in his office. He looked less like a stranger, and more like someone she thought she should know. Only she didn't really. What she did know was he was wrong about her and Hector's relationship, which made her instinctively wary of him.

"Last time I was here, you basically implied you thought Hector and I were lovers."

He held up his hands. "It is what I thought, yes.

It's what everybody thought, but that doesn't mean I think you killed him."

"That wasn't the impression I got."

"Then I'm sorry," Freddy said. "Let me make it up to you. Stay here. In his place. We'll start thinking about your options. I know it's what Hector would have wanted. For me to help you get through this."

Liza looked at Greg who was still staring at Freddy. She could feel the tension in him. Because he was in Atlantic City, because his past was being thrown in his face, or because Freddy was lying. She wasn't sure which. It didn't matter. There was no way she was staying in Hector's penthouse.

"I would rather go back to my place."

Freddy's mouth tightened and he took a step toward her. "Liza, you need help. You need someone you can trust. I know you don't remember me, but you *knew* me. You trusted me for years. How long have you known this guy, a week?"

Liza turned back to Greg, whose hands were shoved deep in his pockets and whose eyes were now on the floor. He seemed defeated to her and she didn't think she had ever seen him that way.

"This guy was a loser. Couldn't quit the game so my boys had to take care of him, send him a message. You understand what kind of sick that is? When you know you're going to get the shit kicked out of you but you go back for it, anyway. Is that the kind of guy you think can help you out of this mess?"

"He's right."

Liza's head snapped to Greg. It was this place, she thought. It was making him act differently. She thought he'd found some sense of peace when he was overlooking the main floor. That he'd realized something he hadn't before. Being with Freddy, here in this room, changed him.

Or maybe it was the two thugs behind Freddy.

Oh God, had they been the ones who sent the message?

"Greg."

"No," he said, shaking his head. "He's right. I was sick. So maybe I'm not the best person to help you through this, but you're basically stuck with me. She's leaving with me."

Freddy's jaw tightened, but he didn't say anything immediately. "I guess that's up to her. Liza, we need to talk. About this place, what you want to do with it."

Liza laughed. Right. She owned a casino. In the midst of all of this she had to deal with that, too. "I sort of have something else I need to deal with right now."

"I get that, but the legal thing is going to take months before they even have a trial. This is business, love it or hate it. People's livelihoods depend on our decisions. We need to have a plan, at least for the interim. Let me come over tomorrow. To your place. We'll talk."

Liza looked back at Greg whose eyes were again pinned on Freddy. A short nod let her know he was okay with the request. "Okay. That's fine."

"I'll be there," Greg told him. "She won't be alone."

"I guess that's her choice, too." Freddy looked over Liza's head to Greg. "Are we going to need to escort you out?"

"No," he said quietly.

"You sure you can resist the temptation?" Freddy sneered.

"Yeah. I'm sure."

"Guess my boys made that message count, huh?"

Liza watched as the two men behind Freddy snickered at each other. It disgusted her to know she was actually responsible for their paychecks. Certainly, if she kept this place, that would change.

"Then I'll see you both tomorrow."

The men left, and the tension in the air dissipated with their departure.

Greg let out a whoosh of air. "Let's get the hell out of here."

"Wait, that's it?" That couldn't be it. She'd come hoping for answers, only there had been no sudden revelations. No outpouring of memories. Greg shouldn't have had to go through what he did for such a measly outcome. It wasn't fair. "But I still... I still don't remember everything."

Greg didn't state the obvious, that maybe she never would. Or maybe it would take years.

Years. That would be too late for her. Too late for them.

He held out his hand and she took it, as he led her out of the casino.

She didn't argue when Greg walked to the driver's side of the car and held out his hand for the keys. She thought to make some joke about men's inability to let a woman drive and how good he'd been by letting her drive them to the casino, but she knew this was about control for him. He wanted some of it back and the least she could do was hand over her keys.

As they drove away from Atlantic City she thought she might feel a change in him, but his knuckles were white against the steering wheel and his expression was grim at best. A heavy silence hung between them as the car ate up the highway in front of them.

"So, what was all that about back there with Freddy?"

"What?"

"About him being right about you. He made you sound like a degenerate. You're not that."

"I was that."

Liza shook her head. "I don't believe it. You're too…you're too…"

"What?"

Liza tried to think of the word that described Greg. For her it was too big. He was a lighthouse in a horrible storm, or a pond of water in the middle of the desert. He was safety and trust and truth. It was why, even when she had sensed his cynicism the first time she met him, she had inherently understood that he would help her.

"Noble."

The word popped out and she thought it was a good description. Like any hero in any story, he may have faced obstacles in his life, but those obstacles were ones he'd created because he felt he hadn't lived up to the person he wanted to be.

She could hear him snicker, and it wasn't a nice sound. He was mocking her, but she knew she was right. Amnesiac or not, she knew how he made her feel.

"Sweetheart, noble is the last thing I am. I'm a washed up ex-psychologist who is hanging on to gambling sobriety by a thread most days."

"You didn't rush off to any table while we were in the casino," she pointed out. "You didn't even look tempted."

"Maybe not. Maybe I finally figured out what the gambling meant to me. Why it was important then and why it's not important now. It doesn't change what I became. It doesn't change the fact that I let it happen. I was a mess and I destroyed things. My practice, my relationships. I'm the last person you should trust to help you out of this, but like I said, it's too late. You're stuck."

Liza tried to understand what Greg saw when he looked in the mirror and how that could be so different from what she saw when she looked at him. "What did you expect of yourself? Perfection?"

His head turned sharply to her and maybe the word hit a chord in him.

"Because if that was the bar you set for yourself then I feel sorry for you, because you were always destined to fail."

"I didn't need to be perfect," he said between gritted teeth. "I just wasn't supposed to be so weak."

"Ha!" Liza burst out. Greg was turning the car into the driveway but she wasn't going to wait to make her point. "Now who's being ridiculous? Is that what you think, because you let the tragic loss of a patient affect you, that you're weak? When you wouldn't let me wallow for one second in the feeling that this freaking condition is a result of my own weakness. That's not fair."

She got out of the car and started down the path to the front door. She could hear the hard slam of a car door and knew he was following her. Holding his tongue until she had deactivated the alarm and the door was closed behind them.

"It's not about fair," he said. "It's about what's right there in front of our freaking faces. You're not weak! Not at all. You suffered significant tragedies in your life yet you grew up whole and sensible. You made a life for yourself and came out stronger. What's happening to you now is because you were a witness to your godfather's killing! Do you know how many people would come through that unscathed? No one! You're the opposite of what I did. I had everything and one failure destroyed me. I'm pathetic."

Liza stared at the man who had saved her from the abyss and struggled with this image he had of himself. Then, suddenly, his words from that morning came back to her, the ones that hurt so much because it had felt as if he was rejecting her.

She thought when he told her what a mess he was that it was a line. A way to back out of something by suggesting it was his fault and not hers and she hadn't really believed him. Now she could see how much he believed it.

"No, you're a hypocrite," she said, suddenly angry at him. Really angry. "It's okay when you're the hero, when you're saving the day. It's okay when someone else needs you and you can be the strong, cool, collected one. But when you make a mistake and when someone wants to be there for you, someone wants to lo… Care for you. Then that's unacceptable. You tell yourself you're not worthy, or you're pathetic, or whatever other word you want to use, but the truth is you're afraid."

She could see his eyes widen and his body jolt as if she had physically hit him. "This morning I asked you what you thought this thing between us was and you panicked!" Liza laughed through the sick feeling in her heart. "You weren't rejecting me—

you're too scared to take a chance on opening your-self up again."

"Why would I do that?" he snapped back. "Why would I throw away everything I know about people, which is that most of them are liars? Why would I let myself trust anyone again when the one time I needed *anyone,* no one was there for me?"

"Chuck was there for you," she whispered, her heart now aching for a totally different reason.

Greg fell onto the seat of her couch and put his head in his hands. "Chuck was there for me when I hit rock bottom. When I had already started to crawl out of the pit. He helped me to keep climbing."

Liza sat next to him on the couch, not touching him but wanting to. Wishing she had known him back then. Wishing she could have been there when he'd needed help. Now, it was too late. She couldn't help him until he accepted he wasn't perfect.

"Would you have let someone help you back then?"

He leaned back, his long body sprawled over the furniture. He laughed humorlessly. "That is a very good question."

"I don't think you would have. You would have seen that as 'weak,' too," she said, using her fingers to make quotes around the word she knew he hated. A word she had hated, too. Because, after all, who wanted to be weak. "Oh Greg, noble was the best word I could have used for you. You made a mistake and you wanted to punish yourself for that. That's why you kept people away, not because you're afraid to trust people. Not because no one was there, because you wouldn't have let them help if they were. Being a hero doesn't mean having to be perfect. You're still a mortal like the rest of us."

She patted him on the leg and stood. He had no words, no comeback. Probably because he knew she was right.

"I believe you now when you say we can't have a relationship. Because I'm decidedly not perfect and I wouldn't want to be with someone who felt so superior. I wouldn't want to be with someone who would always want to be there for me, but would never let me be there for him."

When he looked up at her, she could see the pain in his eyes. The anguish that, until he accepted himself for who he was, including his flaws, he was doomed to be alone.

"I'm going to make some tea and think about dinner. I imagine you'll stay over because that's who you are. Always the vigilant protector. Tonight you can sleep in the guestroom."

Liza made it to the kitchen before she started to cry.

CHAPTER NINETEEN

THE DOORBELL RANG AND Elaine jumped. She'd been so absorbed in the report Mark and JoJo had provided her that she'd lost her sense of space and time. She was at her kitchen table, in her condo, in Society Hill.

She checked the clock on the laptop and saw it was after 10:00 p.m. She didn't really know her neighbors in the building and none of her friends would have come over without calling first. Assuming the visit had to be related to Liza's case, maybe Greg or Liza with some new information, she walked over to the door and checked the peephole. Then she groaned.

"I heard that," Chuck called through the door.

Great. Elaine glanced down at herself. She was dressed in her normal at-home attire. Cotton pajama pants, which were too big for her, and a tank top. And no bra, because no woman ever wore a bra when she didn't have to.

She opened the door, but left the security chain in place and made sure to stay out of his view.

"What do you want?"

She could see his face through the two inches and he looked determined. "For you to let me in."

"Why?"

"Because we need to talk."

"About what?"

"Jesus, Elaine. Will you let me in? Look I brought Chinese from that place you like."

He held up the bag and her stomach nearly growled. Before Chuck showed up, she'd decided it was too late to eat, but her stomach obviously disagreed. She didn't want to think about how he knew about her favorite Chinese take-out place, but the logo on the bag was the right one.

"I've got dumplings…"

Dumplings were her downfall. She closed the door and unlocked the chain. She considered racing to her bedroom to get a bra, but then decided she really didn't care. She was a modest B-cup—her breasts weren't going to fill up the space between them—and besides, it wasn't as if she cared what he thought anymore. At least not when it came to her.

Removing the chain, she opened the door and let him enter. He walked through her living room to the kitchen as if he owned the place. As if he'd been there lots of times before because he was her boyfriend.

Stop. She would not let herself go there. She was officially forgetting him. Putting him behind her. Moving on and concentrating on finding someone else she liked half as much. Right after she figured out how to prove Liza Dunning was innocent of murder.

"Get this," Chuck said as he started pulling out white cartons of food and placing them on her table. Elaine moved her laptop to the counter so as not to risk soy sauce damage. "Guess where Greg was today?"

"I'm going to bet solid money that he was wherever Liza was."

"Yeah, but she was in Atlantic City."

Elaine processed that information. "Why?"

"She probably wanted to go check out her new digs. To make Greg go, that's just wrong. I'm telling you, she is bad news. I mean, I know you're defending her and everything, but who does that? Who makes a guy with a gambling problem go to AC?"

Maybe someone who wanted to help him. "You know Greg's phobia of AC isn't exactly healthy."

Chuck squinted at her as if she couldn't be serious.

"I'm just saying to recover, to really recover, he has to face his demons. All of them. Including being able to walk into a casino and know that he won't gamble. It's possible Liza could see that."

"What the eff? She's known him a week and you think she has a better handle on him than me who's been living with him for the past year?"

Elaine didn't want to argue, but the truth was yes, she did think Liza saw things about Greg that everyone else probably missed. Because she also thought Liza was crazy about the guy and sometimes that went beyond the skin and deep into the soul.

"If you say something like 'bros before hoes,' right now, I'm kicking you out."

Chuck shut his mouth and sat in one of her two kitchen chairs. He popped open a carton, letting the dumpling scented steam fill the air. He fished out two sets of chopsticks and handed a pair to her.

Elaine thought about fetching plates and forks and napkins, but then he handed the carton to her and she forgot everything in pursuit of a pork-filled dumpling. She found the dipping sauce and let it soak for exactly two seconds before lifting the dripping delicacy into her mouth.

Heaven.

"I like to watch you eat."

Elaine chewed and swallowed and tried not to take that as a compliment. After all, what kind of compliment was that?

"You never hold back. It makes me wonder what you would be like… Never mind."

Elaine had this ridiculous urge to tell him, since she knew exactly where he was going, that yes, he was right, she was *great* in bed. Which raised an uncomfortable question. Did everyone think they were good at sex? All she knew was that, because for her it happened so infrequently, she took extra measures to enjoy it while it was happening. She felt fully confident that she would rock his world. Even though it was never going to happen.

"Why did you come here? To tell me you think Liza is a danger to Greg?"

"She's trouble. There's no getting around it."

Elaine nodded. "I think it's trouble Greg needs in his life. I mean, I didn't know him before the whole gambling thing, only since he came to work at the Tyler Group. But I would bet he's different from the guy he used to be. It's like he's developed this really hard shell around him and I used to think if you cracked it, he'd probably be all Cadbury Creme Egg gooey sweetness inside. Only it's like the gooeyness is starting to harden up, too."

"You're comparing Greg to Easter candy?"

"They make it at Halloween now, too." Elaine let herself have two eggs per year. "I'm saying, I see the way he looks at her and it's a good thing. Because instead of being cold and cynical, it's like he finally cares about something. I bet pre-gambling-addiction Greg cared about a lot of things. She's bringing that out in him again. They could be good for each other."

Chuck laughed. "Unless she's a freaking murderer," he said as he stuffed lo mein noodles into his mouth.

Elaine shook her head. "I don't think she is."

"You got proof of that?"

"Not enough. But Mark sent over a report of what he pulled together today. We have access to the surveillance cameras that the police have. You can see Hector walking through the floor and out through a backdoor. A few seconds later you can see Liza following him. She's wearing the dress she was found in, no purse, nothing in her hands."

"Casinos have cameras outside, too."

Elaine smiled. "Shockingly, the one outside the door where Hector left was broken."

"Or tampered with."

"The police don't indicate that in the report, only that it conveniently wasn't working at the time of the murder. Which, of course, given that Liza was an employee of the casino, lends to their speculation that she was responsible for somehow deactivating it."

"Opportunity, motive, she better hope you are a really good lawyer."

Elaine straightened. "I am. However, I might not need to be. Guess what Mark also found. According to the time stamp on the surveillance video, Hector was killed at about 1:00 a.m."

"Yeah?"

Elaine paused for a moment to build effect. After all, she was a trial lawyer. "Well, Mark pulled Liza's phone records. She received three calls originating from Atlantic City late that Saturday night. That's as specific as he can be now, but he's going to run the numbers to see if they came from The Grande."

"So?"

"So…they came in at eleven forty-one, eleven forty-six p.m. and eleven fifty-two. If it was Hector calling, he was probably asking her to come see him. Which means maybe she didn't go down there of her own initiative."

Chuck shook his head. "Lame."

Elaine frowned and opened another carton filled with chicken and broccoli. "It speaks to a lack of premeditation."

"It doesn't speak to anything. You said there were three calls, which means maybe she didn't answer the phone so he kept calling, which means maybe she was already headed down there with a gun strapped to her thigh. What's the trip from her place to AC, about an hour? Plenty of time to get down there, disable the camera, send D'Amato a message that he needs to meet her outside…"

"Let herself be seen on camera practically chasing him across the main floor?"

Chuck shrugged. "I never said I could hack it as a cop on *Law & Order*. I program apps, remember?"

"Yes, the flying squirrels. Such a productive use of your genius."

"Did you just call me a genius?" He batted his eyelashes. "I'm flattered."

Elaine didn't respond. She knew the phone records were weak evidence, but so far they were all she and Mark had. Yet. All they had yet. "There has to be more. A connection between her, the embezzlement and why she went to the casino that night."

"Also why she was covered in blood, and her prints were found on the gun…"

"Whose side are you on?"

"Greg's. And yours, I guess. Not hers until you convince me otherwise, and I'm not convinced."

Elaine studied him over her chopsticks. "You're not jealous of her, are you?"

"Jealous?"

"I mean you can't be oblivious to it. The way Greg is around her. The way she looks at him."

"Yeah, I see it, but I'm not jealous. I just don't think it's a good idea."

"Just because he gets a girlfriend doesn't mean you guys won't be friends."

Chuck rolled his eyes. "Look, if she's not in jail and they want to date, whatever. I'm not jealous of Greg moving on with his life. I worry about him, that's all. He doesn't realize it, but he's the kind of person who puts himself out there. Hell, the fact that he brought her home to stay with us in the first place tells you who he is. If he weren't allergic, I'm positive the loft would be filled with stray animals. Which means somebody has to have his back. That's me."

Elaine nodded. That was the thing about Chuck. He seemed like a complete and total ass up until the point when you knew he wasn't. That he was really a good guy and a loyal friend. Which made her sad because she guessed once this case was over, they probably weren't going to have any reasons to see each other. She probably wouldn't see him until the next time a case came up where both she and Greg were needed. Now that she and Chuck had firmly concluded there wasn't going to be anything between them, they weren't even going to have the chance to be friends anymore. Chuck was a really good friend to have. She wished she had appreciated their friendship more when it had been there.

"That's why you came over here? To tell me you have Greg's back?"

"No," he said around a mouthful of noodles. "I told you, I wanted to talk."

Her stomach got fluttery. "Talk. But if it's going to be about how much sex you're having with all the women you're dating…"

"Look—" He stopped her. "I'm sorry about that. I told you I wasn't trying to brag, but I didn't want you to find out after and think I was a scumbag."

"Indiscriminate sex with multiple partners implies scumbag."

"Are you trying to convict me or are you going to listen?"

"Listen," Elaine muttered.

"I went out with those women because you rejected me. Okay? I wanted to not feel like the biggest loser in the world. I don't think that's a crime."

It wasn't. It hurt on multiple levels, though. The idea of him being with other women. Also, that she made him feel like a loser in the first place. Then something he said earlier triggered a question.

"After what?"

"Huh?" he set down the carton and the chopsticks, which she took to mean he was full. She wondered if he was still going to be around in an hour when he got hungry again.

"You said you didn't want me to find out after... after what?"

Chuck stood and walked to her side of the small kitchen table. He bent down and grasped her wrist as if to keep the chopsticks she held from becoming a weapon.

"After this." His head dropped and before she could even process what was happening, he was kissing her. Actually kissing her. Tongue in mouth kissing. It felt so supremely good. Like a cool shower on a hot day or a hot shower on a cold day...oh hell, she didn't know what it felt like other than good and right.

Chuck had one hand wrapped around her neck and the other still held her hand with the chopsticks, and his lips were doing all the work. To say she was turned on was like saying she breathed. Because Chuck was kissing her and she didn't want it to stop. Ever. Oh, God. She had missed months of this because she thought they were only friends?

Stupid, Elaine. Stupid, stupid.

Then it was over. He was lifting his head away from her and she was afraid it was because of her dumpling breath, but rather than looking disgusted, he looked satisfied.

And also not satisfied enough. As if he wanted more.

"You screwed up," he told her. "Then I screwed up. It doesn't mean we can't have a second chance at this. Think about it."

With that, he left the kitchen and a few seconds later, she heard her door closing.

Oh yeah, she was sure she was going to think about it. Most likely all the lonely night long.

Bastard.

GREG CLOSED THE door of his loft behind him, hoping he would be alone. No such luck. Chuck was sprawled out on the sofa watching a movie with a bowl of ice-cream balanced on his flat stomach.

"Hey, what are you doing here? Shouldn't you be guarding Princess Memory?"

Yes. He should. As he was beginning to shine a particularly bright light on all his worst traits, he realized he was not a man who dealt with tension and awkwardness well. Especially when he was the one causing it.

"I got Mark to come over and watch the place. He

won't let anything happen. Not that I think anything will happen tonight."

Chuck swung his legs off the couch and sat up. "What happened? You guys get into a fight?"

A fight? It was hard to say. Liza had said a lot of stuff, stuff that hurt. She hadn't done it with malicious intent. She'd been telling the truth. That was why it hurt so much, because there wasn't a damn thing he could say in contradiction. Yes, he hated the idea of failing at something. Yes, he strived to be infallible. He was a therapist who used to mess with people's heads. Their emotions, their fears, their goals. He got deep inside them and figured out their problems and fixed their lives. Saved their lives. How many patients had he stopped from committing suicide until he failed with Tommy?

Shouldn't a person with that much power want to be perfect at it? So why had it sounded so ugly when she said it? As if he were some superior bastard with a God complex who thought he was above it all.

"I'm going to go to my room."

Chuck shrugged. "Whatever. You know you can tell me anything."

Yeah, he did. He joined Chuck on the couch and saw the movie was actually a romantic comedy. Chuck did not watch romantic comedies. Chuck watched things get shot, kicked and blown up.

"Are you sure you don't want to tell *me* something?" Greg asked with half a smile.

"Nah, it's too new. Let's say I've got women and romance on the brain and leave it at that."

Romance. Greg shook his head. With everything that had happened between him and Liza, absolutely the last thing he'd shown her was any romance. The backseat of her car, sure. A batting cage.

"Look, let me cut to the chase for you," Chuck said. "You like this girl and it's freaking you out. Probably because you don't know whether or not she's a killer."

Greg sighed. "She's not a killer."

"You don't know that for sure."

Yes, he did. He knew for sure.

"Okay, let's assume she's innocent. That her name gets cleared. Let's even assume Princess Memory gets her memory back. What are you going to do next?"

Nothing. Because he was a coward who had never actually dealt with his failure. Because he was supposed to have been better than he was, only he wasn't. Which made him an ass.

Liza wanted someone who would be there for her, which currently he wasn't, and who would let her be there for him, which he didn't know how to do. He didn't blame her for pushing him away.

He looked at Chuck and thought about what Liza said. Chuck had been there to help him. He'd almost dismissed it at the time, as if Chuck giving him a place to stay and keeping him away from the poker

able hadn't really been all that much. That he'd done
he real work and Chuck had simply been a safety
net. A sponsor of sorts to help him from going off
he deep end when he'd been so much more than that.

"Have I ever thanked you for everything you did
for me in the past year?"

"Oh, here we go. Look man, just because I'm
watching a chick movie doesn't mean I want to
share, okay. If you want to talk about why you're
so bent over the princess go for it, but that's where
I draw the line."

Greg laughed softly. "Got it. No sharing."

"So you going to ask her out when this is over?
Take her on a date? Because you know that's where
it should start. A nice dinner, a movie. Conversation where you don't spend the whole time studying her pupils and her pores to see if she's lying.
Because dude, a woman sometimes lies, even when
she doesn't want to. Even when she doesn't mean it.
Like, if you ask a woman about her weight, sure as
shit she will lie. You got to get over that."

Greg thought about all the times he'd talked with
Liza, how he could count the two times she'd lied
to him, to protect herself and to protect her heart.
Maybe that was why she had drawn him in so deeply.
Maybe, subconsciously, he knew he could trust her.

When this was over? When she had her real life
back? It was going to happen. He knew that now.
Unless he dealt with his shit she would move on with

her life without him. The sharp pain in his head he got just thinking about never seeing her again was something he didn't want to live with.

"When did you get to know so much?"

"Through trial and error." Chuck grinned. "I figured out something tonight, though. You can't let yourself get in your own way. All the anxiety and fear and worries about what might or might not happen in life, you got to let that shit go. Otherwise you'll never get the thing you want."

"Did you get the *thing*—" he coughed "—Elaine …you want?"

"You knew about that?"

Greg chuckled again. "I had my suspicions. I knew there was something behind all that bickering. Pretty good bet it was sexual tension."

"Well, we're still in the feeling-things-out stage, but at least we're being honest about it." Chuck shifted on the couch. "That's a start. You want this to go anywhere with Liza and you're going to have to do the same."

"She thinks I'm a superior bastard."

Chuck laughed so hard that he had to grab on to the ice cream bowl so it wouldn't fall. "Man, you are. She nailed you. But you're also messed up like the rest of us and that's why people like you."

"Do they?"

"Yeah. They look up to you, they respect you. You freak them out with the whole lying thing, but mos people get that's part of your crazy genius. They also know that like everyone else sometimes you're holding on by your fingertips. It's what makes you human. You want to hear the scary truth? The thing I know you don't like to deal with is probably what made you really good at your job. Your real job. Not his lie detector stuff. Practicing psychology."

Instantly, Greg could feel his chest tighten, which was what happened every time he thought about his former life.

God, he'd run from that, too, like a freaking chicken.

"You helped people."

"You didn't know me then."

"Doesn't matter. I can still tell. Look at what you did for JoJo. Hell, look at what you did for Liza. Greg, people have laid off you for a while because everyone knows you were trying to get your shit together, but it's been a year. It's time to go back to doing what you do best."

"What if I don't want to?"

"Then you spend your life not being the person you're supposed to be, and I have to say that would suck."

Greg's eyes shot up. "Oh, really? You were meant to program flying-squirrel apps?"

Chuck laughed and then his face grew more serious. "I was meant to be rich. I have my reasons for that. The squirrels were just the means. But yeah, I hear what you're saying. Elaine says it all the time,

too. Maybe it's time I find something more produc
tive to do with my genius."

"She called you a genius?"

Chuck smiled even wider. "She did."

Greg nodded. "Good for you. Okay, well, I'll think
about what you said. I'm going to catch a few hours
of sleep before I head back over to Liza's."

"To make up with her?"

"To prove she didn't kill Hector D'Amato."

"Okay, but then after that you should make up
with her. Elaine says she's good for you."

She was, Greg realized. She was very good for
him. The question was whether he was going to be
brave enough to accept that.

Honestly, he didn't know.

CHAPTER TWENTY

LIZA HEARD THE KNOCK ON the back door and looked up from her coffee mug. Greg's face was framed by the window and she considered not opening the door. After he'd left, she'd spent the night crying over him, not sleeping, arguing with him in her head until her brain hurt, and now she was flat out exhausted.

Only she knew he wasn't going to go away, and the reason he was there more likely had something to do with Freddy coming by to talk to her than anything to do with them.

Which only made her sadder.

Getting up from the kitchen table, she unlocked the door and let him in.

"Hi."

She offered a weak wave in return. "Do you want some coffee?"

"Sure."

She could feel him looking at her. She could only imagine how swollen her eyes were. She'd taken the coward's way out this morning and had brushed her teeth without once looking in the mirror.

He caught her hand as she moved to get a mug

down from the cabinet and brought his other hand up to cup her cheek. She hated how good it made her feel. How cared for.

"You've been crying. Did I do that?"

"No." It was an instinctual lie. After all, who wanted to admit that to the person they were crying about? She could tell he knew she was lying.

"Oh, babe," he said sadly. "Don't do that. Not with me."

She backed away from him until he wasn't touching her any longer. "Well, it was a stupid question to ask. I can see now where that could become annoying really quickly. You won't let anyone have any secrets."

"I'm not a mind reader, Liza. I know you're lying but I don't know what the truth is."

The truth. To her it was so evident. She'd fallen in love with him. Stupidly, ridiculously, completely in love. Yes, last night she'd spent half the time arguing with him in her head, but the other half she'd argued with herself for being so stupid to fall in love with someone when her life was such a mess.

She tried to rationalize the love away.

Her feelings were a natural reaction given the stress she was under. She was confusing his role as helper and protector with deeper feelings. Love didn't happen in a week. It was the sex. She'd confused physical satisfaction with emotion. The feeling would be fleeting.

All of it made so much sense, except when she stopped offering up logical arguments and let herself feel, she knew it was love. She knew it was love because the thing she most wanted from Greg was not for him to help her, but for him to let her help him. To let her inside his imperfect soul and share all that messy stuff with her. It was when she feared he wasn't capable of letting her inside, that she started to cry.

Greg was capable of loving someone; he just didn't want to do it. And that sucked.

"Well the truth is you hurt me," she said, letting him see her eyes and know she was telling the truth. "I trusted you with so many things, the least of which was my body and, memory or not I know that's not something I do easily or casually. You need to respect the fact that the things you say and do have consequences."

"Yeah, I get that."

"Okay. Then don't ever ask me again if I was crying and if you were the reason."

"I don't want to hurt you. You are the last person in the world I want to do that to."

"Tough. You already did."

He winced and she thought it was cruel of her to be so honest. She could see his turmoil and knew that whatever was going on in his head wasn't any easier to sort through than what was going on in hers.

"Liza, I've been thinking. Thinking and talking a lot. And I want…"

The phone rang and interrupted him. Liza turned to the kitchen phone and debated letting it go to voice mail.

"Go ahead. Answer it."

Liza picked up the phone. "Hello."

"Hey, it's Elaine. I have some news. It's nothing major, but I figured I would share it with you and see if it triggers anything about that day. That is assuming you didn't wake up this morning and remember everything."

Liza grimaced. "No. That didn't happen."

The front doorbell rang then, and Liza turned to Greg with her hand over the receiver. "It's probably Freddy. He called this morning and said he was coming over to talk about the casino. Do you want to let him in?"

The look on Greg's face suddenly scared her. As if he'd changed from the man she knew to a harder, colder person she didn't recognize.

"Yes. I would love to let him in."

He left the kitchen and, before she had time to worry about Greg's reaction, Elaine was talking in her ear again.

"Mark pulled your phone records. The night of Hector's death, three calls were made to your house from AC at around eleven-forty. The surveillance cameras pegged Hector's death as having occurred

fter 1:00 a.m. So I'm thinking maybe he called you
or a reason. Maybe he asked you to come in?"

Liza thought about what Elaine was saying. She
till didn't remember that night at all until the police
officer picked her up on the side of the road the next
morning. But the phone calls, that resonated. That
vas a real memory. Three messages on her phone.
They were from Freddy, wondering where she was.
Worried about her.

But they were left before Hector died, not after.

"Hey, Liza...you still with me?"

Freddy. Who was probably in the living room with
Greg now.

"Elaine, I have to go."

Liza hung up the phone with a strange sense of
nevitability. As if everything that had happened
ince she found herself on the highway with no mem-
ry had led to this moment. All she knew was that
Greg was in the living room with Freddy and that
vasn't good.

Because Greg was alone with Freddy and Freddy
vas...

Liza ran from the kitchen to the living room and
topped when she saw what was happening in front
of her.

"Let's talk about this, Freddy," Greg was saying
n the voice she hated. His calm, soothing voice that
he imagined he used with patients. She was sure

they appreciated it, but when it was directed at her she felt as if he was trying to treat her.

Now she really hoped it worked.

Freddy turned his head slightly as Liza was taking a step backward toward the kitchen. To the phone she'd hung up, instead of telling Elaine that they needed help.

"Sorry, Liza. In here. Now."

In his hand was a gun aimed at Greg. Then Freddy started talking, but the words didn't penetrate.

Freddy didn't want to shoot her, but he had no problem using Greg to get her to do what he wanted.

He was right. She would do anything to spare Greg's life. Cautiously, she stepped into the living room, wondering if Elaine would interpret the abrupt end to their conversation as an indication of trouble. Did a hang-up warrant a call to the police?

Liza stood a few feet away from Greg wondering what the next move was going to be. She'd seen this play out a hundred different ways on television. She couldn't remember specifics about what show or how it worked out, but the good guys always escaped. Somehow.

Did that happen in real life? She hadn't even told Greg she loved him. He should know that before he died. Before he died because of her.

"What are you going to do?"

Freddy actually looked contrite. "I'm sorry. I didn't want it to end like this, but I really can't take

he chance of you getting your memory back. Once
you were charged, I was officially off the hook. Now
I'll set up your suicide, you'll leave a note and the
whole thing will end."

"And Greg?"

"It's going to be sad when his body turns up on
the beach in AC. Gambling relapse turned nasty
when he gets confronted by some not-so-friendly
people who want his cash. Greg understands how
that works, don't you, Greg?"

Liza looked over at Greg who stood motionless.

"Since I knew you were going to be here—and
thank you, by the way, for making this easy—I
brought these." Freddy pulled out a pair of handcuffs and tossed them to Greg who let them drop
on the floor. "Put them on, hands behind you, and
do not attempt to be a hero."

"Or what? You'll kill me? Seems like a pretty
foregone conclusion at this point."

Liza wanted to scream at him to put the handcuffs
on. To obey everything Freddy said so he would live
that much longer. Because with time came opportunity. There had to be opportunity. Because the good
guys were supposed to win.

"Look, I have a bunch of pills for Liza. I can make
her death easy. Or hard, like making her hang herself. You get to pick."

Greg bent down and put on one of the cuffs, then

fastened the other behind his back. He turned around so that Freddy could see they were locked.

"You killed Hector." Liza could feel herself getting dizzy. As if she wasn't in control of her body anymore. She half sat, half collapsed on the couch as the realization of what was happening sank in. Freddy killed Hector and now he was going to kill her and Greg.

They were going to die and the good guys weren't going to win today.

"I figured out it was you. You were the only one with enough access to the accounts besides me…." It was like watching a movie, she thought. The memories started running together and it was as if she was watching her life on a screen. "I could prove to Hector the money was being stolen. I made an appointment for that Sunday. When I figured out it was you, I got worried. Worried because Hector trusted you so completely. You must have found out about the Sunday meeting. That's why you called me."

"It wasn't embezzling, sweetheart," Freddy told her. "It was investing. Hector had this stupid idea he could make the casino a legit business. That's not how this city works. Certainly not when the business you took over was shadier than any place on the boardwalk. Your father built The Grande with illegal cash. Hector wanted out of the drug game, but that left us weak. I couldn't have that. Drugs are money and money is power. What I did, I did for Hector."

"Until you killed him," Greg pointed out.

"It didn't work out for my father so well, either," Liza muttered. The picture of that pool of blood getting closer and closer to her feet flashed behind her eyes. Was that how Greg's blood would look if Freddy shot him? Would it run like a slow moving river out of his body?

She would lose it. This time she knew, if she had to witness his death, she would lose it. And it wouldn't matter if Freddy killed her or not. She was done seeing people die violently.

"Hector trusted me, like your father trusted him. He had no idea it was me. Said it right to my face, 'When I find this guy I'm going to pop him myself.' What I did, man, it was like self-defense."

Liza closed her eyes, but still the memory of the shooting wouldn't come. She remembered going to Hector's office and finding it empty, then seeing him on the floor. She remembered calling to him, but he hadn't heard her over the noise. That was where the memory stopped.

For once she was actually grateful for that. There was no point in remembering now. No reason to re-live it. But if she'd been there, close enough to Hector to have been splattered by his blood, why was she alive?

"I must have seen you. You couldn't know that I was going to lose my memory. Why didn't you shoot me, then?"

Freddy shrugged. "I wasn't expecting you. Figured I would take care of you after the fact. Then you popped out of the door as I shot him. I was about to do you but there was a group of people coming down the boardwalk, probably freaking drunk kids that time of night. I couldn't take the chance so I dropped the gun and split. I wasn't completely stupid. It was dark, I wore a ski mask. You might not have made me, but I wasn't taking a chance. I came around your place that morning to finish the job, but you were gone. Then I came again to wait for you, only he was with you. Next thing I know, the cops are questioning me, but it's not about me or the embezzlement. It's about you and how you don't remember anything, which the cops didn't believe. It was the perfect set up. All I had to do was wait. And when they found the gun, that was the icing on the cake."

"I must have taken the gun with me. I don't know why I would have done that."

Freddy actually looked regretful. Then he reached into his pocket and pulled out a bottle of pills. "I liked you, Liza. You seemed like a nice kid, if a little sheltered. We'll do this the easy way. You write the note and take the pills. I promise you I won't make your boyfriend over here suffer."

"Is that enough?" Greg asked.

Freddy and Liza looked at him.

"Is what eno…"

Freddy barely got the word out before the front

door flew open and four armed police officers entered with their guns directed at Freddy.

"Everyone down! On the floor! Now! Put your weapon down!"

Liza screamed and instantly dropped to the floor as did Greg. She could hear the sound of Freddy's gun falling on the carpet and when she lifted her head it was over. He was handcuffed, face pressed into the carpet and a man in plain clothes was walking over to help Greg up and get him out of his handcuffs.

Greg immediately knelt next to her, but she didn't want to move. She wanted to stay there on the carpet and not think about what had happened.

"Come on, Liza. It's over."

Eventually, she rolled and then sat up. She stared at the man in the jeans. "Who are you?"

"This is Mark Sharpe. I told you he was going to watch the house for you last night. Remember?"

Yes, she remembered. She remembered she'd told Greg he couldn't sleep in her bed and then she remembered him saying he needed to get out and think about stuff, but his friend Mark was coming by and wouldn't let anyone hurt her.

The truth was much more complicated. Greg wouldn't have left her if he thought she was in danger. He only left her because he knew she wasn't. At least not last night. Not when he knew Freddy was coming over today because he'd said so in Hector's suite. That he wanted to talk to her about the casino.

"You knew it was Freddy."

Greg nodded. "I strongly suspected. He was lying yesterday when he said he wanted to help you. When I considered that and started putting all the pieces together, he fit better than Verdi as the killer. As far as the embezzlement, as the person who shot at us. He had access to the camera in the alley. He also knew you had no memory."

"When Greg told me that," Mark said, "I sent JoJo to tail him. He's been under surveillance since last night and this morning, Liza. We knew his every move."

Did they know he was armed? Did they know he would aim that gun at Greg? She looked at Greg. "What if he'd shot you when you opened the door?"

"I didn't consider that," Greg said honestly. "I was only thinking about letting him show up here and play it out. I figured it was the quickest way to end this. I couldn't take my suspicion to the police. It wouldn't have been enough."

Liza shook her head. She was cold and wanted to lie down. "You didn't tell me."

"I didn't know what to say. I didn't know what Freddy was planning. Only that he was coming here to talk to you. I made certain the police could hear everything he said." Greg hesitated and she knew she wasn't going to like what came next.

"What?" she pressed.

"Had I told you, I couldn't be certain you wouldn't tip him off in some way. You're so damn expressive, Liza. If you knew he was the enemy, I think he would have known it, too. I swear I didn't know what he was planning. I took every precaution I could think of so you wouldn't be in any danger. Mark was here, the detective was here, and no fewer than three squad cars were here to make sure nothing happened to you."

"You took every precaution except telling me the truth." Liza looked around the room. The police had already removed Freddy. Others were collecting the recording devices. Bugs she didn't know were there. "How?"

"Sorry," Mark said, raising his hand. "I got in last night after you went to sleep and set up the house."

Got in. Not broke in. "So much for my alarm."

"If it makes you feel any better, I used to do this stuff for a living."

No, it didn't make her feel better. It didn't make her feel anything at all. "I want everyone to leave." She looked up at Greg. "Can I make that happen? Can I make everyone just go?"

Mark and Greg exchanged a look, which basically told her no.

Greg shook his head. "You're going to need to be questioned by the police now."

"Why? They heard everything."

"It's the process they go through," Greg said. "I know this is a lot to deal with, but if you could hang on for a little while longer then all of this will be behind you."

Of course she could hang on for a little while longer. She got to her feet and used Greg to steady herself before she was certain her knees wouldn't buckle. "I'm cold. I'm going to get a sweater, then the police can ask me anything they want. When they're done I want everyone to leave. Do you understand what I'm asking, Greg?"

His eyes darkened, but he nodded.

"I have had everyone I loved in my life die. My parents and my godfather were shot right in front of me. I love you. You must know, I do. It's why you're so scared of it. But you chose to be in this house with me, with a man you suspected was capable of murder. He could have shot you as soon as you opened the door and then I would have watched another person I love die. You're responsible for that."

"Liza…" his voice cracked and she could see him swallow, but he had nothing else to say.

"You're not perfect, Greg. And today you weren't my hero."

CHAPTER TWENTY-ONE

"YOUR HONOR, GIVEN THE compelling evidence presented by the detective, I ask that all charges against my client be dropped."

Liza listened to the judge clearing her of all charges, and then the sound of the gavel hitting his bench confirmed it. Elaine turned to her with a smile and a thumbs-up. She was wearing a charcoal-gray business suit and odd platform shoes that had different colors layered throughout the wedge of the heel.

Liza and Elaine would never agree on their choice of shoes. That didn't mean they couldn't become friends. As soon as everyone left her house that day Freddy was arrested, Greg decided she couldn't be left on her own. He called Elaine and the woman came over and drank wine with her and listened to her cry about what Greg had done. After many tears, chocolate ice cream and a big bottle of chardonnay, they had both agreed that men were stupid.

Elaine had checked in with her every day since, and now that the charges were formally dropped and Liza was free once again, they were going to celebrate over lunch. It seemed like something girlfriends did and it pleased Liza that Elaine had invited her.

They found a spot on the boardwalk overlooking the beach, which offered drinks with umbrellas and great guacamole.

"Here's to your freedom," Elaine toasted.

They clinked their margarita glasses together and watched as the water pounded against the sand twenty feet away. This city, she realized, was such a strange place. With the ocean offering up so much beauty, but the casinos behind them offering up so much sin.

She thought about what Freddy had said, how he was going to kill Greg and let his body wash up on the beach. She shivered and tried to remember that it hadn't happened. That Greg had lived.

"So, what happens now?"

Liza wasn't sure what Elaine meant. With her life, with her heart, with…Greg? Greg, who had called her every day, whose calls she wouldn't return. She didn't know what she would say to him. The level of hurt he caused her, by risking his life like that… What if she'd lost him? What if Freddy had panicked when the police came through the door and shot him?

The what-ifs were killing her.

"With the casino, I mean. Are you going to be the big boss lady?"

That decision had been easy. "No. I don't want

any part of that business. Too many bad memories between my parents and Hector. I'm going to sell it. Technically, I'm not allowed to tell anyone, because he wants the transaction kept private, but let's just say a prominent owner of another casino in AC, with really, really bad hair, has made me an offer I'm not going to refuse."

"Then you're rich! We should go shoe shopping."

Liza smiled. "I don't really know what I'm going to do with the money. I'm sure as hell not giving any to Dr. Verdi, but I thought I would find a charity that helps victims of head trauma."

"What about the doctor you saw? He might have some ideas."

Over the past few weeks she had recovered most of her memory. Still, there were a few blank spots, spots she was happy to leave as is, if it spared her Hector's violent death. She did finally have her appointment with the specialist at Thomas Jefferson. While he couldn't give her any definitive answers about whether everything would come back to her one day, he did recommend a psychologist to help her deal with the trauma she'd experienced. Both in her past and recently. Liza wasn't necessarily ready to commit to therapy, given her past history with it, but she hadn't ruled it out.

After all, it wasn't a weakness to say she needed help. If it was okay to see a medical doctor about her condition, then she thought it was fine to see a psychologist, too. They weren't the enemy. She had grown in that regard because of Greg. She wondered if he knew.

"Maybe. Anyway I'm glad it's finally over. I know what happened to Hector. I've buried him and now it's time to move on."

Liza thought about the funeral. Greg had come. She'd seen him in the back of the church, then again at the gravesite. She'd wanted to run into his arms and have him hold her. Have him stand by her side. If he had come to her, then maybe… But he hadn't.

She was the one who'd asked him to leave her alone, after all. It didn't seem fair to him to say she'd changed her mind. That it didn't matter that what he'd done by not telling her about Freddy was wrong, that it didn't matter that he couldn't accept her love because he was afraid.

Because she missed him.

Because she felt more lost without him than she had in that small interrogation room the police had brought her to when she first realized she didn't know who she was.

"Do you really mean that? About moving on?"

"Yes. I'm going to go back to my life. Hopefully get my job back at McKay and Fitz. Be an ordinary citizen again."

"Are you planning on maybe, I don't know…dating someone? Like a really tall, kind of lanky guy who is into psychology?"

"Elaine," Liza warned. Thinking about Greg hurt enough. Talking about him sent painful spikes through her heart.

Her friend leaned over the table with all the urgency of someone who wanted to say something really important. "He's a wreck. He doesn't eat, Chuck says he isn't sleeping. I think Chuck is really worried he's about to fall off the wagon."

The hurt in her heart only grew, but Liza couldn't let guilt drive her decisions. She needed time to process what he'd done. She needed time to decide if it was worth the risk of giving herself to someone who wasn't certain he could give himself back.

"Elaine, what he did…"

"I know, I know. He was a typical male asshole, but he wasn't necessarily wrong. You had no proof against Freddy. The only way to put the murder on him was for him to confess. In order for the cops to buy that confession, you had to be legitimate. In everything you said and did. He should have told you what he suspected, he should have trusted you, but he did save your ass."

"Nearly at the expense of his!"

"Doesn't that tell you something? He was willing to put his life on the line to save yours."

"Yes, it tells me his hero complex is alive and well. I don't want a hero, Elaine. I want a man. A man with all his flaws, who loves me for all my flaws.

Greg wants to be above it all and I can't go there with him, because I'm not above it all."

Elaine leaned back in her chair and sipped on her margarita. "You're right. Which leads us back to why men are stupid and why women turn to cats out of desperation."

Liza laughed, which she knew was Elaine's point, but the thought of Greg suffering in any way because of her made her lose her appetite for guacamole.

"What about Chuck? Has he asked you out yet?"

"That would be a big fat no. I mean, what the heck? He comes in with his Chinese food and he's all, I screwed up and you screwed up and kisses me, then nothing. It's been weeks!"

"Well, he did tell you to think about it. So the ball is sort of in your court. Why don't you ask him out?"

"Me?" she screeched. "What if he says no? What if this was all some big elaborate plot to pay me back?"

"Do you honestly think that?"

Elaine stirred her drink with the umbrella a few times. "I guess not. I mean, that kiss, it was pretty— wow. That couldn't be all one-sided, could it?"

Liza knew all about wow kisses. She missed wow kisses. She didn't think they could be one-sided. They had to be equally enjoyed by both parties. It was what made them wow. "Ask him out."

"It's scary."

Yeah, it was. Love, putting your heart out there,

risking having someone smash it up or not want it, all of it was scary. But after a bit of time, Liza was certain the week she'd spent with Greg was better than all the weeks she'd spent without him. Which made her think that as scary as it was, it was worth the risk.

ELAINE RANG THE doorbell of Chuck's loft and really hoped he didn't open the door. After two margaritas and a lot of pep talk, Liza had finally convinced her to go for it. Like ripping off a Band-Aid, she needed to get in front of his face, tell Chuck how she felt and ask him out on a real date.

"Please don't be home, please don't be home."

It was amazing what a thirty-minute drive could do to a person's confidence. Maybe she should call Liza and have her give her one more boost of pep. Like a little pep shot. Or maybe she needed another drink.

"Hey, what are you doing here?"

Elaine blinked. How long had the door been open? Chuck was smiling, so she hoped that his question meant he was pleased rather than irritated by her arrival.

"Uh…"

"Come on in." He walked away from her, assuming she would follow. Elaine figured she could turn around right now and sprint back to her car. That wouldn't be weird at all. Okay, maybe a little weird, but Chuck already knew that about her. It was there in her choice of shoes. The weird factor. Running was totally an option.

Then again, she'd found a really good parking spot and the odds of that happening again if she changed her mind and wanted to come back later were pretty slim. So because of the parking space and the fact that she didn't want to be weird, she followed him inside.

"Is Greg here?"

"No, he's out brooding. As usual. I wish he would do something about it, you know? Go to her place, tell her how he feels, tell her he's sorry he messed up but he wants another chance. Instead, he feels like he can't because he blew it. But we all blow it at one time or another, right?"

Elaine pounced on that as it echoed what he'd told her that night he kissed her. About getting a second chance. Maybe she didn't have to do the scary thing after all. Maybe she could tell him she was completely down with second chances, 100 percent on board with them, and he would make the first move. Excellent plan.

"Right! Yes. Everyone should get a second chance. I love second chances. They are great!"

"Yeah," Chuck said, looking at her with a hint of a smile.

Elaine waited for it. Any second now, he was going to pop the question.

"Can I get you something to drink?"

That wasn't the question she was anticipating. "Sure. Soda or something."

She watched him make his way into the kitchen and come back with a soda. She noted it was not diet and thought the two of them really had come a long way. They weren't snarling at each other anymore. They had actually kissed and it had been hot. What was his problem?

"What is your problem?" Elaine shouted, unable to keep it in any longer.

"What problem?"

"Why won't you ask me out? I mean, I've given you all the signs. I kissed you back. We've been talking on the phone. We met up for drinks the other night at the bar you like that I hate because it's filled with college girls who like to show off their midriffs. What more does a person have to do to show you she's interested so that you'll ask her out?"

His smile grew a little deeper. "I already asked you out, remember?"

"Yes, but I thought we were over that. You said we could have a second chance."

"We can. But I went out on a limb the first time. I did the asking and you said no. You want a second chance, I figure it's your turn."

In that moment Elaine hated both Liza and Chuck for being right. "Fine." She took a deep breath, pulled together every ounce of courage she had and let the words fall from her lips. "Willyougooutwithme?"

The way she said it sounded like one really long word. Still, it was out there.

"Yes."

Now it was her turn to smile. "Yes?"

"Yes, Elaine, even though you wear crazy shoes. I mean, seriously, what are those? I will go out with you."

Elaine couldn't say what the emotion was that filled her. Was this joy? Yes, she thought. Pure happiness mixed with the anticipation that something magical was going to happen. Joy.

"I think you secretly like my shoes."

He shrugged. "Whatever."

"I also think you should have to pay. I have to hold on to some old-fashioned standards."

"Deal. It's a good thing I'm rich from the squirrels. I can afford it."

"I'm never going to stop pushing you to be more," she warned. Yes, he'd given her a little inkling of his past and what drove him, but that didn't mean she was going to stop hounding him to fulfill his potential.

"I guess I can live with that. So, I'm thinking we seal it with a kiss?" he offered, wiggling his eyebrows in a way that always made her want to laugh.

Elaine had decided he'd gotten the best of her toight. "A kiss? Well, I guess we'll have to see how the ate goes before we know if that's going to happen."

"Seriously? You're going to make me wait until ur date?"

"Seriously," she told him. "I didn't say the date ouldn't be like…tomorrow."

Chuck laughed. "You are a strange and unusual voman, Elaine, and I can't wait to see where this is oing to go."

"Me, either," she said, still relishing in the glow f success. "Me, either."

GREG WATCHED AS Liza walked into the coffee shop. itting in his car, he considered that following her round on a Saturday while she ran her errands night technically be considered stalking. It probaly was actual stalking, but it wasn't done with the reepy intent, so he decided it was okay. When he'd een her come out of her house in a pair of skinny eans and a flowing yellow top, he'd almost lost his reath.

Missing her was unlike anything he'd ever experinced in his life. It was harder than dealing with the rief and guilt he felt over Tommy's death, harder han not gambling. Harder than anything until fially he woke up and realized he didn't want to do t anymore.

Missing Liza was too hard.

He drove to her house, but he couldn't find the

courage to get out of his car, which was pathetic but real. Then she left to run errands and it only seemed natural that he should follow her to the cleaners and the pharmacy. Then she drove down the main street of her town and parked and so he parked across the street.

Now she was inside the coffee shop, maybe getting a cup of coffee to stay for a while and read, or maybe grabbing something to go and he would follow her to the next place.

Like a stalker.

"Or you can grow a set," he told the empty car. Chuck had given him what had to be the greatest pep talk in the history of the brotherhood. Chuck, who thought Liza was the coolest woman alive now that she was proven innocent.

"Amnesia, man. You know what that means, you can create like every good memory she has. It's a blank slate and you're it. No comparisons to other boyfriends, nothing. Hell, every present you give her will be like the best one, because they are the only ones she remembers. You have to go for it!"

Greg didn't necessarily agree that her condition was what should motivate him. Hell, he didn't even know what her condition was at this point. She'd been remembering so much, even about that night. However, he did like the idea of creating new memories for her. Happy memories, filled with love and fun. He had this crazy idea that he wanted to give her family. His parents and his sister. His nieces and nephews. He wanted to give her children of her own.

That had been the ace in his pocket. If he'd gotten her pregnant then she would have had to reach out to him. Would have had to let him know. As the weeks passed and the phone didn't ring he had to assume she would have known by now, one way or the other.

It wasn't as if she would call him to tell him she wasn't pregnant.

Which meant his only option was to end the stalemate. Stop trying to figure out if what she really wanted was for him to stay away and instead let her know what he wanted.

Her forgiveness. That had to be the first thing. Her love. Which she had wanted to give him, but he hadn't been able to accept. Now he knew differently. He knew what it was not to have her in his life and that was intolerable. So yeah, it was easy to overcome any fears he had about being loved and being able to love back when the alternative sucked that bad.

The alternative had Greg opening the door to his car. It pushed him across the street and made him open the door to the coffee shop. She was sitting at a table against the wall with a frozen something in front of her that was piled with whipped cream and dripping chocolate.

He didn't know she had a sweet tooth.

Her head was down and he could see her hold ing an e-reader.

He didn't know she liked to read. He wondered what her tastes were. Romance, mystery, maybe the serious kind of books. He knew he wanted to know. Needed to know everything there was about her. Every part of her she remembered, and everything that changed about her from here on out.

Suddenly it was the easiest thing in the world to walk across the shop and stand in front of her table.

"Excuse me, is this seat taken?"

She gasped when she saw him. Greg didn't know if that was good or bad, but he didn't want to give her a chance to reject his presence. He sat down on the small chair and tucked his long legs under the table. Their knees bumped, and he was embarrassed to say even that minor contact turned him on.

"My name is Greg Chalmers. I saw you walk into this place, and it's crazy, but something about you.. made me want to follow you. And talk to you."

Her mouth opened but he could tell she still hadn't figured out what to say, so he filled the silence in stead.

"You don't know me, but I'm pretty messed up. was a psychologist, but I lost a patient and it messed with my head. Then I fell into a gambling addic tion that I've been struggling to get out of. It hasn't been easy."

"Sounds pretty bad."

"It is. What made it worse was that I wouldn't accept that it had happened to me. As a psychologist you listen to people's problems and the goal is to fix them. I was crazy good at it, too. I thought that was who I was meant to be. The person who helped, or saved or fixed. When I lost that ability I didn't know who I was anymore. It became easy to keep people away after that. It became necessary, I thought."

"You must have been lonely," she said.

"I was. For a really long time. Then I met this amazing woman and she had all this *stuff* she wanted to give me, but I was too afraid to take it. I wanted to help her. I wanted to save her. But I told myself I couldn't let her do those things for me. Which is stupid, because the whole time I wouldn't admit to it, she was helping me. She was saving me."

He could see her eyes filling with tears, but her lips were curving up. Greg didn't need to be an expert at reading people to understand that she had missed him, too. It was hard to know what emotion was controlling him, relief or love. He decided it didn't matter.

"I loved her, but I screwed up and she kicked me out."

"I'm sorry."

Greg smiled. "Yes, but you see it's all going to

work out. Because I saw you walk into this shop and I had this immediate connection to you. I was wondering, if you're free sometime would you like to go to dinner with me?"

She nodded. "I think dinner would be nice. Nice and normal."

Greg reached across the table and took her hand. Just that, just touching her again grounded him in a way he'd never felt before. He had no idea how lost he was, until Eliza Dunning found him.

"Very normal," he agreed, not letting her go. "Just two people who happened to meet, who might find themselves falling in love."

"What do these two people do next, after they find themselves falling in love?"

He cupped her face in his hand and watched her turn into his embrace.

This is it. The real deal.

"They date for a while and get used to each other. Then he gets down on one knee with a ring and looks like a fool doing it."

She shook her head and he loved the feel of her hair sliding against his wrist. "No, he could never look like a fool doing that."

"She accepts his love…"

He could see tears in her eyes. "Does he accept hers?"

If the joy in his chest was any indication, then he

did. He really did. "Yes. Completely. That's why they get married and live happily ever after."

"That would be a nice ending."

He beamed at her. "That would be the best ending."

* * * * *

LARGER-PRINT BOOKS!
GET 2 FREE LARGER-PRINT NOVELS PLUS
2 FREE GIFTS!

⬧HARLEQUIN®

super romance®

More Story...More Romance

YES! Please send me 2 FREE LARGER-PRINT Harlequin® Superromance® novels and my 2 FREE gifts (gifts are worth about $10). After receiving them, if I don't wish to receive any more books, I can return the shipping statement marked "cancel." If I don't cancel, I will receive 6 brand-new novels every month and be billed just $5.69 per book in the U.S. or $5.99 per book in Canada. That's a savings of at least 16% off the cover price! It's quite a bargain! Shipping and handling is just 50¢ per book in the U.S. or 75¢ per book in Canada.* I understand that accepting the 2 free books and gifts places me under no obligation to buy anything. I can always return a shipment and cancel at any time. Even if I never buy another book, the two free books and gifts are mine to keep forever.

139/339 HDN F46Y

Name _____
(PLEASE PRINT)

Address _____ Apt. # _____

City _____ State/Prov. _____ Zip/Postal Code _____

Signature (if under 18, a parent or guardian must sign) _____

Mail to the **Harlequin® Reader Service:**
IN U.S.A.: P.O. Box 1867, Buffalo, NY 14240-1867
IN CANADA: P.O. Box 609, Fort Erie, Ontario L2A 5X3
**Are you a current subscriber to Harlequin Superromance books
and want to receive the larger-print edition?
Call 1-800-873-8635 today or visit www.ReaderService.com.**

* Terms and prices subject to change without notice. Prices do not include applicable taxes. Sales tax applicable in N.Y. Canadian residents will be charged applicable taxes. Offer not valid in Quebec. This offer is limited to one order per household. Not valid for current subscribers to Harlequin Superromance Larger-Print books. All orders subject to credit approval. Credit or debit balances in a customer's account(s) may be offset by any other outstanding balance owed by or to the customer. Please allow 4 to 6 weeks for delivery. Offer available while quantities last.

Your Privacy—The Harlequin® Reader Service is committed to protecting your privacy. Our Privacy Policy is available online at www.ReaderService.com or upon request from the Harlequin Reader Service.

We make a portion of our mailing list available to reputable third parties that offer products we believe may interest you. If you prefer that we not exchange your name with third parties, or if you wish to clarify or modify your communication preferences, please visit us at www.ReaderService.com/consumerchoice or write to us at Harlequin Reader Service Preference Service, P.O. Box 9062, Buffalo, NY 14269. Include your complete name and address.

HSRLP13R

LARGER-PRINT BOOKS!

HARLEQUIN *Presents*

PASSION
GUARANTEED
SEDUCTION

GET 2 FREE LARGER-PRINT NOVELS PLUS 2 FREE GIFTS!

YES! Please send me 2 FREE LARGER-PRINT Harlequin Presents® novels and my 2 FREE gifts (gifts are worth about $10). After receiving them, if I don't wish to receive any more books, I can return the shipping statement marked "cancel." If I don't cancel, I will receive 6 brand-new novels every month and be billed just $5.05 per book in the U.S. or $5.49 per book in Canada. That's a saving of at least 16% off the cover price! It's quite a bargain! Shipping and handling is just 50¢ per book in the U.S. and 75¢ per book in Canada.* I understand that accepting the 2 free books and gifts places me under no obligation to buy anything. I can always return a shipment and cancel at any time. Even if I never buy another book, the two free books and gifts are mine to keep forever.

176/376 HDN F43N

Name _____ (PLEASE PRINT)

Address _____ Apt. #

City _____ State/Prov. _____ Zip/Postal Code

Signature (if under 18, a parent or guardian must sign)

Mail to the **Harlequin® Reader Service:**
IN U.S.A.: P.O. Box 1867, Buffalo, NY 14240-1867
IN CANADA: P.O. Box 609, Fort Erie, Ontario L2A 5X3

Are you a subscriber to Harlequin Presents books and want to receive the larger-print edition?
Call 1-800-873-8635 today or visit us at www.ReaderService.com.

* Terms and prices subject to change without notice. Prices do not include applicable taxes. Sales tax applicable in N.Y. Canadian residents will be charged applicable taxes. Offer not valid in Quebec. This offer is limited to one order per household. Not valid for current subscribers to Harlequin Presents Larger-Print books. All orders subject to credit approval. Credit or debit balances in a customer's account(s) may be offset by any other outstanding balance owed by or to the customer. Please allow 4 to 6 weeks for delivery. Offer available while quantities last.

Your Privacy—The Harlequin® Reader Service is committed to protecting your privacy. Our Privacy Policy is available online at www.ReaderService.com or upon request from the Harlequin Reader Service.

We make a portion of our mailing list available to reputable third parties that offer products we believe may interest you. If you prefer that we not exchange your name with third parties, or if you wish to clarify or modify your communication preferences, please visit us at www.ReaderService.com/consumerchoice or write to us at Harlequin Reader Service Preference Service, P.O. Box 9062, Buffalo, NY 14269. Include your complete name and address.

HPLP13R